# QUEEN OF LOST STARS

## *A Medieval Romance*

By Kathryn Le Veque

# Kathryn Le Veque Novels

**Medieval Romance:**

**The de Russe Legacy:**
The White Lord of Wellesbourne
The Dark One: Dark Knight
Beast
Lord of War: Black Angel
The Falls of Erith

**The de Lohr Dynasty:**
While Angels Slept (Lords of East Anglia)
Rise of the Defender
Spectre of the Sword
Unending Love
Archangel
Steelheart

**Great Lords of le Bec:**
Great Protector
To the Lady Born (House of de Royans)

**Lords of Eire:**
The Darkland (Master Knights of Connaught)
Black Sword
Echoes of Ancient Dreams (time travel)

**De Wolfe Pack Series:**
The Wolfe
Serpent
Scorpion (Saxon Lords of Hage – Also related to The Questing)
Walls of Babylon
The Lion of the North
Dark Destroyer

**Ancient Kings of Anglecynn:**
The Whispering Night
Netherworld

**Battle Lords of de Velt:**
The Dark Lord
Devil's Dominion

**Reign of the House of de Winter:**
Lespada
Swords and Shields (also related to The Questing, While Angels Slept)

**De Reyne Domination:**
Guardian of Darkness
The Fallen One (part of Dragonblade Series)

**Unrelated characters or family groups:**
The Gorgon (Also related to Lords of Thunder)
The Warrior Poet (St. John and de Gare)
Tender is the Knight (House of d'Vant)
Lord of Light
The Questing (related to The Dark Lord, Scorpion)
The Legend (House of Summerlin)

**The Dragonblade Series: (Great Marcher Lords of de Lara)**
Dragonblade
Island of Glass (House of St. Hever)
The Savage Curtain (Lords of Pembury)
The Fallen One (De Reyne Domination)
Fragments of Grace (House of St. Hever)
Lord of the Shadows
Queen of Lost Stars (House of St. Hever)

**Lords of Thunder: The de Shera Brotherhood Trilogy**
The Thunder Lord
The Thunder Warrior
The Thunder Knight

**Time Travel Romance:** (Saxon Lords of Hage)
The Crusader
Kingdom Come

**Contemporary Romance:**

**Kathlyn Trent/Marcus Burton Series:**
Valley of the Shadow
The Eden Factor
Canyon of the Sphinx

**The American Heroes Series:**
Resurrection
Fires of Autumn
Evenshade
Sea of Dreams
Purgatory

**Other Contemporary Romance:**
Lady of Heaven
Darkling, I Listen

**Multi-author Collections/Anthologies:**

<u>With Dreams Only of You</u> (USA Today bestseller)
<u>Sirens of the Northern Seas</u> (Viking romance)

**Note:** All Kathryn's novels are designed to be read as stand-alones, although many have cross-over characters or cross-over family groups. Novels that are grouped together have related characters or family groups.

Series are clearly marked. All series contain the same characters or family groups except the American Heroes Series, which is an anthology with unrelated characters.

There is NO particular chronological order for any of the novels because they can all be read as stand-alones, even the series.

For more information, find it in **A Reader's Guide to the Medieval World of Le Veque**.

# Author's Note

A very unusual novel....

This is yet another of those novels missing big chunks due to a faulty hard drive, written back in the days before clouds and Dropbox, when every chapter was its own file, and floppy discs were the back-up method. My guess is that this book first saw the light of day back in the late 1990s but I can't be certain. I wrote a lot of stuff back then. All I know is that I was only able to salvage pieces of it. It's an unusual storyline, and far different from anything I've ever written, so I thought I would finally finish it. Every story deserves to be finished! I have a few more that will be finished someday – someday soon, I hope.

Oh, the name changes that went on in this book! I have a confession – my heroine had a different name in the beginning, which I thought was pretty and unusual, but then I worked with a girl (back in the day when I worked in an office) with the same name and far be it from me to judge people, but she turned out to be a terrible co-worker, so I quickly changed the heroine's name. Ha! The hero's name was also different but that, too, changed a few times – yes, a few times – until I settled on the one you see. This novel had a bit of a difficult time finding an identity, but it has finally come into its own and now I am proud to present it to you. One thing that didn't change is the name St. Hèver – our hero, Kaspian, is a cousin to Kenneth St. Hèver (ISLAND OF GLASS) from the Dragonblade saga. Since Kenneth's father, Kurtis, only had one brother, we will assume that Kaspian's father was a cousin to Kurtis and his brother, Keir (FRAGMENTS OF GRACE).

A few things to note in this book – there is a mixture of real and fictional castles as well as real and fictional lords and princes. Some places, like Hawarden Castle and Beeston Castle, are real places that played a role in the Welsh wars, but our main castle, Lavister, is fictional. The location where I placed it, however, really does have a hilly crag, a perfect place for such a fortress to be built – if it existed. There is some adventure in this book, a little bit of politics, and a whole lot of unusual romance.

A little erotic? Definitely. Like I said, very different from my other novels. Keep an open mind and I think you just might like it…!

Love,
Kathryn

# CHAPTER ONE

*Lavister Crag Castle, South of Chester along the Welsh Marches*
*May, Year of Our Lord 1320 A.D.*

"**W**e've got to move, man. Where have you been?"

The question came from a very large man, dressed from head to toe in enough armor and weaponry to single-handedly conquer a small country. He had his helm in one hand, revealing cropped blonde hair and a granite-square jaw, but the light in the pale blue eyes was cold, cold as the snows on an early winter morning.

It was, in fact, an early winter morning and the mighty garrison of Lavister Crag Castle was mobilized, organized and driven by the man with the ice-cold stare. Kaspian St. Hèver was a man not to be crossed or trifled with, and he certainly wasn't a man to be disobeyed. He had the St. Hèver size, command ability, and lack of pleasant temperament. His question was focused on a big red-haired knight who had just emerged from Lavister's significant keep, a man who smiled weakly to St. Hèver's query.

"I wanted to see Madelayne one more time before we left," he said. "Dolwyd will not let her come down to see me off and she is quite upset by it."

Kaspian eyed the man, trying to shift from command mode into some semblance of a compassionate mode. The situation warranted it.

"Is she well?" he asked.

Cairn l'Ebreux nodded his red head, plopping his helm on to cover his skull. "She is," he said. "She is worried, of course. She fears the child will be born whilst we are away. I have assured her that this quest will only take a week at most, but she is still frightened."

Kaspian wasn't one given to fits of mercy or humor in any given situation; therefore, moments like this were difficult for him to gauge. He didn't want to sound completely heartless, but his was a world of battle and it was to battle his men were headed, including Cairn, who was an excellent knight from a fine family. But Cairn was also the husband of a woman who was on her second pregnancy in as many years, the first pregnancy having resulted in the loss of a premature son. The woman was terrified for this child and rightly so. But the fact remained that Lady l'Ebreux's fear and her pregnancy were not his problem.

"The physic is with her," Kaspian finally said, turning away. "Leave Dolwyd to tend your wife. I need you with me. I need your mind with me, Cairn. If you are distracted, you are of no good to me or yourself or your wife. I do not want to return to tell her that you have been killed."

Cairn knew that was about as close to a compassionate statement as Kaspian could make. The two of them had worked together for years and although Kaspian wasn't a man to cultivate friendship, Cairn considered him a friend. But Cairn was far more compassionate and feeling than his big, blonde counterpart and his heart, his soul, was with his wife up in their chamber.

He'd left her weeping, something he hated to do, but she wept a good deal these days. She was frightened for their child and now frightened for Cairn as he left to tend to a skirmish over at Beeston Castle, but the Welsh were on the march these days.

Led by Dafydd ap Gruffydd, or at least led by his supporters, the Welsh had been hitting English castles along the Marches, and inside Wales, more actively this year than in the previous ones. Sometimes they charged with a thousand men and sometimes it was just a few hundred. They weren't particularly skilled for the most part but they could do damage if unchecked and they were bothersome. They tried to gain access to a castle any way they could and had been beaten back by the English time and time again.

They were bothersome and they were time consuming, proven today as the men of Lavister Crag Castle gathered again for yet another show of support against the Welsh. Lavister was a military outpost with a rather small feasting hall and few living quarters, and those quarters they did have weren't very comfortable. The army lived in two big, long houses with pitched roofs on the east side of the bailey, and they also lived in shelters some of the soldiers had built outside of those barracks because they could be very crowded. St. Hèver kept almost a thousand men in this close-quarters castle as the knights and their wives lived in the keep. Thick, moss-covered stone comprised the keep and the small rooms within were cheerless. It was a hellish place for a man much less a woman.

A hellish place for a child to be born.

But Cairn shook off the morose thoughts. St Hèver was correct; distraction in his business could be deadly and he most certainly wanted to return to the wife who was far too beautiful for him. Madelayne Gray l'Ebreux was his everything. He had cherished her since the first moment he'd laid eyes on her, the daughter of wealthy merchant. Even now, on the cusp of battle, he remembered the day he first met her, passing through the town of Wrexham and witnessing beauty such as had never been seen upon the earth. He'd offered for her hand that very day and a month later they had been married. It had been the best day of Cairn's life.

But even as he adored her, he knew that she didn't return the sentiment. She was kind and polite to him, and laughed at his jests, but he knew there was no fire in her heart for him where he was concerned. It didn't bother him too much because he was certain that, someday, he could earn her love. But it was becoming increasingly discouraging. The harder he tried, the more politely she smiled at him. He only wanted her to be happy. But selfishly, he wanted to be the source of that happiness.

He shook himself again, content to reflect upon the sentimental past when St. Hèver was demanding his attention. Sometimes Cairn was too sentimental for his own good.

"You have my full attention, Kaspian," he said quietly, pushing past the enormous knight. "Let us make short work of the Welsh so we can return soon. I promised Madelayne I would."

Kaspian watched the man walk by, knowing that his statement about his attention had been a noble lie. He didn't have the man's full attention and they both knew it, but there wasn't much to be done about it. Cairn was very attached to his beautiful wife and rightly so, but Kaspian shook his head faintly, with regret, for a man who was attending battle without his full focus. That would mean Kaspian would have to keep an eye on him. Kaspian didn't like that because it meant his attention would be divided, too.

"Cairn, wait," he said, watching the knight come to a halt and look at him. "I cannot have you join a battle in your current state. You will not live to see the sun set if that is the case."

Cairn's brow furrowed curiously. "I am quite well," he assured him. "Let us leave now. The longer we delay, the more Beeston is chewed up by those aggravating mites called Welshmen."

Kaspian gave him a long look, one of great doubt. "You are not going," he said. "You are going to get us both killed."

Now, Cairn was becoming offended. "Why would you say such a thing?" he asked. A man of mild temper, he rarely raised his voice or became irate. "Have I ever failed you in battle, Kaspian?"

"You have not."

"This will not be the first time."

With that, he turned and headed for his warhorse, being held steady near the enormous gatehouse by a soldier. In fact, all of the soldiers were milling about, waiting for orders to move out, and Kaspian's three other knights were waiting for those orders as well. Kaspian could see Sir Thomas Allington-More, Sir Ewan de Poyer and his younger brother, Sir Reece de Poyer, already mounted and waiting in the mouth of the gatehouse. Everyone had been waiting for Cairn to say farewell to his sickly, pregnant wife. Now, Kaspian sighed heavily at the sight of Cairn marching for his steed as if charged up for the battle that lay ahead. It was an act, Kaspian knew. The man wasn't charged up for anything.

"Cairn!"

A female voice came from the entry to the keep; the entry was on the ground floor, unusual to most keeps, but the door that held the entry was made of iron that could not be broken, melted, softened, or breached. It was the Door to Hell, as some called it, but now within that door stood a small, titian-haired woman, very pregnant. Even as Kaspian and Cairn turned to look at her, as did most of the other men in the bailey, she lifted her hand and waved at her husband.

"*Cairn!*"

Kaspian was unbelievably frustrated by this point. His jaw began to tick and he turned away from Lady l'Ebreux as her husband, startled by her appearance, began to run in her direction. Kaspian hadn't taken but a few steps when Lady l'Ebreux called to him as well.

"Sir Kaspian?" she said. "May I humbly ask a question, my lord?"

Jaw still ticking unhappily, Kaspian politely turned to her. "My pleasure, my lady."

She smiled, a gesture that Kaspian had always thought was the most lovely smile he had ever seen. Lady l'Ebreux was, in fact, the most beautiful woman he had ever seen and he truly didn't blame Cairn for the way the man fell all over himself when it came to his wife. But Kaspian wasn't in the habit of thinking on other men's wives so his thoughts of Lady l'Ebreux went no further. Still, the shapely figure, auburn hair, and green eyes were quite a glorious spectacle.

"Thank you," the lady said sincerely. "I know you are ready to depart and I am very sorry if I am delaying your army, but Cairn tells me that this skirmish should not be too difficult. I fear he tells me this to ease my mind. Is it true?"

Kaspian cleared his throat softly as Cairn ran past him to his wife. The red-haired knight immediately put his arms around the woman. "What are you doing out here?" he demanded softly. "You must return to bed immediately. Where is Mavia?"

"I am here," a blonde woman emerged behind Lady l'Ebreux. Lady Allington-More, wife of Sir Thomas, gave Cairn a rather remorseful expression. "She wanted to speak with you, Cairn. I could not stop her."

Cairn looked at his wife with as much impatience as he could muster. "What is so important that you had to leave your bed, Madelayne?" he asked. "You should not be here and you know it."

Madelayne returned her attention to Kaspian. "I came to ask Sir Kaspian a question," she said. "Cairn, I fear you would tell me what I want to hear simply to ease me. I want to know the truth."

Everyone was looking at Kaspian now and he felt his patience slip. He should have been on the road a half hour ago and the delay because of Lady l'Ebreux was testing his temper.

"My lady, I have no way of knowing how bad the situation at Beeston actually is until I get there," he said, rather pointedly. "The messenger from Beeston said it was a mild attack compared to some, but I cannot know if this situation has changed. You will forgive me for being short, but the longer you delay us, the more difficult it may become. The Welsh may have time to summon reinforcements, as well. Good day, my lady."

With that, he bowed his head crisply in her direction, spun on his heel, and marched off towards his waiting army. Cairn, frustrated with Madelayne and not particularly pleased at Kaspian's blunt response to her, turned to his wife.

"You see?" he pointed out. "You have upset him. Now I have to go on a battle march with a man who will be annoyed with me. Get back to bed or I will take a switch to you. Do you hear me?"

Madelayne looked up at him with big eyes. "Will the Welsh really call for reinforcements?"

"*Go.*"

He wasn't meant to be disobeyed. Rebuked and upset, Madelayne turned for the keep but not before Cairn kissed her forehead to show he wasn't too entirely angry with her. With Lady Allington-More pulling her back into the darkened, musty keep, Madelayne's last look at her husband was as he followed St. Hèver towards the gathering of men at the gatehouse. Big, broad Cairn, a sweet man of infinite patience and kindness, a man she was fond of.

Perhaps someday she would even grow to love him.

He would be home to her in a week.

C3

*Beeston Castle*
*Welsh Marches*
*Two days later*

The skirmish at Beeston had been much worse than the men from Lavister Crag had been led to believe. Hundreds of Welsh were attacking the place, made difficult by Beeston's position on a rocky hill in the midst of the Shropshire plains. The castle was positioned much like Lavister, built on an elevated position so it could dominate the countryside. There were tunnels and caves beneath it, dug down into the rocky hills, used by men for centuries before the coming of the Normans and the building of the mighty castles that lined the Marches.

Beeston was purely a military fortress with little by way of comfortable accommodations, but it was manned by a big army because of its strategic importance on the Marches. The Welsh knew this, which is why they were quite determined to remove the English and replace them with a Welsh garrison. The English, as usual, resisted the invitation to leave and the battle that ensued was fierce. Kaspian and Cairn saw the ferocity the day they arrived and, two days later, it was still going on although the fervor was weakening. Men were exhausted, dying or dead, and the battle for Beeston was now mostly on the plain below where there were pockets of steady fighting.

There has been cause for English hope that morning when a small contingent of men from Anchorsholme Castle, about a two day's ride from Beeston, arrived on a cold and smoky dawn. Anchorsholme was part of the de Cleveley lands and they were loyal to Edward, so the king staffed a small contingent of crown troops at the castle.

It was this contingent, led by Sir Nicholas de Dalyn, who rode upon the battle at Beeston and immediately began dispatching any Welsh they came across. There were only about two hundred men, however. Not a huge amount of men against so many Welsh, but they had been a fresh and welcome addition to the English nonetheless.

"My lord!" Nicholas called out to Kaspian as he fought his way towards the massive knight. "You have my thanks for holding the battle until we arrived. My men and I have been without action for so long that this excitement is a welcome change!"

Kaspian very nearly grinned at the humor; he knew Nicholas and had fought with him before. De Dalyn was an excellent commander and a powerful knight, which gave Kaspian a good deal of relief to see him. But he was also arrogant and ambitious; Kaspian seemed to remember hearing, long ago, that de Dalyn was one of those men who had no problem stepping on, or eliminating, others in order to see his goals achieved, but Kaspian had never experienced such a thing. He was simply glad the man had come with reinforcements. His character, for the moment, was not at issue, at least not in the midst of the battle.

"We have been holding the battle, indeed," he said, kicking aside a Welshman who had been trying to gore one of his soldiers with a spear. "Now that you are here, we can stop dancing with these fools and go in for the kill."

De Dalyn grinned. He was big, blonde, and handsome. "I would be agreeable to that," he said, holding his big, brown warhorse steady as the animal tried to charge forward. "How long has it been like this?"

Kaspian looked up at the structure of Beeston high on its rocky hill. "The Beeston commander tells me that the Welsh have been at him, periodically, for the entire month but only in the last week has it grown this serious. My men and I have been here for two days and it has been a steady fight, just as you see it."

Nicholas, too, looked up to the castle on the hill as the battle went on up at its gates. "Then I say we end this," he said. "I have been bored out of my mind at Anchorsholme, to be truthful. I would much rather have a command at Beeston or Lavister Crag."

Kaspian smiled, a humorless gesture. "You cannot have it," he said. "It is a prestigious castle and a world of my own to govern. If you want the command, you will have to wait for me or l'Ebreux to be transferred to another post or die. We like it here."

Nicholas had his attention on a fighting group that was moving in his direction. His broadsword was at the ready. "Will you not reconsider?" he asked. "I will gladly surrender Anchorsholme to you."

"I do not want it."

"What about l'Ebreux?"

"I will not let him leave me."

Nicholas shifted his broadsword so that it was closer to the men who were moving in his direction. He seemed to be off the subject of moving to Lavister, at least for the moment. There were more important things at hand.

"I have already seen the de Poyer brothers, somewhere off to the north," he said. "Is l'Ebreux here, too?"

"He is," Kaspian said, eyeing the same group of battling men shuffling towards them as they fought and grunted. "The last I saw him, he was over near the road that leads up to Beeston. He and his men were fighting off a pack of Welsh. Find him and help him."

"How many men did he have with him?"

"Not many. Hurry and find him."

A flash of something dark and calculating moved across Nicholas' features. It was there for an instant and then it was gone; Kaspian never saw it. He was focused on the collection of Welsh and English combatants that were steadily moving in his direction. As he charged towards the crowd of battling men, swinging his broadsword, Nicholas spurred his horse towards the base of the hill where the road led up to Beeston.

There were huge rocks and any number of crevices where men could fight or hide. Nicholas charged towards the mound with several men on his tail, including a few of Kaspian's men, only to find Cairn and the small group of English soldiers with him being swarmed.

It didn't look good. They were back in one of the larger crevices at the base of the crag and the fighting was hand-to-hand. Nicholas paused, watching Cairn as the man struggled to fight off the Welsh from atop his roan charger. It was clear that he was struggling, nearly overwhelmed by the sheer number of Welsh, but he was fighting valiantly. He was swinging his sword and his fists, and even his feet. As Nicholas watched, a Welsh fighter grabbed hold of Cairn's left arm and pulled him off of his charger, back into a cluster of rocks. As the horse bolted off, Cairn was swarmed by men trying to kill him.

This should have been Nicholas' cue to ride to the rescue, but he didn't. He simply watched as Cairn fought for his life. What was it St. Hèver had said? *We shall be at Lavister until we die.* Knights couldn't live forever, after all. One man falling in battle would not a difference make.

*… would it?*

That something dark and calculating flickered in Nicholas' eyes again.

Seeing that the knight was down, the men with Nicholas began to rush in to help him but Nicholas called them off. He held out a big hand, preventing them from charging in.

*One man falling in battle would not a difference make….*

"Nay!" he bellowed. "I will get to the knight! You clear these Welsh out of here! Get them away!"

It was a command that made little sense but the English obeyed. One man, one of Kaspian's men, disobeyed the order and ran for Cairn, but Nicholas intercepted the soldier and kicked him in the head, sending the man to the ground, half-conscious. As the fresh English soldiers went to clean up the Welsh beating up on Cairn's outnumbered and weary troop, Nicholas spurred his horse in Cairn's direction.

But he didn't get too close. He simply swung his sword around and looked as if he were going after the men who were overwhelming Cairn. Nicholas knew l'Ebreux distantly; he didn't know him well. They were not friends. He'd always heard that the man was competent if not a bit too relaxed when it came to his duties. Surely a man like that wasn't worthy to have a post at Lavister. It was an active and prestigious post that had a lot to do with feasting and soothing the local Welsh warlords. There were opportunities for wealth there, too, in the form of contracts and negotiations. Surely a knight like l'Ebreux didn't deserve the post. He was a mediocre knight in a land that was full of such fortunate fools. A knight like Nicholas deserved it more.

Therefore, one knight falling in battle would not a difference make.

So Nicholas remained just out of range as Cairn was thrown onto his back, making eye contact with Cairn and seeing the panic in his eyes. Cairn was giving the fight a tremendous effort but it was to no avail. As Nicholas easily dispatched a few Welsh who had rushed him, he made no effort to assist Cairn, who received a dagger to his chest and neck. The Welsh were vicious and relentless, and yanked his helm off, revealing his bright red hair, as they continued to beat and stab him with their crude iron knives.

It would have been a horrific thing to watch for anyone else, but not Nicholas. He was quite detached. When he finally saw that Cairn was beyond help, he rushed in and chased the Welsh off, looking for all the world like a man who had been too late to save his comrade. He even dismounted and picked Cairn up, slinging him over the back of his horse, and looking heroic as he carried Cairn to safety, but by then it was too late. Cairn had bled out from his wounds and there was no longer anything to be done for him. Nicholas took Cairn away from the fighting, back to where the wounded were being tended.

Nicholas also noticed that Kaspian was with the wounded as well, having been felled by a nasty Welsh spear straight to the lower abdomen. With Cairn dead and Kaspian badly wounded, Nicholas took charge of the battle from Thomas Allington-More. Thomas, a seasoned knight with more battle experience than Nicholas, had been swept aside by the brash and arrogant knight. Nicholas was able to take credit for the victory with his fresh men against the weary Welsh, but it was a victory nonetheless.

As a valiant knight in shining armor, Sir Nicholas de Dalyn emerged from the battle of Beeston as the glorious one.

At least, that was what the Beeston commander's missive to King Edward clearly stated.

The battle at Beeston had a hero, and that hero had a specific request of the king.

*Lavister Crag.*

# CHAPTER TWO

*Lavister Crag Castle*
*Days later*

"**W**hat shall I tell her?" Mavia hissed. "She will want to see her child!"

An old man in smelly woolen robes and a head of stringy white hair simply shook his head. "She will not," he said. "She knows her child is dead. He was born with the birthing cord wrapped around his neck. She'll not ask for him."

Mavia stood at the chamber door, peeking into the small, cramped chamber beyond where Madelayne had recently given birth. She could see the woman lying on the bed, bundled up and lying on her side. Mavia thought she was sleeping. The child had been big enough, unlike the previous child she had birthed who had been born far too early, but this son had been born with the cord wrapped around his neck and his face shades of blue. It was heartbreaking, truly. Madelayne had feared for this child so and her worst fears had come to light. Mavia sighed heavily.

"My heart grieves for her," Mavia whispered. "She wanted this child so badly. Why do you suppose such things happen, Dolwyd? Madelayne is a good woman. She is kind to the poor and she is pious. Why should such bad fortunate befall her?"

The old physic shook his head. He, too, could see Madelayne on the bed through the slit in the door. "It is the will of God," he said simply. "The lass has suffered much loss in her life; her mother dying when she was young, her babes dying last year and this year. Lady Madelayne may have to face the fact that God does not want her to have a child."

Mavia's gaze was intense upon the old man. "After you ripped the child from her, it is a wonder she did not bleed to death," she muttered. "Did you have to be so rough?"

Dolwyd was unruffled by the accusation. There wasn't much in life that excited or upset him anymore. "The child was wedged in," he said. "He was stuck. Would you have me lose both the mother and the child?"

Mavia sighed sharply. "Of course not," she said. "But the way you... God's Bones, Dolwyd. You literally yanked the child from her body. You tore her to shreds!"

"If I had not, the child would not have been born and Lady Madelayne would have eventually lost her strength and both she and the child would have died. Is that what you would rather see? There is no place for your proprieties, lady."

"It was not a matter of propriety! It was a matter of your being quite rough with Madelayne. She is not one of the soldiers you tend, you know. You did not need to be so forceful with her."

As Mavia and Dolwyd whispered outside of the chamber door, Madelayne was very much awake even though she was motionless, facing the wall. She could hear every word spoken, angry whispers from her friend and the calm response of the old physic. As if they thought she couldn't hear them. Tears trickled from Madelayne's eyes and onto the pillow beneath her; aye, she knew her son was dead even without the whispers outside her door. She hadn't even seen the little lad when he'd been born but the way Dolwyd had handed the child off and the receiving female servant had fled, she knew.

Another dead son.

She didn't know why she was being punished so. Death had always been part of her life; when she was young, her mother and grandmother died within a few days of each other of a malady the physics could not explain. She's been raised by house servants after that because her father, a wealthy man, had been too busy with his business to tend to his only child. There really hadn't been anyone for Madelayne to love or feel close to; with a distant father and no other family, there hadn't been much to cling to.

But there had been plenty of lost stars in the heavens above to keep her company. That was what her mother had once called dead family members – fathers, grandmothers, and even her mother's own two brothers had passed on. *Lost stars*, Madelayne's mother had called them. Elisabet Gray had been a lost star for many years, too, and was joined by her two grandsons. Madelayne's babies had become lost stars, now watching over her from above. It gave her some comfort to think that her sons had their grandmother to tend them. That was perhaps the only thing that gave Madelayne comfort, for life on earth was certainly a hellish existence now.

God's Bones, what was she going to tell Cairn? How was she to face the man and tell him that his second son had died? He had, perhaps, been more excited about the children than she was. He was a man who had married later in life and was thrilled to finally have a family. Only he had no family at all, only a wife who had thus far managed to bear him two dead children. She felt useless, worthless, and sad. The tears began to fall faster onto the pillow.

"Lady l'Ebreux?"

Dolwyd's dull voice filled the air and Madelayne stirred, wiping at her face as the old man came around the side of the bed to look at her. Their eyes met and Madelayne could feel the weight of the news the old physic bore. Therefore, she spoke first.

"He is dead," she muttered. "You do not have to tell me. I know."

Dolwyd simply nodded his head, moving to pull a stool next to the bed as Mavia came to stand at the foot of it. Mavia had a kerchief to her nose and it was clear that she was very upset. Madelayne was somewhat resentful for the woman to be so distraught; it wasn't her child, after all. It wasn't her loss. In her grief, she begrudged her friend some grief of her own. At the moment, Madelayne's grief was the only one that mattered.

"He was born with the birthing cord wrapped around his neck, my lady," Dolwyd said in his dull, raspy voice. "There was nothing to be done. He had been dead for a while."

Madelayne looked at the old man, frowning. "But I felt him move only two days ago," she insisted. "He had been moving the entire time."

Dolwyd shrugged. "He was more than likely going through his death throes," he said cruelly, causing Mavia to gasp in horror. "When he was born, there was nothing to be done. 'Tis God's will that the child be born dead. God has taken him home again."

Madelayne shifted on the bed, causing herself great pain as she did so. Everything from the breasts down was horrifically sore. She grunted softly in pain as she moved. "Speak not to me of God," she said. "God is cruel for taking my son away before I was given the chance to feel him tug hungrily at my breast, or before I was able to see the color of his hair. Was it red, Dolwyd? Did he look like Cairn?"

Dolwyd hesitated a moment before nodding his head. "He was a fat baby with Lord l'Ebreux's hair," he said. "I had him wrapped carefully and put in the cold of the vault. You may see him if you wish."

Madelayne thought on that prospect, of seeing the child she had prayed so hard for lying dead in her arms. As ghastly as it sounded, something deep inside her needed to see him and hold him. She needed to see this child she had felt growing inside of her for the past several months. She knew him, when he liked to sleep and when he liked to wake. He was always awake at the oddest hours, kicking her belly in the middle of the night. The thought made her smile but just as quickly, the tears came again. She would miss those little kicks.

She would miss *him*.

"I will see him," she whispered. "Have someone bring him to me. I will see him."

Dolwyd looked at Mavia, who nodded quickly and fled the chamber. She still had her kerchief to her nose. When the woman was gone, Dolwyd seemed to grow serious, which was odd for the usually unemotional physic.

"The birth was difficult," he said. "The lad was stuck inside of you and I had to fight to free him else you would not have survived. I have sewn you up as best I can but I do not know if you will be able to have more children after this. Mayhap you were not meant to. After two dead sons, mayhap it is a blessing that you cannot."

He was always frank in his words, lacking the tact to relay them sometimes. Madelayne looked at him, aghast. "How can you say such a thing?" she hissed. "Of course there will be more children for me. How can you so carelessly take away the one ability that makes me a woman? If you take that ability away from me, there is nothing left. I will be useless."

Dolwyd lifted his eyebrows as if to agree with her. "You have your beauty and your vigor," he said. "Cairn will not find you useless, I think. He is far gone in love with you so your inability to bear him a son will not matter. I would not worry over it."

It was a careless thing to say and Madelayne had enough of the man's tactless manner. He may have been an excellent healer, but he was brash and cruel. At this moment, she didn't like him at all.

"Get out," she hissed. "I do not want to see you anymore."

Dolwyd wasn't insulted in the least. Women, in his opinion, were often irrational and fickle creatures, especially when it came to childbearing. He simply stood up and pushed his stool over to the wall, tugging on his dirty, smelly robes as he moved for the door.

"As you say, my lady," he said. "But I will be back later to bind your breasts. Without a child to nurse, they will produce milk and it will become painful for you. Binding them will dry your milk."

Madelayne didn't even know what to say. She was overwhelmed with the old physic's assessment that she may never bear children again and now he wanted to dry up her milk. She didn't want to surrender to that dismal prediction, not yet. Not now. As Dolwyd quit the chamber, she put her hand to her breasts, which were sore and engorged, and squeezed. Pulling at a nipple immediately brought forth a stream of milk. It stained her gown. She kept her hand on her right breast and began to weep, squeezing the breast and causing more and more milk to leak out. There was something therapeutic in it, something that convinced her that she would still be able to produce a child someday. But if not a child, then this would be the last of it. The last milk she would ever produce.

Milk for a son who was not to be.

Dolwyd could hear Madelayne weeping as he shut her chamber door. He sighed faintly, indeed dredging up the will to feel the least bit sorry for her because after two dead children, surely the woman had a right to be distraught. In time, she would understand that his forthright bedside manner and his inclination to bind her breasts were for the best. As he headed for the narrow stairs that would take him down to the keep entry level, his mind lingered on the lady. He was so distracted with her that he was nearly bowled over by Mavia as she burst out at the top of the steps.

"Great Gods!" Dolwyd hissed, grabbing his chest to still his startled heart. "Are you mad, woman?"

Mavia's face was white. "The army," she gasped. "I saw them entering the bailey as I was going to the vault! Dolwyd, they have wounded!"

Dolwyd was on the move.

## ❦

"Is he still alive?"

Thomas was nearly shouting the question at Reece and Ewan. The big de Poyer brothers, grizzled with stubble and exhausted from having transported Kaspian from Beeston, both lifted a hand to Thomas' inquiry.

"Aye," Ewan, the older brother, answered. "He is alive, but barely. Did someone send for Dolwyd?"

The bailey of Lavister was chaotic as men poured in through the gatehouse, both the wounded and the able-bodied. Clouds of dust were kicking up in the air as men shuffled around, disorderly, although Thomas was trying very much to control the throng. Unfortunately, he was more focused on the wagon being driven into the bailey by Ewan that contained not only Kaspian's, but Cairn's body as well. Kaspian had been in and out of consciousness, lying next to his dead second in command, as Thomas and the other knights returned the army home.

"I will find the old man," Reece said. He had been in the bed of the wagon, now leaping over the side. "I will see where he is!"

Thomas let him go, watching the young knight rush towards the keep. Meanwhile, he directed Ewan off to the left, over near the stables, to get the wagon out of the way as more wounded were brought in. Out of the nine hundred men Kaspian had taken to Beeston, they'd lost seventeen men and had one hundred and three wounded. Those were fairly significant ratios considering their initial information on Beeston had been that it was a small skirmish. It hadn't been small in the least and it had been a very costly one.

"Thomas?" Kaspian's weak voice began to call out to the knight. "Thomas, where is my horse?"

Thomas, hearing his name, bailed from his steed and rushed to the edge of the wagon where Kaspian was squirming about, listlessly.

"Your horse is safe, Kaspian," he said. "The soldiers are already taking him to the stables to be tended."

Kaspian kept kicking a big leg, an involuntary action because he had so much pain in his torso that it was radiating down his right leg.

"Have him prepared," he mumbled.

"Aye, Kaspian."

"I must go to Chester."

"Aye, Kaspian."

After that, Kaspian seemed to drift off again, uncomfortable, feverish, and injured. Thomas simply stood there, looking at the man, before his gaze drifted to Cairn. The big, red-haired knight was wrapped up in a roll of oiled cloth that they used for shelter. He had been dead these two days now and had moved beyond the stiff stage and was now simply limp. He was also changing color, as Thomas could see one of his big hands sticking outside of the material. The bottom of the hand was purple while the top was ghostly white. As he stood there looking at the pair, Ewan came up beside him.

"What will we do when Lady l'Ebreux wants to see her husband?" he asked grimly. "The man is already starting to smell. This is not for a lady to see."

Thomas simply shook his head; although he was a man of considerable experience as a knight, he'd always been more of a follower than a leader, which was why de Dalyn had been able to take over the battle at Beeston so easily. Being in command of Lavister's army was an overwhelming experience for Thomas and he wished to heaven that he could push the duty off on someone else. But there was no one else. Ewan was a good knight but too emotional in his command ability and Reece was simply too young, so the duty fell on Thomas as next in the chain of command behind Cairn. He sincerely wished it wasn't so.

"We have little choice," he said. "Find a couple of men to take Cairn down into the vault. It is cold down there and should keep the man from putrefying too much before we bury him. Wrap him up so only his head is visible; the lady need not see all of the blood on his body."

Ewan's dark gaze moved to Cairn, all covered up with the oiled cloth. He grunted with some regret. "I can still hardly believe it," he said quietly. "It was supposed to be a small skirmish, Thomas. A small skirmish! Small skirmishes do not kill one of the best knights I have ever seen!"

"I know."

"Nor do they wound, inarguably, the best knight on the Marches!"

He meant Kaspian. Thomas was simply nodding his head, feeling Ewan's angst. "I know," he said again, patiently. "You remain here for Dolwyd. Help the man transport Kaspian any way you can. I must find Madelayne and deliver the news."

Ewan sighed heavily, rolling his eyes. "This will make her child come," he said. "It will throw her into fits and cause her child to come."

Thomas' gaze was on the keep as he put a hand on Ewan's shoulder. "That cannot be helped," he said steadily. "I will do what I can to ease the blow. Meanwhile, you make sure that Cairn is taken to the vault and properly presented so that his wife can see him."

Ewan nodded in agreement, watching Thomas as the man made his way towards the squat, green-stoned keep of Lavister. There was such shock in the air right now, shock at what had happened at Beeston, but Ewan knew that the shock would soon turn to grief and the grief to rage. For the past two days, the men had only been concerned with returning to Lavister with their dead and wounded as the Welsh had scattered back to their mountains beyond the Marches.

But the threat of the Welsh was still very much prevalent, still lurking in their minds even as they made haste back to Lavister. Now that they were back within the tall walls and strong gates, the thought of the Welsh threat faded but the realization that they'd lost their two commanders was sinking in. Ewan looked around him; he could see that realization on the face of every man in the army. Lavister, in fact, was devastated. Ewan wondered if they would ever be able to pull themselves back together again, strong as they had been when Kaspian and Cairn commanded. It was difficult to shrug off the gloom.

Thomas felt the gloom, too, as he made his way towards the keep. He was nearly to the door when he ran into Reece, who was flushed and winded. He indicated that Dolwyd was on his way down from the top of the keep. As Reece ran off, Thomas entered the low-ceilinged entry of Lavister's keep, and nearly plowed into his wife as she came down the stairs with Dolwyd on her tail.

Mavia's eyes widened at the sight of her husband and she threw her arms around his neck, squeezing tightly.

"Thomas!" she gasped. "God be praised! You have returned safely to me!"

Thomas hugged his wife, accepting her kisses to his cheek. But her affection made him uncomfortable, as it always had, so he tried to discreetly push her away. "I have returned safely," he said, looking between Mavia and Dolwyd as the old man hovered on the steps behind his wife. "But Cairn and Kaspian have not. Dolwyd, Kaspian is badly wounded. He is in the wagon. Ewan is standing guard. You must go to him right away."

Mavia's expression slackened with horror. "Sweet Jesus," she breathed. "What happened to him?"

"He took a spear to the abdomen," Thomas said with a surprising lack of emotion. "And Cairn is dead. Where is Madelayne?"

Mavia's hands flew to her mouth to stifle the sobs but they came anyway. Tears filled her eyes. "It cannot be!" she said through her fingers. "Please say it is not so!"

Thomas nodded, unable to keep the grief from his features. "I wish it was not true, but it is," he said. "I must tell Madelayne before she realizes the army is returned and goes looking for him."

As Mavia struggled not to openly weep, Dolwyd pointed to the floors above. "She will not," he said because Mavia was unable to speak. "Lady l'Ebreux delivered a dead son this morning and is confined to her bed. It will be difficult for her to hear that her husband is dead as well."

The grief on Thomas' features deepened and he shook his head sadly. "That is unfortunate," he said. "Was there no hope for the child, Dolwyd?"

The old physic shook his head. "Born with the birth cord wrapped around his neck, he was," he said. Then, he pushed Mavia aside so he could finish descending the steps. "When you tell Lady l'Ebreux, be kind about it. She has suffered great loss."

That was a fairly compassionate statement coming from the usually tactless physic. Quickly, he shuffled past Thomas and out into the bailey beyond. Thomas turned to watch him as he made his way over to the wagon with Ewan and Reece encouraging him onward. Reece even took him by the arm and began pulling, simply to make him move faster. Dolwyd slapped the young knight's hand away. He was moving as fast as he wanted to move. Thomas returned his attention to his wife.

"Come with me," he muttered. "This is an unhappy duty that I must share with you. Madelayne will need your comfort."

Mavia was wiping her cheeks as she allowed her husband to direct her back up the stairs. "This is tragedy beyond reason," she said softly. "First the child and now Cairn. I do not know how Madelayne will take the news. What happened to Cairn? How was he killed?"

Thomas was weary, so very weary. Cairn's death was dragging at him tremendously, made worse because it was now his job to inform the man's wife. He hated the responsibility and he hated emotion of any kind. This situation called for both and he wasn't good at either.

"He was pulled off of his horse and set upon by many Welsh," he said. "At least, that was what I was told. Another knight saw it happen. He managed to pull Cairn away from the attack but by then it was too late."

Mavia shook her head sadly. "And Kaspian?"

Thomas sighed heavily as they reached the top of the stairs. "His injury was unexpected," he said. "He was fighting a group of Welsh who only seemed to be armed with clubs and daggers, but a spear was thrown and hit him in the lower torso. It went through his mail and tore into his belly. But he did not go down; he simply yanked the spear out and tossed it aside. He kept fighting before eventually making it back to the wounded under his own power but by then, his blood loss was great. Had he not insisted on staying in the battle even with that great wound, it might have gone better for him, but as it is, he compromised himself with his sense of duty."

Mavia pondered the information. "He believes that he is invincible," she said quietly. "He always has. Everyone says that about him."

Thomas grunted. "It is that arrogance that may cost him his life," he said. They were at the top of the stairs now, right outside of Madelayne's closed chamber door. He took a deep breath and pointed at it. "Knock, if you will. I cannot delay this."

Mavia felt the tears again but she fought them. She needed to be strong for her friend. With a soft knock on the door, she admitted both herself and her husband, and closed the door softly behind them.

## ♋

Madelayne heard the footsteps enter behind her but she didn't move. She was certain it was a servant, perhaps even someone with her dead son in their arms. Perhaps they'd come to show her, as she'd requested. Sick to her stomach, she didn't want to turn around and look. Now she was suddenly afraid to look, panic welling in her chest. Perhaps if she didn't look at the baby, he really couldn't be dead. She could pretend that someone had stolen him away and she would always hold out hope that, someday, he would come back.

But those were foolish thoughts. Deep down, she knew she was being ridiculous. Taking a deep breath, she forced her bravery and turned around, surprised to see that Mavia had entered the chamber. Right behind Mavia came Thomas, dirty and exhausted from days of fighting. As soon as Madelayne saw Thomas, fear welled in her heart and she struggled to sit up. She felt a good deal of angst at the knight's appearance.

"Mavia, *nay!*" Madelayne hissed weakly. "You did not tell Thomas, did you? I do not want him to tell Cairn. I must do it!"

Mavia went to her, quickly, trying to soothe her. "Do not trouble yourself, darling," she said, taking one of Madelayne's hands and squeezing it. The other hand was on her shoulder, trying to keep the woman on the bed. "I swear to you that Thomas will not... darling, he has come to speak with you. Please be calm. You should not trouble yourself so."

Mavia was being insistent and soothing, but to Madelayne, she came across as demanding. She was practically pushing her back onto the bed. Madelayne frowned, trying to push the woman away because she seemed too eager to put her hands on her.

"Did Mavia tell you?" Madelayne asked the weary-looking knight. "My son was born this morning. He is dead. I will tell Cairn myself so you must not tell him. Please, Thomas. Do not tell him!"

She was pleading with him. Thomas sighed heavily, mentally preparing what he had to say. Lady Madelayne was pale, her lovely eyes dark-circled, and she had a rather wild-eyed look about her at the moment. He simply couldn't get past that panicked expression, terrified with the thought that Thomas was going to tell Cairn of his dead son before she could. He held out a hand to her, silently begging for calm.

"I will not," he said, his voice dull and hoarse. "Lady, surely, I cannot. I wish to God that I could. I wish to God that *you* could, but you cannot. Lady l'Ebreux, God has taken Cairn to heaven to be with him. He fell in the battle at Beeston and he is gone. It is my wholly unhappy duty to tell you this news, especially in light of what happened this morning, but I have no choice. I pray that you can forgive me for the news I bear and understand that your husband died a glorious death."

Madelayne blinked as if she didn't quite understand what she was being told. She had not slept in almost two days, long days of laboring to bring forth her dead son, so her mind was muddled. She stared at Thomas as Mavia kept trying to squeeze her hand. She yanked her hand away from the woman, unwilling to be comforted. Her gaze upon Thomas was intense.

"That cannot be," she said with an odd calm. "He assured me that he would be home in a few days. He assured me that it was a light skirmish. Surely he is coming home; you must be mistaken, Thomas."

Thomas shook his head sadly. "Alas, I am not," he replied. "Cairn was set upon by rebels and they took his life. I have brought him home to be buried, now with his son that did not survive. I am so very sorry for your losses, Madelayne. Cairn was a good man."

Madelayne stared at the man as she came to realize what he was telling her. The news suddenly hit her like a hammer, colliding with her fragile mind, and her eyes widened and the breath left her. She couldn't breathe at all, now clutching at her throat.

"Nay," she gasped. "It cannot be true!"

"It is."

"It is not! He promised to return to me!"

Thomas sighed heavily, hanging his head. "I have brought him home for you to see him," he said, rather coldly. "He is being taken to the vault. I will take you there when you are strong enough to bear it."

Madelayne was looking at him but she wasn't really seeing him; she was looking through him, perhaps seeing all of those dreams she'd had with a happy husband and family, now gone forever. Swept away by the winds of fate, up into the heavens where memories and souls were kept. Cairn was now one of those lost stars, too, those dead souls that nearly everyone she had ever loved had become.

Now, she was truly alone.

Dear God, it couldn't be true!

*... could it?*

It was too much to bear. Madelayne fell back onto the bed, closing her eyes tightly and trying to bury herself in the coverlet. She didn't want to see anyone or face anyone. She didn't want to see their expressions, an agonizing reflection of what her life had now become in the pitiful trappings of sorrow. Was it really true? Had Cairn really left her alone in this terrible world?

"Madelayne, darling," Mavia was standing over her now, trying to comfort her friend. "I am so sorry for Cairn but it is as Thomas said; God has called him to heaven. It is God's will, my darling girl. You may find comfort in that."

Madelayne was shutting down; her mind, her eyes, her body. Everything was shutting down, buried beneath that coverlet. It was far too painful to face the truth, too painful to realize her husband would never return to her.

"Go away," she groaned at Mavia. "Go away and leave me!"

Mavia had her hands on Madelayne again, stroking her through the coverlet. What was meant to give comfort only gave pain, the lashings of pity swept upon a woman's flesh.

"But...!" Mavia gasped.

"*Go!*" Madelayne screamed. "Go away! Go, I say!"

She was growing hysterical and Thomas reached out, grabbing his wife's hand, pulling her from the room. Madelayne was beyond rational thought at that moment and he knew it. Better to remove his wife so if

Madelayne was going to go mad and destroy the room, or worse, even herself, Mavia would not be caught in the maelstrom.

Sometimes, those in grief simply needed to be left alone. Surely none of them could comfort a woman who had lost her husband and son on the same day. Surely there was no relief to be had from that particular brand of anguish.

Even as Mavia and Thomas emerged into the landing beyond the chamber and shut the door behind them, they could hear Madelayne's mournful sobbing through the very walls.

"You will remain here in case she needs you," Thomas said to his wife, his voice dull. "I must go see to everything else now. This has been a costly battle, indeed."

Mavia simply nodded, leaning against the door and hearing her friend weep. As Thomas walked away and headed back down the stairs, Mavia found herself wishing she could give her friend more comfort. It was sad misfortune that the news was delivered by Thomas, a cold and unemotional man. Perhaps if it had been delivered by someone else, someone with feeling, the impact upon Madelayne might not have been so great.

But Mavia knew the truth; the news would have been terrible regardless of who delivered it.

The young, childless lady was now a widow.

# CHAPTER THREE

Kaspian was in terrible shape.

Dolwyd knew that from his first glimpse of the man lying pale and limp on the wagon bed next to Cairn, who was wrapped up in an oiled cloth. The old physic climbed into the wagon bed with surprising ease, pulling back the tarp to look at Cairn first before moving to Kaspian.

The man was essentially stripped from the waist down and the top of his leather breeches had been cut away where the spear had entered the lower right portion of his abdomen. The weapon had pushed leather and chain mail and dirt into Kaspian's bowels and Dolwyd knew that, more than likely, they were going to lose the man to fever and poison. When the abdomen was compromised, and especially the bowels, that was almost always the case.

But the man wasn't dead yet. Dolwyd put his hand to Kaspian's face, feeling the fever, and he inspected the wound that was festering. He caught a whiff of bowel as well, telling him that it had been perforated. It wasn't a strong smell, but it was there nonetheless. There was no time to waste.

"Take him to his chamber, quickly," he instructed the knights standing around the wagon. "I must get my medicament bag. Move him quickly and I will meet you in his chamber."

The knights began to move. Ewan whistled between his teeth, a shrill sound, and a handful of men ran over from the gatehouse to his summons. Soon enough, Kaspian was being carefully moved off of the wagon bed and carried by his men into the keep. He was a very large man, and heavy, which made it difficult for his men to easily carry him. There were five of them doing the heavy lifting with Ewan following along behind. Reece remained back with Cairn and had four soldiers move the man's body out of the wagon for transport to the vault.

Once inside the keep, it was even more difficult to move Kaspian. His quarters were on the top floor of the keep; literally, the entire top floor because that level only had one chamber and it was a very big one. The spiral stairs that connected the levels were narrow and steep, so it was slow going as they lifted Kaspian up one step at a time. At one point, Thomas met them on the stairs and they actually had to set Kaspian down and drag him up the central portion of the flight leading to the third floor because it narrowed so much. Once he was on the top level, however, the men picked him up again and carried him into his chamber.

His bed was big and messy, as was the chamber in general, the functional abode of a military commander. It smelled like soot and an unwashed male body, typical of a man who lived by himself and wasn't particularly concerned about hygiene. The soldiers lay Kaspian upon his bed, sweaty and grunting with the exertion of having carried the man up two flights of stairs. Thomas then ushered all the men out but Ewan remained behind to help Thomas strip Kaspian of his boots. They also moved the bed away from the wall so that Dolwyd could get to either side of Kaspian with ease. When all of that was finished, the knights waited uneasily for the old physic to make an appearance.

It wasn't a long wait, fortunately, for Dolwyd could move quickly when he wanted to. He appeared in the chamber with a satchel full of medicaments and instruments he used in the course of his healing. Already, he began snapping his fingers and issuing orders.

"Ewan," he said. "Start a fire in the hearth; be quick about it. And Thomas – you will help me with my instruments. Take them out of my bag and set them on Kaspian's table. Hurry!"

There was a sense of urgency in the room as the knights began to move. Ewan quickly stared a fire in the hearth, igniting the kindling with a flint and stone, as Thomas cleaned out Dolwyd's bag and set everything upon the big table in Kaspian's room as he'd been instructed. A small oil lamp with an iron frame on it was set up and upon the frame, over the flame, was a small iron pot that Dolwyd began to immediately put ingredients into. A bit of wine and powder went into it and he stirred it with his finger. Thomas also pulled forth a mortar and pestle, and any number of small sacks containing mysterious and magical ingredients, as least as far as Thomas was concerned. What Dolwyd did had always fascinated him. The man had limitless knowledge, which was going to be put to the test now in the case of Kaspian.

As Ewan's fire began to blaze and he went to fetch water to boil in the hearth, Dolwyd was busily working at his table, surrounded by his ingredients. Thomas watched over Dolwyd's shoulder curiously.

Dolwyd brewed and mashed, and then he carefully pulled forth an earthenware jug that wasHe is corked tight with a wooden plug. When he popped it open, even Thomas could smell the putrid scent. He pointed in disgust.

"What is *that?*" he asked. "It smells like a man's arse!"

Dolwyd grinned, unusual for the old man. "It is called rotten tea," he said. "It is brewed with bread and left to sit and fester in the warmth. It smells horrible and tastes even worse, but if a man has a fever, it will cure him. It will kill whatever poison ails him."

Thomas watched the old man pour a measure of the black liquid into a cup. "And a man must drink this?" he asked, appalled.

Dolwyd nodded. "Aye," he replied. "You must help me get some of this into St. Hèver. His wound is already festering and if we cannot cure it, he will die."

Thomas followed the old physic as the little man shuffled over to Kaspian, who was unconscious on his bed. They both paused a moment, looking down at their once-mighty commander.

"He has grown very weak, very quickly over the past day," Thomas said grimly. "We have withheld all food and water from him because of his wound."

Dolwyd nodded faintly, his gaze lingering on the powerful commanding officer. "As well you should have," he said. "With a belly wound like that, he cannot eat anything. It will only make it worse."

"What of boiled water?"

Dolwyd simply shook his head. "I fear it will only hurt him."

Thomas looked at the physic. "Then what?" he demanded. "Do we simply let him starve to death? If the fever does not kill him, the lack of food will."

Dolwyd started to reply when an idea suddenly hit him. Food for St. Hèver was out of the question because of the belly wound; more than that, the man was too weak to eat. He could take liquids, however, yet they needed to be nourishing if that was his only way of gaining strength. And they needed to be particularly gentle on a man's system, something as bland and soothing as mother's milk.

… *mother's milk!*

Aye, a grand idea came to Dolwyd, one that made the most sense in the world as far as he was concerned. In the chamber below them was a lady full of milk for a dead infant, a nourishing liquid that was meant to sooth and fill a hungry belly. It was the perfect food for an infant and the perfect food for a dying man with a belly wound. He could think of nothing better for St. Hèver.

"We have food for him," Dolwyd said, the light of excitement in his old eyes. "The food God has intended for man from the beginning of time."

Thomas looked at him, puzzled. "What food?"

Dolwyd pointed to the floor as if indicating the lady beneath them. "Lady l'Ebreux is producing milk for a dead child," he said. "It is nourishing and gentle and will aid St. Hèver in his quest to heal."

Thomas' eyebrows lifted in surprise and perhaps some outrage. "Milk?" he repeated. "You intend to feed Kaspian *milk*?"

Dolwyd nodded eagerly. "Indeed," he said. "It is a perfect solution. In fact, perhaps it is God's intention all along. He has given us a wet nurse for St. Hèver – if Lady l'Ebreux cannot nurse her child, then she can nurse a man back to health."

Thomas was dumbfounded. "But a lady…," he sputtered. "Nursing a grown *man*?"

"What is your issue with such a thing?"

Thomas threw up his hands. "It is improper to say the least!"

Dolwyd waved him off. "Pah!" he spat. "'Tis foolish to stand on such proprieties, Thomas. Shall we let St. Hèver die simply because you are uncomfortable with what will cure him? Pah, I say!"

The old man was shuffling towards Kaspian again, cup of rotten tea in hand, as Thomas stood there with his mouth open. "But…," he said, moving forward to help lift Kaspian's head when Dolwyd motioned to him. "But what will Lady l'Ebreux think of such a thing? She has only just lost her husband and…."

Dolwyd put the cup to Kaspian's lips, tipping it, as he cut Thomas off. "And what?"

Thomas was growing frustrated. "*And* she may take issue with putting a grown man to her breast," he pointed out. "It is not only improper, it is unseemly and uncivilized. A man does not nurse from a grown woman's breasts!"

"Would you rather have St. Hèver die, then?"

Thomas backed down. "Nay," he muttered after a moment. "Of course I do not, but…"

Dolwyd finished pouring the rotten tea down Kaspian's throat as the man coughed and choked on it. "Silence," Dolwyd hissed at Thomas. "Bring me Lady l'Ebreux immediately. Carry her up here, for it should be difficult for her to walk after just having given birth. Tell her I am in need of her."

"I will not!"

"Unless you want St. Hèver to die, you will."

Thomas took the cup from the old man and set it aside as Dolwyd carefully laid Kaspian's head back down to his pillow, peeling back the eyelids and looking at the man's eyes. All the while, Thomas stood there, uncertain and uncomfortable. When Dolwyd realized the man was still standing there, he snapped his boney fingers at him.

"What are you waiting for?" he asked. "Bring me Lady l'Ebreux. This shall help her as well; it will help her heal if the breasts are stimulated. It heals the womb. She needs this as much as St. Hèver does so stop acting like an embarrassed child and bring me the lady. Time is of the essence."

With a reluctant sigh, Thomas finally did as he was told. But upon collecting Madelayne from her bed chamber, for she was still deeply grieving and did not wish to leave, he only told her that Dolwyd needed her and nothing more. He would leave it up to the old physic to inform Lady l'Ebreux that she was to become a lifeline for St. Hèver. That she was about to become a wet nurse for a grown man.

Once he carried the woman up to Kaspian's chamber, he didn't stay to see the end result. He was already too uneasy with the entire situation. Setting Lady l'Ebreux on unsteady feet, he fled the chamber and went in search of his wife, who would want to hear of Dolwyd's outrageous scheme of forcing a woman to feed a grown man from her breasts.

Oddly enough, however, Mavia wasn't as outraged as her husband was. Something about Kaspian St. Hèver suckling on her breasts rather excited her, but Thomas never need know that.

The mere thought brought a smile to her lips.

She envied Madelayne.

# CHAPTER FOUR

"**I** am to do *what?*"

Madelayne wasn't sure she had heard correctly but Dolwyd was quite calm, and quite firm, in his reply.

"You will get into bed and nurse the man as you would an infant," the old man explained again. "My lady, you have milk in your breasts that will keep him alive. He has a belly wound and cannot eat. He cannot take any food at all. But you have food within you, meant for your dead child, that will help him survive. Will you not do this for St. Hèver?"

Madelayne had entered Kaspian's chamber as a woman in the throes of grief. Grief for her dead son, her dead husband. All about her was pain. But Dolwyd's unconventional request had her full attention, enough to momentarily push her grief aside because the request was so shocking in nature. To *nurse* a grown man? She had never heard of anything so outrageous in her life.

Still, the way Dolwyd had explained it made perfect sense. Her milk would keep the man alive. Pushing aside the shocking nature of the request, it did, in theory, make utter sense. Still, her initial reaction was to refuse. Staunchly so. But the more she thought on what Dolwyd was trying to accomplish, the more confusion she began to feel. His only goal was in healing St. Hèver and she was the means to an end. Her wary gaze moved to St. Hèver, lying still and pale upon his bed. A very big man, a very handsome man… who needed her breasts.

She was stunned.

"He is to… to…?" she stammered, motioning hesitantly to her breasts.

Dolwyd nodded patiently. "Suckle you," he finished for her. "Please, my lady… St. Hèver's life depends upon you. Will you not save his life?"

Madelayne didn't know what to say. She gazed at the unconscious man, mouth agape, wondering how she could decline such a thing.

Increasingly, she knew she couldn't, not after the way Dolwyd had put it. St. Hèver's life depended on her, so he said and in looking at the man, she could believe it. He looked terrible. But the grief in her heart, the sorrow for her son and husband that had consumed her, was wreaking havoc with her generosity.

"How can you ask me such a thing?" she demanded. "It is because of St. Hèver that Cairn is dead. Now you would have me save the life of the man who saw my husband to his doom? I will not do it, I say!"

Dolwyd remained surprisingly patient with her. "Cairn is not dead because of St. Hèver," he said. "Cairn is dead because of the Welsh. It has nothing to do with Kaspian at all. The Welsh have already claimed your husband. Will you now let them claim St. Hèver as well when you have the power to save him?"

Madelayne looked at the man, fury in her eyes. "You cannot put this all on me," she said. "It is unfair of you to put his life in my hands. I do not want the responsibility!"

Dolwyd sighed. "Lady, the milk in your breasts was put there by God," he said. "It was meant to feed your child, who is dead. That milk has the capability of sustaining life. It would be a sin for you to deliberately withhold it from someone who needs it."

Her eyebrows furrowed. "Speak not to me of God," she hissed. "He took my son and my husband on the same day. I am not particularly grateful to God at the moment so it would be wise to keep Him out of this conversation."

Dolwyd could see the fire in her eyes that had often frightened Cairn. The man had spoken much about his wife's iron will, something he was subjected to but something he *willingly* subjected himself to. It was well known that Cairn was deeply in love with his beautiful wife but it was also quite clear she had never returned those feelings. She had been kind to him, and dutiful, but there had never been a spark in her eyes when it came to Cairn. The man knew it but it didn't seem to matter; she was his wife and that was all he cared about. And Madelayne had always treated him with polite regard, as an obedient wife would.

But the lust for him, the passion, had never been there.

Still, Madelayne respected her husband and she was fond of him in a brotherly sort of way, which made completing her physical wifely duties something of a task and not a desire. Cairn's lust for his wife had been insatiable and she would never deny him his wants; she simply laid on the bed and spread her legs as any good wife would. Dolwyd knew this because he could hear Cairn bedding his wife nightly. He would grunt and gasp in his fervor but she never uttered a sound. That was what told Dolwyd, and most other inhabitants in the keep, that her passion never matched his.

A sad but true fact.

In spite of her lack of passion, she had obeyed him, as her husband, and that was all that truly mattered. A wife was only meant to be obedient even if she never loved him. Even now, Dolwyd knew she would have still obeyed her husband had he been standing next to her. Therefore, he made a calculated move to that regard.

"What would Cairn tell you to do?" he asked pointedly. "Would he tell you not to give St. Hèver that which would keep him alive?"

It was like a shot to the heart for Madelayne, whose gaze trailed to St. Hèver once more. Dolwyd could see the defiance drain out of her face, leaving sadness and indecision in its wake. After several long moments, she hesitantly shook her head.

"He would not be so selfish," she said. "He considered Kaspian his friend."

"Would he tell you to help the man, then?"

She nodded faintly before averting her gaze, ashamed and embarrassed at what had been asked of her, of what she realized she would have to do.

"He would," she said softly.

Dolwyd didn't want to give her any more time to think on it. He grasped her arm and pulled her towards the bed. "Then you must help him," he said. "Get into the bed next to him and offer him your breast, as you would offer it to an infant. The instinct to suckle is a strong one. Do this, Madelayne. *Help* him."

Madelayne didn't acknowledge that he'd called her by her given name. Dolwyd was usually much more formal but this circumstance didn't call for formality. It called for action. She was moving stiffly, however, because her legs hurt and everything between her legs hurt even more. It was difficult to walk but she did so, allowing Dolwyd to lead her towards Kaspian as the man lay, wounded, upon the dirty bed linens. When Dolwyd pulled back the coverlet, Madelayne could see the bandage around the lower part of his abdomen. He smelled of urine and infection.

With great uncertainty, she sat on the bed and Dolwyd helped her lift her legs onto the mattress. She shifted around, uncomfortably, trying to find a good position to do what needed to be done as Dolwyd stood over her and watched most attentively. But his attention was quite embarrassing to Madelayne, given what she had been asked to do.

"I will not do this with you watching," she said flatly, unlacing the top of her shift. "If you want me to do this, then you will give me privacy to do it. I'll not have you watch."

Dolwyd snorted. "I would say your modesty at this point is misplaced."

She turned to glare at him. "Look away or I'll not do this."

He sighed heavily. "When I had my hands betwixt your legs delivering your child, you said naught about it. And one breast looks like all the rest."

She continued to scowl at him, so much so that he eventually turned away in a huff of annoyance. But the truth was that he understood somewhat; he was viewing the situation from a completely clinical standpoint but she was viewing it as something rather intimate. Since he wanted her to tend St. Hèver very much, he didn't want to agitate her. He would give her some privacy.

So he returned to his table and focused on his medicaments as Madelayne returned her attention to the knight breathing heavily beside her. *St. Hèver.* She'd never had much thought about the man other than the fact he was very cold, very serious, and very handsome. All of the women thought so. But his manners were so icy that it precluded any manner of attraction any female might have for him. Some would even say he was terribly unpleasant, but Madelayne didn't give the man much thought one way or the other. She never really had.

Until now – now, she was looking at this cold, serious soldier who was very badly wounded and needed her help. Truth be told, she began to feel some pity for him, injured as he was. She supposed that it was, indeed, her duty to help him however she could, as Cairn's friend, and if her milk could not do her child any good, then perhaps it could help St. Hèver. Looking down into his pale and stubbled face, she was a bit more apt to try now than she had been before.

With a faint sigh, because she was still rather embarrassed to be offering the man her breast, she finished unlacing the top of her shift and she pulled it aside, off of her right shoulder, to expose an engorged right breast. He was flat on the mattress next to her, his face turned in her direction, and she shifted so she could put a nipple by his half-open mouth. Since he wasn't conscious, she wondered if it would even work, if he would sense the nipple by his mouth, so she sought to help him along.

Gently, she rubbed her nipple against his lower lip, hoping he would get a feel for it or at least sense that she was there. When that didn't work, she squeezed her breast slightly and allowed drops of milk to fall into his mouth. She did it a few times before he reacted, licking his lips, tasting the sweet milk on his tongue. She did it again, creating a bit of a stream into his mouth, and this time he reacted faster. He licked his lips again and it seemed to her that he was trying to wake up a bit. She lowered the nipple into his mouth and put her hand on his cheek, as one would do when trying to coax an infant into suckling.

"Drink," she whispered, tickling his cheek. "Drink and regain your strength, St. Hèver. Take what I can offer."

The stimulation to his cheek and mouth brought him around and without even opening his eyes, he latched on to her nipple with surprising strength and suckled so hard that he brought pricks of pain shooting through her breast. Madelayne gasped at the force of it, yelping softly when he suddenly grabbed at her and pulled her against him. She was sore and stiff, and St. Hèver might have been on death's door, but he was still quite strong in moving her towards him. He suckled her hungrily, his hands moving from her torso, where he had grasped her to pull her against him, to her breasts where he started kneading her.

Madelayne was overwhelmed with his innate response, for it was an instantaneous sexual response, much as Cairn had responded to her in their love making. She was trying to keep his hands off of her breasts but she couldn't quite keep them both off of her, and when one wasn't on her breast, he was grasping her bottom through her heavy robe. Every motion St. Hèver had was sexual, an innate response of a man to a woman, and Madelayne was becoming quite embarrassed as she tried to, literally, fight him off. But even as she struggled to keep his behavior proper, something else was happening, an innate sense of sexuality that surprised her.

Something she never knew she possessed.

She had just given birth but there was no mistaking the fire in her belly. She was cramping up, terribly, as he nursed at her breasts and she was torn between the pain of it and the powerful sense of lust the man seemed to spark in her. It was the oddest thing, really; she'd never experienced anything like it. The more St. Hèver suckled, the stronger the sensations became. The more she wanted him to suckle.

"Is he feeding, then?" Dolwyd asked, still over by his table.

Hugely embarrassed at what was taking place, Madelayne answered. "He… he is," she said, grunting when he grabbed her bottom again. "But he cannot seem to keep his hands from me. He is much stronger than you think he is, Dolwyd."

She said it with some panic in her voice and Dolwyd continued on with his medicaments. "There is nothing like a firm young lass in a man's bed to bring him to life," he muttered. "As long as he is feeding, give him all he will take."

Madelayne was now trying to keep Kaspian from putting his hand between her legs, at one point, slapping his hand and yanking on a finger, nearly pulling it off of his hand, to keep him away. He simply went back to her breasts, now suckling on the left one because he's suckled the right one dry. He seemed to have calmed down a bit at this point, simply settling in to nurse rather than trying to grab her. A bit frazzled, Madelayne sighed heavily with relief.

"He seems quite hungry," she said, holding his head against her breast as a kind of instinctive motherly action. "It pains me when he suckles, Dolwyd."

"Where?"

"My belly."

The old man nodded as he measured out a cup of wine. "That is good," he said. "It is your womb, healing itself after the birth. In a sense, St. Hèver is doing you a favor just as you are doing one for him. His suckling is bringing about the healing of your womb. It was what your child would have done, had he lived."

Oddly enough, Madelayne was starting to see what Dolwyd had been trying to explain to her from the beginning – the benefits of this odd and somewhat embarrassing situation. Kaspian needed her and she needed him, and once he'd stopped grabbing at her, they settled in to a kind of fragile peace. Madelayne gazed down at the man as he suckled, feeling her heart flutter, just a bit.

"The pain in my belly is most strong," she said.

"Is it uncomfortable?"

"It is bearable."

"You will feel the pain for the next few days as your womb regains its size again."

After that, Madelayne didn't say much more. She continued to hold St. Hèver's head to her breast as he nursed her dry on both breasts and finally fell into a deep and satisfied sleep. Madelayne remained next to him, wrapped up in his big arms and trapped against him, unable to move. She thought she might leave his bed and return to her own, but the truth was that she was exhausted from the day and, in fact, nestled in St. Hèver's warm bed had her very drowsy.

She hated herself for thinking that she liked it. The only man she had ever lain next to had been Cairn and he never much allowed her to move away from him. His arms were always around her and it was something she'd become accustomed to. There was comfort there, that was true, but sometimes she didn't want to sleep with the man all wrapped up around her. There were even times she had wished she could sleep alone, somewhere else.

Therefore, lying next to Kaspian was something of a new experience altogether. His arms around her weren't cloying or needy; there was something strong and powerful and protective about him, even in his wounded state. And there was a scent about him... something musky and manly – that filled her nostrils in a not unpleasant way. In fact, she rather liked the smell. It was new and different.

And his warmth... aye, it was more than likely the fever that made him so warm, but, God's Bones, there was such comfort in it. She never knew there could be such comfort in a man's arms.

As Dolwyd continued to tinker with his medicaments and the fire in the hearth snapped and hissed, Madelayne fell asleep next to Kaspian, as fine and deep a sleep as she'd had in many a night. Somehow, sleeping next to the man brought her some comfort, as odd as it seemed.

When she awoke later on, near dawn, it was to Kaspian nursing on her again.

# CHAPTER FIVE

*Five days later*

**K**aspian was aware of a body next to him and soft, gentle singing.

*So softly sings, the wind, my babe; On the wings of angels, may you sleep, my babe; God watches over you, my arms embrace you; never are you more content than now; Sleep, my lovely, sleep....*

Whoever was singing had a lovely voice, but he wasn't interested in that as much as he was the soft, warm, and small form next to him. He simply lay there, trying to orient himself and wondering who was in his bed, singing to him. He shifted slightly; his body was sore and it hurt to move. His mind, foggy, tried to recall his last memory. Something about a battle... through the mists of his brain... he remembered leaving Lavister for Beeston. *Beeston!* Such a brutal attack, with Welsh as plentiful as ants, swarming Beeston and the English who came to help. God, there were so many of them.

Memories came falling down upon him, pouring down like a waterfall. He well remembered the Welsh bastards who fought without honor. Surely, some of them could be skilled fighters but they fought dirty, cutting men's legs out from underneath them and killing horses to get to the mounted riders. All signs of bastards without a speck of honor amongst them.

Bastards who had, nonetheless, managed to cut him down. He closed his eyes, remembering the spear that pierced his gut. He had removed the weapon and tried to ignore the bleeding, but bright red blood streamed from him and he knew that he had been badly wounded. With the greatest reluctance, he had turned for the rear of the battle where the wounded were being gathered. He remembered riding into the midst of the wounded and falling from his horse. He tried to walk under his own power but he couldn't seem to do it; men were carrying him, taking him somewhere to lie down.

And then he caught a glimpse of a red-haired knight, lying dead and beaten. *Cairn*. Horror had swept him when he realized that Cairn had been struck down. The man was lying away from the wounded with the dead, but Kaspian had recognized him. His heart sank. And that was about the last thing he remembered until this moment. Grunting with the pain that even lifting his hand caused, he wiped at his crusty eyes.

"St. Hèver?" a soft, sweet voice floated into his ear. "Can you hear me?"

He stopped rubbing at his eyes, turning with some shock towards the sound of the voice. It was coming from that soft, petite body next to him. Just about the time he laid eyes on Lady l'Ebreux who was, in fact, in his bed, he also caught sight of Dolwyd. The old man was over near Kaspian's work table, now evidently cluttered with the old physic's possessions. When Dolwyd saw that Kaspian was actually looking at him, he came away from the table and towards the bed.

"So you are awake?" the old man said, sounding surprised. "I was coming to think you might never awaken. How do you feel?"

Kaspian looked at the old man, puzzled by the comment, but he was even more puzzled by the fact that Lady l'Ebreux was in his bed. He was so muddled that it was difficult to form a coherent thought and he struggled through the cobwebs.

"Weary," he said. "I feel… very weary. And sore. I am at Lavister?"

Dolwyd nodded. "You are," he said. "Your men brought you back from Beeston. You were wounded there. Do you remember anything?"

Kaspian nodded, faintly. "I remember being wounded," he said. "I remember being taken to the wounded and I remember seeing…."

He suddenly looked at Madelayne, flicking his eyes up in her direction. He didn't want to mention what he saw, which was Cairn's battered body, but he was more than interested in the woman's close proximity to him. God's Bones, if the woman wasn't lying in his bed! What was going on here, anyway?

Dolwyd saw where Kaspian's attention went, straight to Madelayne. He suspected the man was hesitant to speak of the battle, and of Cairn, so he hastened to reassure him.

"Cairn came back with you as well, but there was nothing to be done for him," he said quietly. "He has been put in Lavister's vault. It is Lady l'Ebreux's wish that he be buried in Shrewsbury with his sons."

Kaspian's brow furrowed. "Sons?"

"Cairn's second son was born the day you were returned from Beeston," Madelayne said. She could see the confusion in Kaspian's dazed face. "He did not survive his birth. I wish for Cairn to be buried with both of his sons, in the yard at Shrewsbury."

Kaspian felt a great deal of sorrow at the news. He well remembered the day they had departed for Beeston and how Cairn had lingered long enough to anger him, lingering with a pregnant wife who was frightened of birthing yet another dead son. In fact, Kaspian felt like an ogre for having been so impatient with Cairn but he'd had a battle on his mind and not a pregnant woman. Now, he was coming to regret his behavior a great deal.

"I am very sorry, Lady l'Ebreux," he said, somewhat awkwardly. "It would seem that you have had two very unhappy events in your life recently and I am quite sorry to hear of the child's passing. As for Cairn... I will miss him. He was a good man."

Madelayne simply nodded her head and averted her gaze, unable or unwilling to speak more on her husband. Kaspian's attention lingered on her for a moment, his thoughts shifting from Cairn's death back to the fact that the woman was in his bed. Never one to skirt a subject, he looked the old physic in the eye.

"Dolwyd," he said. "I cannot help but notice Lady l'Ebreux is lying next to me. I would assume there is a reason for this?"

Dolwyd gave him a half-grin, acknowledging the tone of his voice. As if Kaspian was both suspicious and afraid, but perhaps even interested, to know the answer to that question.

"Not for anything so scandalous, I assure you," he said. "She has been feeding you."

Kaspian was more puzzled than he had been before. "Feeding me?" he repeated. "I do not need for her to get into bed with me in order to feed me."

Dolwyd nodded. "You do," he replied. "With your belly wound, you cannot take solid food. Lady l'Ebreux has graciously been feeding you that which was meant for her child and, along with the medicines I have been giving you, I believe you are on the path to healing. The poison in your belly has diminished and you have awakened. That is the sign that your strength is returning."

Kaspian stared at him. "Feeding me that which was meant for her...?" It suddenly occurred to him what Dolwyd meant. "Feeding me... *that*?"

Dolwyd snorted at the expression on Kaspian's face. "Milk, good knight," he said. "You have been fed milk. It is the best thing for you in your condition."

Kaspian didn't know what to say. He still wasn't over the part where Cairn's widow had been feeding him... milk from her *breasts*? Shocked, he turned to look at Lady l'Ebreux and suddenly, a host of murky memories collapsed around him. He thought he had been having erotic dreams of making love to a woman, nursing against her breasts, but it was coming to occur to him that perhaps those weren't dreams at all.

Somehow, his subconscious mind had been feeding him these memories of things he had done, of what had occurred when he had been in a delirious state, and now he found himself looking at Lady l'Ebreux and thinking very naughty thoughts. Was it really true?

Had he really been suckling milk from her beautiful breasts all this time... and loving it?

He cleared his throat softly, unsure and embarrassed, noticing that Lady l'Ebreux wasn't looking at him, either. Perhaps she was as embarrassed as he was about it. But on the other hand, she'd given him some of the more pleasurable erotic dreams he'd ever had. She was a beautiful woman, after all... stunningly so. He'd always thought that. And she was a widow, which meant she had no husband. She was unattached. And so was he. So there really wasn't anything wrong with what she had been doing other than the fact that it was highly improper from a social standpoint. And, more than likely, from a religious one, too.

But the fact remained that she had selflessly given of herself to him, a man who had barely spoken ten words to her in the two years they had been acquainted. She had fed him the nourishment meant for the son she had so badly wanted. He'd never heard of such a sacrifice. Now, he was starting to feel rather guilty for his lack of regard for her all of this time. It hadn't been deliberate... *or had it?*

Gazing at the woman, he wasn't entirely sure that his ignorance of her hadn't been deliberate. She was so beautiful that he knew he was attracted to her, so his lack of attention towards her was probably to keep him from thinking about her. She was, after all, Cairn's wife. He would never violate that trust. But the truth was that she wasn't Cairn's wife any longer. That was over with, a barrier removed. That being the case, he wasn't sure he could stop his interest now.

Remembering the warmth and sexual satisfaction over the past several days, he wasn't entirely sure he wanted to stop anything. Out of respect for Cairn, he knew he needed to give the woman time to grieve and he fully intended to do so. But after that… he couldn't make any promises about his attention towards her.

Caddish thoughts, but he couldn't help it.

"Lady l'Ebreux," he said in his deep, husky voice. "I believe gratitude is in order. What you have done for me… it is quite selfless. I do not know if I can ever thank you."

Madelayne had been gazing off into the room, perhaps too embarrassed to look at Kaspian when he realized what she had been doing for him. As if it was a dirty secret they shared. When he spoke softly, in a tone that sent shivers up her spine, she turned to look at him.

"It was no trouble," she said, smiling weakly. "It is what Cairn would have wanted."

Kaspian's eyebrows lifted in surprise. "He would have wanted me to… you to…?"

He was motioning in the general direction of her chest and her smile turned genuine. "He would have wanted me to assist you in any way I could," she said, giggling when he rolled his eyes as he realized what she meant. "Cairn always thought quite highly of you, my lord. He would have wanted me to help you."

Kaspian gazed up at her, a faint smile on his lips. "His generosity is beyond measure," he said quietly. "As is yours. You have my thanks."

The gratitude was genuine and Madelayne flushed, looking away again because the expression on his face was more than gratitude; there was something warm there as well. She felt quite hot and bothered by it, but the truth was that she had spent the past five days with the man suckling at her breasts and she had come to look forward to it. He may have been delirious, but there was an innate sense in him that cuddled up to her every time she fed him, his powerful arms going about her and his heated mouth on her nipples. It had been cozy and intimate.

He would lick her, too, lapping at her nipples to harden them so he could feed. It was so incredibly personal that she was now coming to have trouble separating her duty from her want. Twice, in fact, his suckling had caused her to climax without him so much as touching the dark curls between her legs. His suckling had so highly aroused her that her sensitive body had responded in kind. Even thinking about him suckling on her made her feel warm and giddy, wanting that heady human contact. God's Bones, it was wrong. It was so very wrong and she knew it. But she was coming to crave it nonetheless.

Upon the heels of those thoughts came the guilt she'd been wrestling with for five days as well, guilt over Cairn's death. She felt horrible that she was experiencing excitement with another man so soon after Cairn's death, even if that excitement was in the course of her attempts to help the man. She felt disrespectful to Cairn's memory, tortured by her sexual response to St. Hèver's mouth upon her breasts, but the fact of the matter was that Cairn never gave her such excitement. She had been fond of him, as one would be fond of a friend, but there had never been anything more than that. She'd never loved him. He'd never given her the sensations that St. Hèver had.

Still, she had to mourn the man. She couldn't simply sully his memory by thinking lustful thoughts of another man, and her duty to Cairn, at the moment, was very strong even if her body felt no such loyalty. Therefore, she found herself in a torn and terrible position.

"St. Hèver," Dolwyd said, breaking whatever the spell of silence between Madelayne and Kaspian held. "If you can take some nourishment now, do it. I must give you more rotten tea and it goes down easier if there is something already in your belly."

Kaspian simply nodded, looking to Madelayne almost apologetically. She forced a wan smile. "You and I have been doing this for the better part of a week," she said. "You were simply unaware. If it helps to close your eyes so you cannot see me, then close them."

He frowned. "Why would I not want to see you?" he said. "Although I will admit this feels a bit... strange."

Madelayne nodded in understanding. "I have had five days to overcome the strangeness," she said. "You have not. I simply tell myself that Cairn would have wanted this and it is much easier for me to do my duty. Mayhap if you think the same thing, it will go easier for you as well."

He wasn't sure what to say to her. She was speaking as if this were a very reluctant chore, which he took as an insult. He knew he shouldn't feel that way, but he couldn't help it. He could see that she didn't feel nearly the same attraction to this duty that he did so he was coming to think that perhaps she had something against him personally. *She is in mourning*, he told himself. Of course she would think this distasteful.

So he closed his eyes and lay there, listening to her fumble with the top of her shift. Something warm and sweet was put to his lips and he immediately latched on, suckling firmly, drawing out her sweet liquid. He couldn't help the hand that lifted, going to her breast, squeezing and kneading it. God's Bones, it was the most wonderful sensation in the world, and she was sweet and soft beneath his calloused hand. He could feel himself becoming aroused.

*Is she trembling?* He swore he could feel her quiver and it fed the lust he was trying so hard to keep at bay. He squeezed harder, putting the palm of his hand against her other breast, through the material, and rubbing at it. He could hear her gasp as that nipple, stimulated, began to leak milk and with his eyes still closed, he yanked that portion of her shift off of her right shoulder, exposing the right breast, and he began to suckle back and forth between the two.

Caught up in the maelstrom, Madelayne braced herself against his shoulders as he suckled from both breasts. He was creating such a fire within her that it was an extreme test of her willpower not to give in to his power. Back by the table, Dolwyd said something about retrieving more medicines from his chamber and she heard the door shut behind him, but her mind was in such a state that she really didn't hear what he said. She was singularly focused on Kaspian as he drained her breasts and trying very hard not to climax. But it was a monumental struggle. At one point, he suckled her hard enough to cause her to gasp. He froze.

"Did I hurt you?" he asked huskily.

Madelayne was startled by the sound of his voice, as if reminding her that he was conscious and aware. She'd gone the past five days in a fantasy world where only she was aware of the intimacy of their act.

"A little," she admitted. "They are rather tender"

*They*, as in her breasts. Kaspian immediately took his hands away from her. "I apologize," he said. "I... I believe I have had enough. Thank you, my lady."

Quickly, Madelayne covered herself up and climbed out of the bed, keeping her back turned to him as he watched. Kaspian's gaze trailed down her torso, thinking of the curves and sweet skin the fabric covered up and feeling like a monster for thinking such thoughts.

"Mayhap we should speak on a few things now that I am coherent," he said to her. "It seems that quite a bit has happened since I was rendered unconscious."

Madelayne finished tying up the top of her shift and pulled her robe over her body, covering herself up, as she turned to him.

"Aye," she said honestly. "A good deal has."

He shifted on the bed, realizing he was very sore from having lain in one position for some time. He tried to find a comfortable spot.

"First," he said. "Who returned from Beeston? Where are my knights?"

Madelayne thought on the question as she went to sit on a stool next to the table. "Thomas, Reece, and Ewan returned," she said. "Thomas has been in command but it is my understanding that he sent a missive to the king to inform him of your injuries and Cairn's passing."

Kaspian thought on that. "Good," he said. "When I am finished with you, I shall want to speak with Thomas. You will send him to me."

"Aye, my lord."

He looked at her for a moment, thinking many different things. Mostly, he was focusing on Madelayne and her situation. For Cairn's sake, he needed to be concerned with the widow.

"Let us discuss you," he said. "Please let me once again express my sorrow at Cairn's passing. I do not have many friends but I considered Cairn one. His death leaves me greatly saddened."

Madelayne looked to her hands, fidgeting. "As it leaves me."

"And the passing of your child," he said quietly. "Quite terrible."

"Aye, my lord."

His gaze lingered on her lowered head. "What do you intend to do now?" he asked. "With Cairn gone, surely you have plans."

Her head came back up to look at him. "Plans?" she repeated, somewhat confused. "I do not know what you mean."

"What will you do now? Where will you go?"

Madelayne had no idea. "I... I do not know," she said. "I had not thought on it. I have no family other than my father and he was more than happy to be rid of me when Cairn and I married. I have not spoken with him in two years. But... but I suppose I should return to him. There is no need for me to remain at Lavister. Surely you do not want a widowed woman hanging about."

Kaspian realized that he didn't like the idea of her leaving. "You and Lady Allington-More have been my chatelaines for the past few years," he said. "Lavister is very well run thanks to the two of you. I would not want to lose that efficiency."

Madelayne cocked her head curiously at his attitude. "But I cannot remain," she said. "I have no husband here; it would not be right.

Mavia is more than able to assume the duties herself. You do not need me."

He shook his head, faintly. "That is where you are wrong," he said. "You are far more efficient than Mavia is and if it is a choice between the two of you, I should choose you. Besides, it would be uncharitable for me to insist you leave Lavister after all of the loss you have suffered and I do not wish to be uncharitable. 'Tis a cruel fact that a widowed woman such as yourself will face a bleak outlook on your life without a husband to take care of you."

He may have been trying to convince her that remaining at Lavister as the chatelaine was the best course of action, but he was only succeeding in making her feel worse about the entire circumstance. She had been feeling enough self-pity about her situation without him being so brutally frank about it.

"As I said, I can return to my father," she said, embarrassed that he was making it clear that he viewed her as a charity case. "I worked with him before and I can do it again. You need not keep me at Lavister simply because you feel as if you should."

Kaspian wasn't catching on to the fact that he had insulted her. He had never been very good with women in that sense. "As I said, you are efficient as chatelaine and that is why I would ask you to remain," he said. "Surely you would rather remain here with people that you know. And Mavia is your friend, so surely you do not want to leave her."

Madelayne shrugged. "I do not, but that does not change the fact that with my husband dead, it simply would not be right for me to remain here alone."

"Then I will insist you stay."

She looked at him pointedly. "My lord, I do not need your charity," she said frankly. "I will return to my father and you do not have to worry about me telling others that you turned me out. I would say no such thing."

He was finally coming to see what she thought of the conversation and of him, as if he were asking her to stay purely out of pity. He hastened to assure her that was not the case. "You would be doing me a favor by remaining," he said. "You will become my ward and everything will be proper. Or do you wish to return to your father so much?"

She shook her head hesitantly. "I do not, my lord, but...."

He cut her off. "Kaspian."

She had no idea what he meant. "My lord?"

"You may even call me Kaspian. Addressing me formally seems strange under these circumstances. May I call you Madelayne?"

She nodded before she could even think about what he had asked because the conversation had her muddled. "You may," she said. "But… are you certain I will not be a burden?"

"You let me worry about that," he said. "For now, you will continue to sleep in the chamber you shared with Cairn and you will continue with your chatelaine duties. It is the least I can do for Cairn, Madelayne. You will remain here with us until the situation must be addressed again."

Madelayne had no idea how to respond to him. She simply nodded her head, feeling confused and strange about the entire conversation. In fact, she didn't want to talk about it any longer, knowing that he was allowing her to stay because he felt pity for her. She didn't like that at all. She didn't want to be a charity act for him.

"You said that you wished to see Thomas?" she said, rising off of the stool and heading for the chamber door. "Would you like me to send him to you now?"

Kaspian watched her move, stiffly, and he remembered she had given birth days before. "Send a servant for him," he said. "You will not go. Return to your chamber now and I will send for you when I need you."

*When I need you.* More suckling, more touching, more silent fantasies in her heart about the man. A cold, impersonal man who made her feel more alive and excited than Cairn ever had. It was terrible and unhealthy for her to think that her association with St. Hèver could be anything more than what it already was. The man only needed her breasts. He didn't need, or want, anything else about her. She was a burden but he was too loyal to Cairn to say so.

A burden. *A widowed woman will face a bleak outlook.*

As long as she remained at Lavister, that was all she would ever be.

Silently, she quit the chamber and sent a servant to find Thomas. As she slowly descended the stairs and entered her chamber, she looked at the four walls around her and realized that she couldn't bear to remain. She only had horrible memories of this room, where she had birthed two dead children, and where her dead husband had lived with her. As she looked around, all she could see was pain. She couldn't stay no matter what St. Hèver said.

She had to go.

Before the hour was out, she did.

# CHAPTER SIX

*W*rexham.

It was where her father lived, the one she rarely spoke to, but it was her destination. It wasn't too far from Lavister, to the south about ten miles, so she knew she could make it in a day. She knew that she could have made it faster had she been feeling better, but she was still rather stiff from having given birth a scant five days before.

In the days when women were kept in bed for weeks after giving birth, the fact that she was up and moving, and determined to walk to Wrexham no less, would classify her as something of an idiot, but Madelayne didn't particularly care. She simply wanted to get away from Lavister where the commander of the keep viewed her as something to be pitied. It was better for them all if she left and she kept telling herself that with every step she took.

This month had been oddly dry which meant the roads were in decent shape to travel upon. Usually, May was a very wet month but this year had seen the anomalistic dry weather pattern. It wasn't particularly cold, either, but Madelayne was wrapped up in a dark cloak against the weather and also to keep herself covered up. She felt exposed enough, a woman on foot, without announcing herself to anyone she passed. On this main road, she had passed several people, traveling out of Wrexham to points north, but most had been farmers or merchants who hadn't give her much notice. She wanted it that way.

*Foolish wench!*

She could hear her father now when she showed up at his door. He'd never much cared for his only child and had been quite happy when Cairn had offered for her hand. Melchoir Gray was a cousin to the Northumberland Grays, an offshoot of a big family who had become wealthy from transporting fabrics and oils from France. Melchoir's father had started the business, eschewing his family ties because he fell in love with a peasant woman. That woman had been Madelayne's grandmother, a woman she remembered well and a woman she greatly favored, but a cancer had taken her grandmother away just as a cancer had taken away Madelayne's own mother away. Two women in the family taken by a cancer. It was something Melchoir had never been able to rectify in his mind.

So he ignored his daughter and spent his time on his business or whores. There was no kind way to put it – he spent his money on women, sometimes two at a time, and Madelayne had grown up in a fine house in Wrexham, ignoring the trollops who dined with her father and stole from him. On more than one occasion, Madelayne had caught the women stealing plate from the feasting hall and she'd taken a broom to them, beating them soundly as they fled the house empty-handed.

It was her duty to tend the house, and the contents, and she wouldn't tolerate thievery from her father's companions. Madelayne had been the keeper of the home as well as of the business books, as she had been educated in her youth and knew how to cipher. It was only through her that her father's business survived, for he spent money foolishly, so she wondered what she was going to find upon returning home.

It made her sick to think about returning to that home where her father cared nothing for her and she lived in loneliness. Perhaps that had been her main reason for marrying Cairn; to get away from the loneliness. But at least in her father's home, she wouldn't feel as if she were a burden like she would if she remained at Lavister.

The morning progressed as she continued to walk, moving along the edge of the road, trying to keep her head down and not make eye contact with anyone. It was incredibly foolish to be traveling like this but she had little choice. Her body hurt badly but she ignored it, trudging along, trying not to think on what she'd left behind. *A dead husband, dead sons…* that was all she had left behind. A life that was over before it ever really got started. She missed Cairn's guidance and protective instincts but, strangely enough, she also missed the feel of Kaspian's arms around her. Those few short days with the man, sleeping alongside him, knowing he was dependent upon what she could provide… instead of bonding to her child, she had bonded with a grown man.

And she felt guilty as hell about it.

So she moved quickly down the road, scurrying along, praying to make it to Wrexham before dark. All the while, she kept her thoughts on what lay ahead, on what she would say to her father when he saw her standing on his doorstep. But no matter what she said to him, she knew what he would say to her…

*Foolish wench!*

She thought on resuming her old life, on seeing her old friends, friends she hadn't seen since she had married Cairn. There were the baker and her daughter, and the butcher's wife down the avenue. Round women with lips that were perpetually blabbing everyone's business. She thought on what she would tell them about her life at Lavister, being married to a powerful knight. She knew that whatever she told them would make it all over town in minutes. She was thinking so much on seeing her old friends again that she failed to notice a farmer and his son who had been trailing her.

The pair had passed her going the opposite way about an hour earlier and they had eyed her with great interest. A lone woman traveling down the road. The farmer had been more interested in her than his son had been, for the farmer had recently lost his wife and had been on the hunt for a new one for some time. This lone woman traveling might be the perfect wife for him. A lady that surely had no one, for no man would allow his woman to travel alone as she was. He had caught a glimpse of her face beneath her hood and from what he had seen, she was pleasant enough to look at. And that gave him an idea.

So he turned the wagon around and began following her, far enough back so she couldn't hear noise from the horse or the creak of the wagon wheels. Surely she didn't have any kin or even a husband if she was traveling alone, which was why the farmer thought he might very well like to pluck her right off of the road and take her home. The son wasn't so keen in abducting the woman but the father was. He needed someone to cook and clean and sew, and he'd been unsuccessful in finding a wife candidate on their weekly visits to town. Some women seemed to react adversely to his one brown eye and one milky eye, and also the fact that he reeked of cheese. It was an appalling smell but the farmer had never really noticed. He didn't particularly care.

If he couldn't find a wife, then he would take one.

Unaware of the danger behind her, Madelayne's pace was slowing as her exhaustion increased. Her legs hurt, her belly ached, and the area between her legs was sore and chaffing. She could see Wrexham in the distance, nestled amongst the green Welsh hills, so her goal was in sight. Just a little further and she would be able to rest under her father's roof. Already, she was thinking ahead to what possible mess might be facing her in the two years since she left. She would be surprised if her father was still in business. Therefore, she tried to work up the focus to face what was to come and not think about what she left.

*Who* she left.

But those were her last coherent thoughts as someone grabbed her from behind. Strong, sinewy arms went around her ribs, lifting her off the ground, and she immediately began to scream and fight. Caught off guard as she was, all she could feel was utter terror. Cowering in fear, or surrendering to whoever had overwhelmed her, never came to mind. She screamed her head off, trying to kick whoever held her, and she was lucky enough to make contact with a bony knee. With a curse, the man dropped her and she fell to her hands and knees. Before she could pick herself up again, he grabbed her once more and dragged her backwards. Madelayne could see a wheel and part of a wagon bed from the corner of her eye.

"Enough with ye!" a male voice in the wagon hissed. "Put her in the wagon and let us be off!"

Panicked, Madelayne continued to twist and fight, knowing that whoever had her was strong and obviously male. There was a second man in the wagon. Put her in the wagon and let us be off! Obviously, they had wicked intentions. God help her, she was in the exact situation she had strived not to fall in to during her journey from Lavister. She'd covered herself up, tried to move swiftly, but in spite of her precautions, she had been set upon. She could only scold herself at the moment, much in the words of her father.

*Foolish wench!*

Aye, she was foolish. Foolish to let herself fall into lascivious hands. But she had fight in her and unless they tied her up or killed her, she would continue to fight. She wouldn't make an easy victim. So she continued screaming and fighting with her overtaxed and sore body, even as she was dragged into the bed of the wagon and the entire vehicle lurched forward, nearly spilling her and her abductor off of it. Madelayne tried to climb off of the wagon bed but bony, strong fingers held her tight.

She kept screaming even as the wagon bounced off the road and headed west, hoping someone would hear her and help.

Praying for a miracle.

*God help me!*

"Get back into bed! Are you mad?"

Dolwyd was shouting at Kaspian, who had just risen to his feet from his deathbed. Thomas and Ewan were standing in the chamber, watching him, their expressions grim. It was grim news indeed that Ewan had just brought to Kaspian, enough to propel the man out of his bed. Even as he rose to his feet, he staggered and Thomas reached out to grab him. Dolwyd was flitting around, shouting.

"You are not well, St. Hèver, not in the least!" he said. "You must get back into bed!"

Kaspian was gray with pain and exertion, holding on to Thomas so he wouldn't fall down. Ignoring the furious physic, he looked at Ewan.

"I saw her in my chamber this morning, a mere few hours ago," he said, hunched over with a hand over his injury. "Have you looked everywhere? She did not simply disappear."

Ewan shook his head, glancing at Thomas and conveying the fact that he was most reluctant to continue speaking. He'd entered the chamber with the news that Lady l'Ebreux was missing, but that was as far as he'd gotten before Kaspian was struggling up from his deathbed as if the news somehow meant something to him, deep and personal. Now, Ewan had to tell him all of it. The man was on his feet, demanding answers on the whereabouts of the missing widow.

"She did not disappear, my lord," Ewan said hesitantly. "None of the sentries saw her leave, but the cook said that Lady l'Ebreux passed through the kitchens sometime this morning before leaving from the postern gate."

Kaspian's eyebrows lifted in alarm. "So she has left Lavister?" he asked. "And not one of my sentries saw this?"

"I have not questioned everyone, but those I was able to ask did not see her."

"What of the cook? Why did she not tell us sooner?"

"Because she is a drunk, my lord, and has been sleeping most of the day. You now that the cook drinks too much. She did not think to tell us."

Kaspian was quickly growing infuriated. "Damnation," he growled. "So Lady l'Ebreux left us some time this morning and we are just now finding out about it? God's Bones, she could be anywhere by now. Did she take a horse?"

Ewan shook his head. "It was my impression that she was on foot."

Kaspian was genuinely at a loss. He was also quite concerned for Madelayne's sake, for obvious reasons, but there was more to it than that. There was an odd fear in his belly, something he'd never experienced before. It was something that suggested his concern went beyond simple compassion. He shook his head, baffled.

"But why would she leave?" he asked, a rhetorical question. "Why would she do it? She was in my chamber this morning and made no indication that she wanted to leave. What would make her leave and not tell anyone?"

Thomas was still holding on to Kaspian as the man tried to gain his bearings. "You spoke to her at length this morning, did you not?" he asked. "What did you say to her that might cause her to flee?"

Thomas didn't say it in an accusing manner and Kaspian didn't take it that way. It was a logical question considering Kaspian had been the last person to speak with her. He thought very hard on his conversation with Madelayne and of what he could have possibly said to upset the woman enough to cause her to run off. Usually a man of sharp recall, his mind was still muddled a bit from his injury and weakness. He struggled to recall every word.

"I asked her to remain at Lavister as chatelaine," he said. "It is the least I can do considering her husband met his death under my command. She seemed agreeable to it."

"Is that all you said to her?"

Kaspian shrugged. "I expressed my sorrow at Cairn's loss," he said. "I asked her to remain as my chatelaine because it is a cruel fact that a widowed woman faces a bleak outlook on life without a husband to take care of her."

Thomas lifted his eyebrow rather dubiously. "Did you tell her that?"

"I did," Kaspian said, then noticed something odd in Thomas' expression. "Why?"

"Well...."

Based on Thomas' hesitant manner, Kaspian was beginning to catch on. "Could she have possibly been insulted by it?"

Thomas shrugged, glancing at Ewan, who was still looking quite serious about the entire situation. "Mayhap," he said. "It was probably not something she wanted to hear."

"It was the truth."

Thomas scratched his head at Kaspian's blunt manner. "Truth or not, I would imagine it upset her to hear such a thing from you," he said. "But in any case, it does not matter. The fact remains that she has fled. It matters not why. Did she give you any indication where she might go if she left Lavister?"

Kaspian nodded. "She said she could return to her father," he said. "I was with Cairn when he first met Madelayne and, at that time, her father lived in Wrexham. I do not know if he is still there or if that is where she would go, but it seems like a logical place to start."

"Then Wrexham is where we shall go," Thomas said, motioning to Ewan, who fled the chamber with the intention of forming a search party to recover Lady l'Ebreux. "Thank God it is not far. Return to your bed, Kaspian. We will find the lady and bring her back."

Kaspian was shaking his head. "Nay," he said. "I must go. You may have trouble convincing her to return and, obviously, I said something to send her away. I must be the one to bring her back."

Thomas glanced over at Dolwyd, who was standing by his medicament table shaking his head in distress. "Kaspian," Thomas said, lowering his voice. "You have only just awoken from a grave injury. You are not well in the least. Exerting yourself in your search for the lady could make your injury far worse and you may never recover."

Kaspian ignored him for the most part. "If I can stand, I can ride," he said flatly. "Where is my armor? Where is my sword? Bring them to me, Thomas. And have my steed prepared and waiting for me. We have no time to waste; a woman traveling alone could find herself in all manner of danger."

It was clear that Kaspian would not be kept down. He was stubborn that way. He was also brave that way. It seemed as if he were most determined to save Lady l'Ebreux from danger and determined in a way that Thomas had never seen from him before. The Kaspian he knew would have cursed Lady l'Ebreux for her stupidity but he would have done his duty nonetheless. But in this case, Kaspian wasn't cursing the woman at all. In fact, he seemed quite concerned for her to the point of panic, which was exceedingly odd. But Thomas attributed that edginess to the fact that Kaspian felt responsible for the woman on Cairn's behalf.

As Thomas wrestled with Kaspian's determined manner, Dolwyd was watching the scene closely. He wasn't at all happy with what was going on, distressed that Kaspian should think of the lady's safety over his health. He had a host of knights ready to ride to her aid but that evidently wasn't good enough; he had to ride, too.

"St. Hèver," the old physic grumbled, a far cry from the shouting he had been doing earlier. "You will do yourself far more damage than good if you go. Your body needs rest, man. Do you not understand that?"

Kaspian fixed the old man in the eye as he let go of Thomas and tried to stand tall, to prove he was fit to ride. "I understand," he said steadily. "But this is something I must do. I cannot fail Cairn in such a way. His son was lost and now is wife is missing. Surely I must have sent her away with something I said."

"But you cannot be sure of that. Women are strange creatures not given to the rationalities of a man."

"Be that as it may, it is my duty to bring her back, Dolwyd. If you cannot understand that, then I cannot explain it any better."

Dolwyd sighed heavily and turned away, mostly because he knew there was nothing he could say to change Kaspian's mind. In his opinion, the man was as good as dead. This trip to find Lady l'Ebreux was going to be the death of him and Dolwyd resigned himself to that fact. But there was nothing he could do. He could understand the man's sense of responsibility towards his dead friend's wife, but there was more to it than that. Dolwyd sensed that beneath all of that knightly duty and honor, something in Kaspian's expression suggested that perhaps he *wanted* to go after the woman for reasons that had nothing to do with Cairn.

Therefore, he shut his mouth. It wouldn't do any good, anyway, to argue with the man. But he collected his worn, torn satchel and began piling stuff into it.

"Then if you must go, I will go, too," he said, thrusting a finger at Kaspian when the man lifted an eyebrow at him. "Like it or not, you are a sick man and if you intend to do this foolish thing, I will go with you to make sure you survive it. Do not argue with me, St. Hèver. If you go, I go."

Kaspian frowned, conveying his displeasure without actually speaking. Thomas was already at the man's wardrobe, pulling out clothing he could wear considering he was still in the breeches he had been wearing when he was injured.

As Dolwyd fumed and didn't lift a finger to help, it was Thomas who helped Kaspian dress, very slowly, in a fresh pair of leather breeches and a clean tunic. Even though they kept squires at Lavister,

Thomas didn't want anyone to see Kaspian in his lowly state in order to preserve the man's dignity. All the while, Kaspian kept trying to keep his bandage from slipping but Dolwyd still wouldn't help. At that point, he seemed to be busy with something on his medicament table and by the time Kaspian was finished, the old man came to him with a small cup and handed it to him.

"Drink this," he told him.

Kaspian did but the moment it passed over his tongue, he choked and sputtered. He handed the cup back to the old man, a disgusted expression on his face.

"What in the hell is that?" he demanded.

Dolwyd took the cup and set it down on the table, his manner casual. "Rotten tea," he said. "I have been giving it to you since you were injured. It is what has cured you. Now I give it to you as a precaution since you are determined to go riding out to save a foolish lady."

Kaspian made a face as Thomas pulled a pair of boots out from the wardrobe and indicated for Kaspian to sit. "I think I recall that taste," he said, lowering his body onto a stool next to the table and perching on the edge of it gingerly. "What a cruel man you are to force such poison down my throat when I cannot fight back."

It was unexpected humor, mostly to ease Dolwyd's frustration, and it worked. At least marginally. The old man smiled, briefly, but it quickly vanished. He finished packing up his satchel and tied it closed.

"I am going to fetch my steed," he said. "I will leave you with Thomas and meet you down in the ward."

Kaspian watched the old physic shuffle out as Thomas helped him pull on his boots. Kaspian grunted in pain, more than once, but the pain was secondary to the thoughts rolling through his head, thoughts on Dolwyd and Madelayne. He didn't exactly feel up to this duty, but he wasn't going to let injury and weakness stop him. Secretly, he was glad the physic was coming along in case he needed the old man and his talents. He'd always respected Dolwyd for his knowledge but now he was coming to appreciate him just a little more. Something about this injury was making him come to appreciate everyone just a little more, including Thomas, who had helped him dress. It was a kind gesture from the loyal knight.

"Dolwyd never left your side," Thomas said as he finished with the ties on the boot, securing them because Kaspian couldn't bend over. "He slept on the floor next to you the entire time. I am sure he is quite insulted that you are determined to go after Lady l'Ebreux and not heed his advice."

Kaspian sighed faintly. "I must go after her because she kept me alive," he said quietly, glancing at Thomas and seeing the man's odd expression. "Aye, I know what she did for me. I woke up and the woman was lying next to me. And I recall the times she fed me, although I thought I was dreaming them until Dolwyd told me otherwise. I would be far less of a man if I allowed her to run away and suffer danger without trying to bring her back. I owe her a great deal."

Thomas came to understand all of Kaspian's motivation in that softly uttered statement. "I see," he said, standing up and reaching out a hand to help pull Kaspian to his feet. "So you feel obligation to her, then."

Kaspian nodded, grunting at the pain in his groin when he stood on his feet. "Obligation and gratitude," he said. "Moreover, she was Cairn's wife. I already allowed harm to befall him. I cannot let it befall her."

So he felt some guilt for Cairn's death. It was natural, Thomas supposed, but he said nothing more about it. Time was of the essence and they needed to be on their way. Slowly, he led the man from the chamber and preceded him down the narrow stairs, moving slowly and making sure Kaspian was able to keep his balance, before making their way out into the bailey of Lavister.

The men were already gathered near the gatehouse, a party of twenty men, along with Ewan. Reece had been commanded to remain behind on guard. The mood around Lavister had been gloomy since the return from Beeston, gloom and doom because of the condition of Kaspian, but once the men saw him emerge from the keep, it was, to many, as if watching Lazarus emerge from the tomb. Everyone was watching, marveling at the strength of Kaspian, marveling at the determination that he should ride to the aid of l'Ebreux's widow. Aye, they all knew about her escape and there wasn't one man that didn't feel guilty about it. Somehow, they'd missed a lone woman walking away from Lavister. But watching St. Hèver come alive to ride to her rescue gave them all a measure of hope and admiration.

Hope for Lady l'Ebreux and admiration for St. Hèver.

But, in spite of Kaspian's appearance, it took both Thomas and Ewan to help him mount his horse. Once he was in the saddle, he was there for good. He sat like a stone atop his big, brown beast, ready to take charge. With St. Hèver in command again, every man at Lavister had all of the faith in the world that everything was right again. That Lavister was strong again. Watching the man ride from the gatehouse, the confidence of Lavister was restored.

As Lavister's men basked in the joy of St. Hèver's return, Kaspian realized, about twenty feet from the gatehouse, that it was taking all of his strength not to fall from his horse and land in a heap. He was putting on an excellent front, but inside, he was struggling. As the horses were spurred into a gallop, Kaspian was slowly sinking.

He prayed he could find Madelayne before his strength gave out completely.

ᘓ

Madelayne had managed to throw herself off of the wagon bed when it got stuck in some dark, slick mud near a lively brook. She had stopped fighting for a while as the wagon lurched across a meadow, away from the main road, lulling her abductors into a false sense of security by pretending to faint. But that act was cut short when the wagon became stuck in a quagmire of soppy earth. Feeling the wagon falter, she came to life, slugging her captor in the face and throwing herself off of the wagon bed.

She had stunned the man enough so that she could get a good start on him but she didn't head back towards the road. She ran into a grove of trees to the south, a thick smattering of foliage that the brook ran through, and tried to hide. She could hear two men coming for her, speaking angrily to each other as they drew near, and she hunkered down in the thick bushes, trying to stay low and out of sight.

God help her, she was terrified. Moreover, her bruised body was rebelling and everything about her hurt desperately. Her thighs and torso ached from the exertion and she was physically incapable of running for very long and certainly not for very far. Walking had been difficult enough, but she feared she had truly hurt herself by fighting off her attackers. It was her own damnable fault and she knew it, but there was nothing to be done about it now. She had gotten herself into this situation and she was determined to get herself out of it. Wrexham wasn't far off but she realized she wasn't going to make it there by dark. She was fairly certain her abductors weren't going to give up on her so easily and she didn't want to chance coming out of her hiding place any time soon.

She was in a thick cluster of branches and bushes, tucked down by the base of a tree. It was the perfect hiding place, actually. It also gave her a chance to rest, something she desperately needed, so she sat low against the tree trunk, rolled up in a ball, and listened as her abductors began searching close to her. They were shaking bushes; she could hear them, which worried her when they would come to her bush. She was thickly protected but if they took a good look between the branches, they might very well see her. She was still in her black cloak, which was good camouflage in the dim light of the forest, but there was still a chance they might see her.

Therefore, she couldn't rest completely. Her ears were attuned to what was going on around her and even as her abductors moved in her direction, shouting and poking sticks into thick clusters of bushes, they suddenly veered off and headed away from her into an area that was evidently more thickly clustered with trees and growth. Madelayne could hear the men speaking of the perfect hiding place and they even began calling out to her, telling her to show herself because they would beat her if they found her. Relieved they were moving away, Madelayne considered moving out of her hiding place and making a break back towards the road in the opposite direction.

But it was sheer exhaustion that kept her where she was. She was horribly sore and weary from the fight and from the walk, and her legs were cramping up from the position she was sitting in, but still she was afraid to move, afraid that she wouldn't be able to run fast enough if the abductors happened to see her flee. They were still far enough away that she might have a chance to escape them and she seriously weighed her options at that point. She was afraid of what would happen if she left her hiding place and she was afraid of what would happen if she did.

After careful consideration, she decided that it would be better if she tried to run because she could hear them in the distance, beating bushes and she knew, eventually, they would make it over her way. Therefore, she had to run. She couldn't simply wait for them to find her.

Unwinding her legs from beneath her body, she slowly rolled onto her knees, trying to keep abreast of where, exactly, her abductors were. She could hear them, over towards the west, so she crawled through the damp brush, getting her hands and knees dirty, until she emerged from the brush and into a thick bank of trees.

Carefully, she stood up and slipped behind the trees, using them as cover, as she tried to keep an eye on her abductors in the distance. She could still hear them and it gave her confidence. She was putting space between them and her. It gave her such hope and nearly brought tears to her eyes, hoping that, for once, God was looking upon her and would protect her from harm. God had never paid much attention to her in the past, but it would seem that was about to change. She found herself praying fervently for His protection.

The road to Wrexham was just across the meadow in front of her, the same meadow they had crossed in that ramshackle wagon. The grass was waist-high in some places, knee high in most, and she thought she would do better – and not be seen – if she stayed on her hands and knees. So she dropped down and began to crawl across the ground again, grinding mud and rocks into her hands and knees. She left the shelter of the trees and proceeded into the wet grass, continuing to pray for God's help in escaping those who sought to do her harm. Her praying was silent for the most part but when she entered the grass, it became a fervent whisper, as if that would help God hear her better. She didn't dare look back.

It was difficult to crawl in the garment she was wearing and, more than once, her feet became tangled in her cloak, but she continued on, pushing through the wet grass, heading for that road to safety and freedom, or so she hoped. She was determined to make it to the road and run, run as fast and as hard as she could, in the direction of Wrexham. Surely by the time her abductors discovered she had eluded them, she would be to safety.

God, let me get to safety and I swear I will never do anything so foolish again!

She was midway between the trees and the road and she could no longer hear her abductors in the woods behind her. That concerned her somewhat and as she was contemplating turning to see if she could spot them back in the overgrowth, she heard what sounded like thunder. It was coming from the direction of the road, south to be exact, and it grew progressively louder.

Curious, she lifted her head slightly to see where the noise was coming from and was immediately confronted with knights on horseback, dressed for battle, accompanied by at least twenty soldiers who were also on horseback. The knights were on fat, well-fed horses and wore tunics of blue and yellow.

She knew those tunics very well.

*Lavister!*

Madelayne forgot all about the men beating the bushes looking for her. At the sight of men from Lavister, she suddenly bolted to her feet and began screaming. She waved her arms and began to run, trying to catch their attention, but they didn't seem to notice her. Perhaps she was too far away because no one slowed down; no one even looked in her direction. Still screaming, she ran towards the road, waving her arms wildly. While she didn't yet catch their attention, she had caught the attention of the men who had been trying to abduct her.

Madelayne heard a shout behind her and turned to see the two slovenly men burst from the trees and head in her direction. Terrified, Madelayne picked up the pace and, in a burst of speed, tore off towards the road. The collection of knights and soldiers were nearly past her now but she continued to wave her hands and shout, praying someone would see her. Praying that just one man would happen to look over and see her racing across the meadow. All she needed was one man.

Just one.

*Please, God... just one!*

God must have heard her because the very last soldier in the group happened to look over and see a woman running across a field with two men after her. Fortunately, the man was a senior soldier and recognized Lady Madelayne right away. With a piercing whistle, he caught the attention of several men in front of him, who in turn caught the attention of the rest of the group. Kaspian, who had been in the lead with Thomas and Ewan, turned to see what had his soldiers so excited and he was seized with relief and terror to see Madelayne running across a field of blue-green grass with two men in pursuit of her.

The battalion from Lavister turned their mounts for the field and, suddenly, horses were plowing into the grass towards Madelayne. She was so relieved that she started to cry and her legs, so achy and weary, buckled. She fell to her knees as men on horseback charged past her, heading for the two men who had been pursuing her, men who now realized they were in a great deal of trouble. The farmer and his son tried to run but the son was cut down by Ewan while the father was cut down by Thomas. Thomas then ordered the soldiers to go into the trees to see if there were any more men as Kaspian and Dolwyd converged on Madelayne.

On her knees in the wet grass, she wept loudly. Kaspian could hear her crying as he drew near. He was shaky and in great pain, but he managed to pull his steed up a few feet away from her and bail from his horse. In truth, he literally fell off the horse and had to catch himself on the saddle. His legs were quaking and his entire body was screaming with agony. But he ripped off his helm and made his way to Madelayne, taking a knee beside her as she wept and grasping her face between his two big hands. There was great emotion in his expression as he spoke.

"Madelayne," he said earnestly. "Are you well? Have you been injured?"

Madelayne shook her head, sobbing. Tears cascaded down her creamy cheeks. "I am not injured," she wept, his big hands on her face causing her heart to pound against her chest. There was such warmth in his expression. "I am so sorry, Kaspian. I did not mean to cause you such trouble that you would ride to my aid. You should not be out of bed!"

That was very true and he was feeling rather lightheaded now, but he didn't speak on it. He would not acknowledge it. He didn't want to admit that coming after her had been more taxing than he thought it would be. But the fact that she should be concerned for him in the midst of her danger touched him deeply. He'd never had anyone care for his well-being like that before and that endeared her to him even more than she already was.

"It does not matter," he scolded softly. "All that matters is that you are not injured. But why did you leave? What happened that you would run from Lavister and risk yourself so?"

Madelayne was trying very hard to stop her tears but it was difficult. Along with her relief at finally being safe, her sense of embarrassment was great. Gazing at the man, she could feel those torn feelings rising up again, feelings of warmth and excitement for Kaspian against feelings of mourning for Cairn. It was an internal struggle that was only growing worse as Kaspian gazed at her almost as if he were glad to see her.

*Almost as if he cared.*

"I... I would be a burden to you if I remained," she sniffled, trying to fight off the idea that the man might actually care about her. "You were simply being kind by asking me to stay at Lavister, Kaspian, but the truth is that I do not belong there. You were right when you said a widowed woman would face a bleak outlook and it is not your responsibility to provide for me. You are too kind to send me away so I had to leave."

He just looked at her, greatly disheartened by her words. "So I did say something to chase you off," he muttered, realizing his sense of lightheadedness was growing worse. "I suspected as much. Why did you not simply come to me and speak to me of your fears? I did not mean to offend or hurt you, Madelayne. Surely you know that."

Madelayne nodded, her tears calming and nearly gone by now. "I know you did not mean to intentionally offend me," she said. "I never thought that."

His gaze turned soft and a gloved thumb stroked her cheek, ever so faintly. It was a gesture that sent a wild chill up Madelayne's spine.

"Then why did you run away?" he asked quietly.

She averted her gaze. "I told you why. Because you were too kind to send me away."

That thumb stroked her cheek again. "I did not mean to…mean to…."

He suddenly trailed off and his eyes took on a rather glazed look. As Madelayne and Dolwyd watched, Kaspian suddenly pitched right over into the grass and passed out cold.

# CHAPTER SEVEN

*Two days later*

*So softly sings, the wind, my babe; On the wings of angels, may you sleep, my babe; God watches over you, my arms embrace you; never are you more content than now; Sleep, my lovely, sleep....*

Madelayne finished the lullaby, a whispered sonnet. She had become accustomed to singing it to Kaspian over the past two days and it was coming to tenderly suit the man who had probably never known any tenderness at all. He had always seemed hard and cold that way. She gazed down at him, so still and silent on the bed, and her heart twisted with concern.

"He hasn't awoken," she said. "It's been so long, Dolwyd. Why doesn't he wake?"

The old man sat upon a stool and scratched his spotted scalp. "Because he did too much damage to himself riding about the countryside looking for you," he snapped. "Had you not been so stupid, he would be well on the road to recovery now."

Madelayne turned her face from the churlish physic. She was feeling guilty enough without his added anger. "What's done is done and yelling at me isn't going to help."

"It helps me a great deal," the physic exclaimed. "Maybe you won't do anything like that again and wreak havoc all about Lavister."

Madelayne's jaw was tight. "I know what I did. I do not need your lectures."

"'Tis not enough lecture you've had," Dolwyd pointed a finger at her. "If Kaspian has any sense when he awakens, he'll thrash you soundly."

Madelayne visibly perked. "Then you reckon he'll awaken soon?"

"I didn't say that!" he barked. "I said you need thrashing!"

"You'll not speak to her like that."

It was a very faint, very muffled voice. It took both Madelayne and Dolwyd a moment to realize it was coming from Kaspian. With a gasp of delight, Madelayne bent over the supine form and pulled the pillow away from his face, giving him plenty of air to breath. He was horribly pale and licked his dry lips, but the blue eyes were open.

"Kaspian," Dolwyd leapt up and hovered over him. "How do you feel, man?"

"As if I need to stay in bed for the rest of my life." Kaspian blinked up at the physic. "But if I hear you speak to Madelayne like that again, the only person thrashed around here will be you. Is that clear?"

The old man merely grunted. "If you can get up and catch me, you are welcome to try. But I'd advise against if for now, so I suppose I'll keep my mouth shut."

Kaspian didn't say anything as Dolwyd checked his wound again and tightened the bandages. "Well? Are my innards still intact?" he finally asked.

"Enough so," the old man replied. "I do not think you did any real damage, but you tore some of my stitches."

"Then I'll recover?"

"More than likely. But you cannot take any more strain, Kaspian. You need to stay in bed and rest and eat. Only then will you fully recover."

Kaspian's eyes moved to Madelayne, her angelic face looming above him. "Do you hear that? No more running off with you. I'm too old and weak to be chasing around after you."

She smiled at him, vastly relieved he was conscious and speaking. "Old? You cannot possibly be that old."

Kaspian sighed faintly, closing his eyes. "Old enough," he muttered. "Christ, I probably look every year of my thirty-seven years and then some."

"Damn old for a fighting man," Dolwyd concurred. "You should have retired years ago."

Kaspian grunted. "I choose to ignore you. Be gone with you now. I feel as if I could sleep for a hundred years."

Dolwyd lifted an eyelid, studying the eyeball, before standing back. "Aside from the fatigue, nothing is paining you?"

Kaspian inhaled deeply, feeling for any aches or pains he might have. "Not too terribly."

"You are damn fortunate, Kaspian. Need I say more?"

"You do not. Get out of here."

The old man grinned, heading for the door. Madelayne began untying her bodice. "You must be famished," she said softly. "Here, take some sustenance before you sleep. I've been full to bursting for two days and it has been most painful. You would be doing me a favor, really."

Kaspian put his hand up to stop her; the contrast in size of his hand against hers was striking. He looked at her a moment, studying her fine features. "In truth, I only wish to sleep. But I thank you for your concern."

Madelayne gazed at his hand over her own, fighting off a tide of warm, giddy feelings. Two days of fighting off those same torn feelings had seen her leaning more and more towards Kaspian and the excitement of his touch. The truth was that Cairn had been more like a brother to her, a protector and provider, and she had been fond of him. Aye, she'd done some soul searching in the past two days since her return to Lavister and she knew, in her heart, that she had never loved Cairn. That was well known.

But what she hadn't expected was her response to St. Hèver, the thrill of his touch and her lust for the man. She felt guilty for allowing her sense of excitement for him to overwhelm her mourning for Cairn. Was it wicked? Perhaps. But all she knew was what she felt every time Kaspian touched her. She couldn't ignore it. For her own sake, she simply couldn't.

"Then I shall leave you to your sleep," she finally said, retying the bodice. "I... I am glad you will recover. I shan't be far should you require me."

Kaspian's fingers curled around her hand, preventing her from leaving. "I would ask you to stay," his voice was soft. "To call out to you would require too much effort. If you simply stay here, I won't need to exert myself."

She eyed him, feeling the warmth of his tone, reluctant to admit that she very much wanted to stay. Slowly, she captured the stool Dolwyd had been sitting upon. An awkward silence prevailed until she pierced it.

"I am sorry," she said softly. "For leaving, for causing your strain... I am truly sorry."

He stared at her for a moment. "'Tis I who should apologize, madam." His voice was husky from fatigue and disuse. "I did not mean to upset you so with my careless words."

Madelayne looked at her hands, fumbling in her lap. "It was a foolish reaction. I must harden myself to the facts of my desolate situation."

He was watching her like a hawk, his blue eyes intensely penetrating. "I would ask a question, Madelayne."

He used her Christian name, soft and sweet, and her head came up, her gaze locking with his. "What is that?"

"What were you going to do once you ran away?"

Her cheeks flushed. "The only thing a person in my circumstance can do. Go back to my father and, presumably, find another husband."

"You would leave us, then?"

"Who is 'us'?"

He seemed suddenly reluctant to answer. "Those... well, those of us at Lavister."

She lifted her shoulders. "My husband is dead," she said. "I have said this before – with Cairn gone, there is no reason for me to stay."

Kaspian knew this but he didn't want to agree with her. "But you are my chatelaine," he insisted. "Did you not stop to think that I need you here, now, more than ever? With my injury and the chaos going on, you are more valuable to me than ever."

She was dubious. "I am?"

"Of course. How could you believe otherwise?"

She shrugged lamely. "Because Mavia is here and...."

"Must we have this discussion again? You are a far better chatelaine than she is."

He was flattering her but it was also the truth. She cast him a sidelong glance, reluctant to believe him even though she wanted to. "But I do not wish to be a burden."

"Upon whom?"

"Well... *you*, my lord."

"Kaspian," he reminded her.

She shook her head quickly, forgetful. "Kaspian."

He struggled not to smile. "Why do not you let me make that determination? You are worth your weight in gold at this moment and I've no intention of letting you slip away. Is that clear?"

Madelayne felt as if a huge weight had been lifted off her shoulders. She opened her mouth to thank him, but instead, tears filled her eyes. Kaspian caught them immediately.

"What's the matter?" he demanded. "What have I said now?"

She shook her head and wiped, embarrassed, at her eyes. "'Tis nothing. I... I'm simply overwhelmed with your graciousness."

He watched her, feeling the pangs of uncertainty. He was trying to reassure her that she was not a burden, but instead, perhaps he had been selfishly demanding. He realized that for quite some time he did not want her to go, albeit because he felt responsible for her since Cairn's death, or perhaps because he didn't like the thought of not seeing her about the castle, he wasn't sure. She was a fixture here, a radiant bit of light in the midst of smelly, fighting men, and he very much wanted her to stay.

"If you do not want to remain, I will not force you," he said, though it was difficult for him to say. "But we need you, Madelayne. *I* need you. I hope you will consider staying with us."

Madelayne was feeling terribly foolish for all of the misconceptions she'd had in recent days. She hadn't given Kaspian enough credit for his compassion. *I need you*, he had said. She wondered if she was reading too much into his statement.

She hoped not.

"Thank you," she whispered. "From the bottom of my heart, I thank you."

He turned his head, looking at her. Christ, she was an incredibly beautiful creature. "'Tis I who am thankful, madam," he said softly. He suddenly realized that he very much missed her presence beside him. The need for her was suddenly an overwhelming urge. "Now, if your offer for sustenance still stands, I find that I could probably take a bit of nourishment."

Madelayne smiled and rose from the stool, sliding down next to him in the bed. His hands were shaking as he helped her pull away the bodice, but not for the reasons of weakness and hunger that she thought.

It was anticipation.

## ○ಙ

**1.**     *Eight days later*

"Nicholas de Dalyn is on his way," Thomas said. "He should be here by the end of the week."

Over a week had passed since Kaspian's second brush with mortality. True to Dolwyd's prediction, his recovery had been much slower this time around. He could sit up in bed and take a bit of solid food, but he didn't eat much. He slept mostly and was able to walk the chamber slowly. Dolwyd wouldn't even let him take the stairs yet. Even now, he sat in bed, propped up with several pillows, listening to Thomas' grim voice.

"You really cannot blame Edward," he finally said. "He has a great deal at stake here at Lavister. To send de Dalyn to help oversee things until I fully recover is not the insult you seem to think it is."

Thomas, Reece and Ewan were visibly displeased. They shifted uncomfortably on their feet or crossed their arms like stubborn children. Since receiving the missive from the king that morning, they'd done nothing but stomp about the castle in fits. Having caught wind of their behavior, Kaspian had called an impromptu meeting to quell the rising rebellion. When de Dalyn arrived, he had to be shown united support.

"Thomas is perfectly capable of leading Lavister's troops," Ewan said. "We do not need an outsider."

Kaspian snorted softly. "I would hardly call Nicholas de Dalyn an outsider. He was present at the battle of Beeston and he knows the situation here at Lavister with my injury and Cairn's death." He shifted in the bed, trying to sit more upright. It bothered him that his men had to see him in his most desperate shape. "And I need not remind any of you that we have all fought alongside de Dalyn. We know his capabilities. If Edward was going to send someone to support our ranks while I am recuperating, he could have done far worse than Nicholas."

Thomas laughed bitterly, softly. "That is true, Kaspian. There are any number of knights I would sooner slash as they come through the gates than allow them to lead Lavister's men."

"But not de Dalyn."

Thomas shook his head reluctantly. "Nay, not de Dalyn," he said. "He is arrogant and assertive, two qualities I am not particularly fond of, but unfortunately for you, he's nearly as capable as you are."

Kaspian cocked a blonde brow. "What does that mean?"

"That he could easily replace you here at Lavister. Edward could then recall you to him to fight wherever you are most needed."

Kaspian put an arm behind his head. His arm was a massive thing with veins and muscles evident. "That is always a possibility, no matter what," he said, thinking back to the battlefield conversation he'd had with de Dalyn at Beeston. "In fact, back at Beeston, he told me he wanted Lavister's command. I thought he was jesting but mayhap he was serious."

Reece and Ewan could sense that the senior knights were not all that incensed over de Dalyn's assignment. In fact, they were rather casual about it. Ewan finally crossed his fuzzy, thick arms stubbornly.

"I fight with St. Hèver," he said flatly. "If he leaves Lavister, I go with him."

Thomas cocked an eyebrow at the young knight. "You'll fight for whomever you are told to fight for, St. Hèver or de Dalyn. You are not of St. Hèver's personal knight corps; you belong to the king. All of us do and we must do as we are told."

The younger knights remained unconvinced but said nothing further. Kaspian looked at Thomas, noting the man was trying to pretend that he was disappointed at not being allowed to lead Lavister's troops. Thomas was an excellent knight, almost as good as Cairn had been, but there had always been something with Thomas that suggested he'd rather have someone else take the command. Kaspian was well aware of that trait. In that sense, perhaps it was better that de Dalyn was coming.

With nothing more to be said, Kaspian dismissed his knights. They understood well what was to happen whether or not they approved. Just as Ewan opened the chamber door, Madelayne blew into the room in a cloud of blue brocade and rose scent. She was looking absolutely exquisite these days, healed from her bout with childbirth and mentally stable. The first few days of doubt and grieving after Cairn's death were gone now; she was much stronger. She brought with her a tray with Kaspian's nooning meal upon it and, immediately, Reece and Ewan stumbled over themselves to assist her.

"My lady," Reece reached out and practically snatched the tray from her. "That is too heavy for your delicate hands. Allow me."

Madelayne smiled at him and attempted to reclaim the tray. "Thank you very much, Reece, but I can manage."

Reece wouldn't hear of it. Not to be outdone, Ewan raced to the corner where a small stool sat and he placed it next to the bed. "Here you are, my lady," he said gallantly. "A throne for Lavister's queen."

They had been acting the idiots for the better part of the week, ever since Kaspian had brought her back from her little misadventure. It was as if they had suddenly realized she was a widowed woman and they were, of course, unmarried knights. Oh, how they fussed and flirted with her, drawing a smile or a polite word, something they would have never done if Cairn were still alive.

But Madelayne didn't want any part of their chivalry. Her patience was thinning. "Truly, good knights," she said, her humor gone. "I can manage well enough."

"But it is our pleasure to assist you," Reece said, holding her arm as if she were incapable of sitting on the stool by herself. "Allow your poor, humble servants the opportunity."

"Wait!" Ewan practically shouted. Madelayne jerked unsteadily, afraid she was about to sit on a viper or something equally as terrible, but Ewan merely snatched a linen rag from the food tray and dusted off the stool. "There we are. Nothing to soil that lovely gown."

Madelayne was struggling with her tongue. Kaspian watched the knights make arses out of themselves and endeavored not to laugh at Madelayne's reaction. But he really couldn't blame them; she was a delightful piece of eye candy. Her silken hair was pulled softly away from her face and her green eyes were large and bright. However, along with all of the tolerance he was feeling, he also felt a good deal of possessiveness.

"De Poyer," he finally snapped at Reece, "stop smothering the lady. Set the food down and be gone with you, all of you."

Thomas grinned at Kaspian, winking as he herded the two younger knights from the room. When they were gone, Madelayne let out a harsh breath that lifted the tendrils of hair off her forehead.

"God in Heaven, when did they become so… so…."

"Cloying?"

"No. So… so…"

"Irritating?"

She jabbed a finger at him. "Exactly. What on earth has happened to them?"

Kaspian tried not to smile as she sat beside the bed with a bowl of gruel in her hands. "I think they are merely showing their appreciation for you," he said neutrally.

She stirred the porridge and held up a spoonful for him. "Well, I wish they would go appreciate someone else. They're driving me mad, I tell you."

He took a bite of the hot food. "They're young. You must take that into consideration."

She shook her head, stirring the steaming contents of the bowl. "They never used to act like that," she said. "Do they actually believe that... with Cairn gone... that I would...?"

Kaspian allowed his smile to break through; she seemed quite baffled by the whole thing. "Perhaps they are hoping. Any man in his right mind would, you know."

She looked at him, feeling a strange tingling in her stomach that spread through her limbs. It even made her hands hurt in an odd, wonderful way simply to look at him, to feel the warmth from his eyes. She wanted so badly to ask him if he was a man in his right mind, too, but the words wouldn't come. She couldn't force them out. Lifting her shoulders, she concentrated on the porridge.

"I cannot think on such things," she said. "'Tis far too soon after Cairn's passing to think on another husband."

Kaspian lifted an eyebrow as she spooned another heaping into his mouth. "You were thinking on it a week ago."

Her cheeks, predictably, flushed. "I wasn't thinking clearly then, not at all. I was confused."

"And now?"

"I have my senses."

"What are they telling you?"

She was preoccupied with stirring the rapidly cooling gruel. "To stay where I am needed. I can be chatelaine at Lavister Crag forever, always serving you and the household."

He wiped a bit of mush from his lips. "But I shan't be at Lavister Crag forever."

A bolt of distress shot through her. "Are you leaving, Kaspian?" she asked anxiously.

His name sounded so smooth and sweet on her tongue. "Not right away. But someday."

Madelayne looked unsettled. "But what if the new liege does not need me? What if he has a wife? I'll be cast aside, consigned to the kitchens, or worse than that, he'll simply send me on my way." Before he could reply to her tirade, she rapidly stood up and set the bowl back on the tray. Her hands went to her mouth as if attempting to quiet her own blathering tongue. "I'm sorry, please forgive me. 'Tis not your responsibility to plan for my future. I should not rattle on so."

"Hold, madam." He wanted to get a word in before she jabbered off again. "You are, indeed, my responsibility. Cairn was my knight and my friend. It was under my command that he was killed. That, indeed, makes you my charge."

She paused, looking at him with those magnificent eyes that took his breath away. "If you'll forgive me again, that is a ridiculous statement."

He looked at her, dumbfounded at her response. "Why would you say that?"

She cocked an eyebrow. "Because you will have a wife someday. Do you really think she'll allow you to keep a full-grown woman as a ward?" She shook her head again. "No, Kaspian, I cannot ask this of you. You have your own life to lead."

He crossed his massive arms, giving her that disapproving look Cairn gave her so often when she was obstinate. "Your selflessness is touching," he said dryly. "But the fact remains that you are still my charge. And as for any wife I might have in the future, who is to say that, purely out of convenience, I will not marry you? That way, both of our problems will be solved."

Now it was Madelayne's turn to be dumbfounded. "What... what problem?"

"The fact that you are so concerned over your future."

She snapped out of her daze, shaking her head irritably. "I know my problem. I meant your problem. What problem could you possibly have that marrying me would solve?"

He looked thoughtful, trying not to appear as if his suggestion was anything other than practicality. Truth was, he was very much concerned with her reaction to his suggestion. He'd been thinking it for days now. Every time she entered his chamber, his heart leapt. Every time she spoke, it was like the dulcet tones of angels speaking. He couldn't get her out of his mind, an obsession he had never before experienced. His response to her was physical; he knew that. It had been from the onset. But as the days passed and he began to come to know her, really know her, now there was an emotional attachment as well. For a man who had never known much emotional attachment, to anyone, it was an astonishing realization. He had no idea he was capable of such feelings.

But he was quite capable, as he was proving daily. Still, he was afraid to say anything to Madelayne, afraid of her reaction. With Cairn so recently deceased, what would she think of him if she knew he wanted to marry her? He didn't want her to think he was an opportunist. That was the furthest thing from his mind. In fact, it had everything to do with his heart and not his mind at all. Now, they broached the subject but he couldn't yet gauge her reaction to it.

"I am a warring man," he said after a moment. "I am thirty-seven years old. I've never had a wife, but there are times when one would be beneficial. Our marriage could be a sort of business arrangement."

Madelayne, who had been stunned and overjoyed at his initial suggestion, now felt her heart sink at his words; they sounded so very cold.

"Business arrangement?" she repeated.

He nodded, pretending not to be too committed to the idea one way or the other because she didn't seem overly receptive. "Aye," he said. "You would take care of my house and hold, and I, in turn, would provide for you. Sensible enough, really."

Her brow furrowed and she turned away from him, pondering his words with a soaring range of emotions. On one hand, she could imagine spending her life as Kaspian's chatelaine without a good deal of distress to that thought. But on the other hand, his suggestion of marriage was cold, without any thought to affection or warmth. She didn't know why it bothered her, but it did. Marriage was foremost a business arrangement anyway, not a love match. But suppose he found a woman later that he wanted, a mistress kept on the side while his dutiful wife went about her duties? Madelayne shuddered; Kaspian wasn't the type, she knew, but she couldn't shake the feeling that he was offering to marry her out of pity. And that, in her opinion, was the worst possible reason.

"I do not believe that would be wise, Kaspian," she said softly. "I'm not a suitable wife for you."

He looked at her as if she had gone daft. "Now *that*, madam, is the most ridiculous statement I have ever heard. You are more than suitable."

She shook her head. "You will want a young virginal wife from a good family to bear you many strong sons."

"You are being fool...."

"Kaspian," she spun around, her voice sharp and soft at the same time. "I cannot bear you children. You need a wife who can bring your sons into this world and I, as we know, am incapable of that. Twice I have tried and twice I have failed. I could not put you through what I put Cairn through. It would not be fair."

He froze, staring at her, the mood of the room suddenly becoming grim and serious. "You are not certain that you cannot bear children," he finally said, his voice steady. "The premature birth of your first son was…."

"God's will."

"Aye, it was. And you should not blame yourself for it, nor should you blame yourself for the second son so recently…"

"Born with the cord wrapped around his neck?" she shook her head, the pain of her son's death still quite strong. "Once is an act of God, but two dead babies are something entirely different. God doesn't want me to have any children."

"That's ludicrous."

"Is it?" There was bitterness in her tone. "Dolwyd tore me asunder trying to take the last child from me. He told me that my womb was ravaged. Believe me, Kaspian, when I say that I cannot bear children. You'd be better off forgetting about marrying me and find yourself a woman who can provide you with a legacy."

He sat silently, watching her pale face. She was obviously very ashamed to tell him her innermost problems, her physical limitations. No wonder the woman had been acting so foolish after the death of her family; she had good reason to on many fronts. But it didn't sway his determination.

"Madelayne," he said softly. "I understand what you are telling me. But hear me well; Dolwyd is not God. He may tell you that your womb is useless, but he does not know for a fact. There is only one way to find out if he is correct."

She knew what he meant and her pale cheeks flushed at the thought of intimacy with him. "And if he is?"

He shrugged slightly. "Then so be it. I have never been one to long for heirs. In fact, children rather frighten me."

"Why on earth?"

"Tiny, fragile things that scream and cry and run about like animals. I've never been particularly fond of them."

Madelayne gazed at him, unsure what to say. She didn't know what to think, for that matter. But one thing was certain; he seemed far too unconcerned about the matter. "But what if, by some miracle, we do have a child?" she asked.

"Then no child on this earth will ever be welcomed more."

She stared at him, rivers of emotion coursing through her. His final statement told her volumes of what was in his heart and she, furthermore, realized that he was lying to her. He wasn't frightened of children; he wanted them, as every man did. She didn't understand why he should lie to her just to convince her to marry him.

Madelayne's feelings were strong for Kaspian. So strong that she couldn't let him make such a miserable mistake by giving in to his pity for her. The man deserved more in life.

"Nay," she finally said. "I will not."

"Will not what?"

"Marry you."

His expression was impassive, though inside he felt as if he had been struck. "Why not?"

She couldn't give him an answer. It was too painful to do so. Turning back to the table that held the now cold gruel, she picked up the bowl. "I shall tend your house and hold, and nurse you until you return to health. But I cannot marry you."

"That is not an answer."

"It is enough of an answer. I do not want to be married, not to you, not to anyone. Please respect my wishes."

Her refusal cut him. When she tried to, very businesslike, feed him the rest of the porridge, he shook his head and lay back down on the bed.

She watched him, wondering what he was feeling. "You must eat, you know that."

"I haven't the strength to eat."

He was lying again, but she didn't say anything. Her heart was heavy as she set the gruel back on the table. "Can you drink, then?"

"Perhaps."

"Ale? Watered wine?"

He didn't say anything for a moment. Then, the pale blue eyes focused on her. "You."

She knew what he meant. She didn't know why her hands were shaking as she stood and unfastened her bodice. Climbing onto the bed beside him was an experience like nothing else she had ever known, making her heart race and her palms sweat. He never took his eyes off her as she pulled her clothing aside, exposing a rosy nipple. He put his hand on her breast, kissing it, very tenderly, before he began to suckle.

It was too much. Madelayne let out a sob, pent-up emotion exploding at the significance of his touch. Before she could take another breath, Kaspian's mouth was on hers, kissing her so deeply, so sweetly, that she instantly gave herself over to him as if she had been doing it her entire life. His kiss was strong and insistent, yet so delicious and gentle that Madelayne thought she would faint. She could taste her milk on his lips and it was wildly erotic. But as quickly as he claimed her, he left her, back to her breast and suckling furiously. Madelayne could only lay there and weep.

Kaspian could only lay there and hold her.

# CHAPTER EIGHT

*Seven days later*

Astride a big dappled charger, a very expensive and hairy beast that had come all the way from Saxony, Nicholas rode into the bailey of Lavister Crag Castle with the air of an arriving hero. He was exactly where he wanted to be, thrilled that Edward had moved him out of hellish Anchorsholme Castle, and thrilled that he was finally on the Marches where the action was. His victory at Beeston had only whetted his appetite more for a border command and he'd waited with great anticipation for Edward's decision to his request to be moved to Lavister. With l'Ebreux dead and St. Hèver injured, Edward had agreed to the transfer and Nicholas had made all due haste to his new post.

Finally, he had arrived.

But there were drawbacks to the Lavister appointment. The castle wasn't nearly as large as Anchorsholme Castle and there weren't nearly as many women. In fact, there were none at all that he could see, so he was a bit disgusted at the fact that it was a true military installation with only smelly men about. Still, it was better than where he'd been so he accepted the fact that there were no women other than, he was sure, servants or whores. He would have to live with it.

As he reined his steed over near the stone-and-wood built stables, a skinny young groom came out to collect his mount. Nicholas dismounted into the mixture of mud and straw that comprised the stable yard, collecting his saddlebags as his gaze moved about the fortress. A great hall with a steeply pitched roof, two stone bunkhouses, a squat-like keep, and not much else, but the place had massive walls around it. Not that it would matter if the Welsh took it into their minds to try and overrun the place, but it seemed fairly well fortified. He grinned, thinking on the action he would see here. He was looking forward to the battles.

As Nicholas stood there and inspected the walls as his horse was led away, Thomas saw him from the keep entry. He had seen the man ride in and was coming forth to greet him, but he paused before doing so, watching Nicholas as he surveyed Lavister as a king would survey his kingdom. There was something haughty in Nicholas' manner as he drew in the walls and watched the men move about. Although Thomas had told Kaspian that he wasn't opposed to Nicholas being there, the truth was that he wasn't much looking forward to it. He didn't particularly like the man. As he took a deep breath and prepared to go forth, Mavia came up behind him.

"Who is that?" she asked.

Thomas turned to his curious wife. "That," he said, "is Sir Nicholas de Dalyn. He will be with us for a time while Kaspian heals. Edward has sent him to reinforce our ranks with Cairn's death and Kaspian's injury."

Mavia squinted at the knight in the stable yard; her eyes weren't very good and it was difficult for her to see at a distance.

"Did you know he would come today?" she asked.

Thomas shook his head. "I knew he was coming but I did not know when."

"Who is that?"

Same question, different voice. Both Thomas and Mavia turned to see Madelayne standing in the keep entry, looking at Nicholas near the stables. She had an apron over her surcoat and she was wiping her hands on it, having come from helping the cook prepare the evening meal. Lavister's keep had two ground floor chambers, a large one and then a very small one, like a guard's room, and Madelayne had been in the larger room cutting up pears to be sauced. Hearing the commotion at the entry had brought her out.

"Sir Nicholas de Dalyn," Thomas said again for Madelayne's benefit. "He is a new knight to be stationed at Lavister while Kaspian is injured. I must go and greet him now."

Madelayne merely shrugged and turned back for the keep, returning to her duties, but Mavia put her hand on her husband's arm. "I will go with you," she said. "Where would you have him housed?"

Thomas started to walk with his wife beside him. "In the gatehouse," he said. "He can have the chamber opposite Ewan and Reece's chamber."

He was pointing to Lavister's gatehouse, which was big and block-like, with an enormous portcullis slicing through it. There were two guard rooms on the bottom and then two additional rooms on the second level where the wall walk was. The knights usually slept in those second floor rooms although one of them was empty and used for storage. Mavia thought on the room her husband was referring to, the storage room, and scratched her head.

"That chamber?" she said. "It is a mess, Thomas. You should have told me sooner that Sir Nicholas was coming so I could have had it prepared for him."

Thomas waved her off. "You can still have it prepared for him," he grumbled. "He does not need anything fancy, simply a room with a bed."

Mavia eyed her husband with some disapproval as they came upon Nicholas, who was still looking up at the parapets. Thomas called out to the man.

"De Dalyn," he said loudly. "Welcome to Lavister."

Nicholas turned around to see Thomas and a blonde woman approach. He forced a smile at Thomas but his attention was really on the woman, who was average in height with a somewhat attractive face.

"Thank you," he said to Thomas, his gaze inevitably moving to the lady at Thomas' side. "Greetings, my lady."

Thomas indicated Mavia. "My wife, Lady Mavia," he said. "She is chatelaine and will be of assistance to you."

Mavia dipped into a polite curtsy for the handsome blonde knight. "Welcome to Lavister Crag Castle, my lord," she said. "My husband tells me that you are to stay with us for a while."

Nicholas smiled at the woman, turning on the charm. He always did when women were around. "Permanently, I hope," he said. "I cannot tell you how happy I am to be away from my previous post. A terrible place with terrible weather, year 'round. And full of Irish!"

Mavia smiled at the man with the bright personality. "God's Bones," she exclaimed softly. "Were you in Ireland?"

Nicholas laughed softly. "Indeed not, my lady," he said, pushing between Thomas and Mavia and extending his elbow to the woman. "I was at a terrible place called Anchorsholme Castle north of Liverpool. An awful place with Irish conscripts, as the Lord of Anchorsholme has lands in Ireland and he ships them over to serve him. But Lavister seems quite impressive, so would you be good enough to show me around?"

Mavia was already under his charming spell. "It would be my pleasure, my lord."

She led him away and began to give him the grand tour as Thomas tagged along behind, shaking his head at his giddy wife. She was such a silly woman, easily flattered by a smooth-talking man. She was a foolish woman in general, he'd always thought, but it wasn't of great concern to him. Neither was Nicholas. Leaving his wife in charge of Nicholas, he headed to the gatehouse to tell a few soldiers to clean out the second floor storage room.

After his business in the gatehouse, he headed back to Lavister's keep, noting that Mavia and Nicholas were over by the bunkhouses now. But he didn't give them a thought as he entered the keep to find Madelayne sitting at the scrubbed feasting table in the large, ground floor room with bowls of fruit around her. This room always smelled heavily of damp earth for some reason, as it did now. When he entered the room, Madelayne looked up from her knife as she sliced pears.

"Where is the new knight?" she asked.

Thomas gestured in the general direction of the bunkhouses. "My wife has him in-hand, showing him Lavister," he said. "I am having the second floor storage room in the gatehouse cleaned out for him. Can you have the servants take a bed to the room for him?"

"Indeed I will," she agreed.

Thomas nodded. "My thanks," he said. "Where is Kaspian?"

The mere mention of Kaspian's name brought a smile to Madelayne's lips, one that she quickly suppressed. "Dolwyd permitted him to walk today," she said. "The last I saw, they were over near the stables. I am surprised you did not see him when you were out in the bailey."

Thomas saw the flash of a grin on Madelayne and knew it was for Kaspian. He wasn't surprised. In fact, they all knew that there was something in the air between the pair although no one would dare speak of it for fear of upsetting Kaspian, who tried very hard to pretend that he held nothing but polite esteem for Lady l'Ebreux.

But it was clear that there was more to it. At Cairn's burial in Shrewsbury nearly a week before, Kaspian had been unable to attend and had been very concerned for the party taking Cairn's body into the town. He had sent three hundred men as an escort, which was excessive, but with the Welsh unstable, he had insisted on the massive escort. Moreover, he had explained, Cairn deserved such an escort and so did Lady l'Ebreux. He'd been particularly clear about protecting the lady and that was when Thomas began to suspect that his stone-faced commander was feeling more than simply gratitude towards the lady who had virtually saved his life. That "something more" had been clear in everything about him.

So the party from Lavister had proceeded into town with their enormous escort, frightening the villagers half to death, thinking they were being overrun by soldiers, and continued on to the cathedral where mass was said for Cairn and his lost son, and the two of them were interred together in the church yard next to the baby that was born prematurely the year of Cairn and Madelayne's marriage. It had been a solemn but rather bittersweet ceremony in that the father was now protecting his children in death as he was unable to protect them in life.

Madelayne had wept at the mass, of course, but no one knew that she was weeping for her children far more than for her lost husband. She was sorrowful for Cairn's death, of course, but it wasn't as if she had lost the love of her life. She'd lost a man who had been very kind and attentive to her, and she would miss the man she was fond of. She had enough guilt over her growing feelings for Kaspian versus the fact that she needed to mourn for Cairn, so she wept quietly for him, thanking him for watching over their sons in death. Still, no one knew the true reasons behind her tears and no one ever would.

But Thomas suspected what lay in her heart when, upon their return to Lavister, she went into Kaspian's chamber and didn't come out until the next morning. He thought it in rather bad taste, in fact, that Cairn's widow was showing such attention to Kaspian on the day she buried her husband, but it wasn't her fault. The truth was that Dolwyd had forced her into the unsavory task of tending Kaspian with his distasteful use of her breasts. It was no wonder the woman was confused in her weakened mental state, and if her heart was compromised because if it, she wasn't to blame. Thomas also suspected that was the reason she had run away, trying to get free of Dolwyd and Kaspian's clutches, but they had brought her back and enslaved her once again even though Kaspian was starting to eat regular foods again.

It was all very confusing, this odd triangle of affections between Cairn and Madelayne and Kaspian, but it truthfully wasn't any of Thomas' business. What Kaspian did with Cairn's widow was his own affair. But whatever it was, shockingly, she seemed to be liking it.

"I did not see them in the stable yard," he replied belatedly to her statement. "I will go and look again. Meanwhile, please have the bed taken to the gatehouse."

Madelayne sliced through another pear. "I will," she said. "The evening meal will be in about an hour. If you see Dolwyd and Kaspian, please tell them."

"I shall."

Thomas wandered out of the chamber, leaving Madelayne to her pears. She had almost the entire bowl cut and peeled, as the old cook would make a compote out of them with currants and cinnamon, cloves and honey. She didn't mind doing labor like this; she'd been doing it her entire life so cutting pears wasn't troubling to her. Moreover, Lavister mostly had male servants except for the one old lady who did the washing, and male servants weren't fond of kitchen work. Even the cook was male, a big man with only one eye who had been at Lavister for years. He was Welsh and had been helpful in the past when the harsh Welsh language needed to be translated. Cairn hadn't spoken Welsh and Kaspian's knowledge of it was limited, so Ioin the cook was often called upon for his translating services.

Even now, the fat man lumbered into the keep with his heavy leather apron, dragging a swollen gout foot behind him, looking for the pears he was soon to boil. Madelayne turned over nearly everything she had, still working on the last few, but the cook took a big bowl of peeled and cut fruit. As Ioin shuffled away, Madelayne continued cutting until she heard voices at the entry. Looking up, she could see Kaspian and Dolwyd enter the keep.

Madelayne's heart leapt at the sight of him; ever since that precious moment seven days ago when he'd kissed her so passionately, it was as if their relationship had transformed into something else, something deeper and warmer. All guilt for Cairn aside, whatever she was feeling for Kaspian was beginning to overwhelm her to the point where she was eager to see the man, any time and in any fashion. He still nursed against her at night, as Dolwyd was still convinced that the organic nourishment was helping Kaspian heal, and Madelayne was more than willing to continue doing her duty, which wasn't so much a duty any longer as it was the thing she looked forward to the most. Kaspian would wrap his big arms around her and suckle her breasts tenderly until she was dry on both of them. More often than not, they fell asleep in that intimate and compromising position and she would awaken to him suckling her again.

God help her, she craved it.

But he never tried anything more than that with her, anything more suggestive, but the gleam in his eye had told her he very much wanted to. He showed remarkable restraint. But she was coming now to frequently climax as he suckled her and she knew he was aware of it because her breathing would come in rapid pants no matter how much she tried to suppress her reaction, and he would suckle harder as she tried to bite off her cries. What had been an embarrassing happenstance the first few times was now becoming a regular part of their time together, as odd as it seemed. And she knew for a fact that she didn't imagine his rock-hard arousal against her leg, but he never tried to do anything about it. It made for a very strange situation between them but something that wasn't unpleasant in the least. It was simply the way of things between them.

And as terrible as it seemed, as unholy and wrong, she loved every minute of it.

But it was her naughty pleasure and hers alone, so she shook herself from her reflections of suckling and climaxes as Kaspian and Dolwyd entered the room. They made quite a pair; Kaspian was a few inches over six feet with enormously wide shoulders and big arms, while Dolwyd was no larger than a child as he stood next to him. With Kaspian's injury, his bulk had diminished somewhat but he was still a very large man.

He looked much healthier than he probably felt because he was still having trouble eating solid foods and his guts pained him a good deal at times, especially if he ate food that was difficult to digest. For the most part, however, he was recovering surprisingly well. The past few days, he was concentrating on standing up straight when he walked because it was an instinct, with a sore gut, to hunch over. As he walked into the keep, he was, indeed, hunched over with his hand over his wound area. Madelayne set down the fruit and knife.

"What is wrong?" she asked with concern, standing up from the table and making her way to Kaspian and Dolwyd. "Why do you look so pained?"

"Because he *is* pained," Dolwyd said before Kaspian could answer. "The man still has a great deal of recovering to do, but no one listens to me. They do whatever they wish and ignore the old physic."

Madelayne focused on Kaspian's hunkered-over form. "You have done too much," she said quietly. "I will help you up to your bed."

Kaspian rubbed at his wound and grunted before standing up straight as if to stretch himself up. "I do not need to be helped to my bed," he assured her before changing the subject because he didn't want to discuss his physical state. "I saw de Dalyn outside. Did he just arrive?"

Madelayne was puzzled at first but then realized who he was speaking of. "Aye, he came a few minutes ago," she said. "Mavia has been showing him the castle but it would be more appropriate for a knight to show him about, I am sure. There will be much he needs to know that Mavia cannot tell him."

Kaspian couldn't disagree with her. "Where is Thomas, then?"

Madelayne shrugged. "He was in here a few minutes ago to tell me that he is making a place for the new knight in the gatehouse," she said. "I am to send the servants with a bed for him."

Kaspian frowned; he wasn't sure why Thomas wasn't showing Nicholas about and, instead, leaving the duty to his wife. He turned to the physic.

"Find a soldier and have him send de Dalyn to me," he said. "I will be here with Lady Madelayne."

Dolwyd watched the man slowly make his way over to the table with the fruit and bowls strewn about it before turning to leave the keep in search of a soldier. It wouldn't do any good for him to stay and lecture Kaspian on how he should be in bed now because the knight wouldn't listen to him, anyway. As he departed in an insulted huff, Madelayne followed Kaspian over to the table, all the while watching him closely.

"Are you sure you are well?" she asked.

"I am well."

"You do not look well."

He glanced at her, eyebrow cocked, before claiming a seat at the table. "Then why did you ask?" he asked as he lowered himself down, grunting at his discomfort. "I said I am well and I am. If you think you already know the answer, then do not ask me the question."

Madelayne fought off a grin at his annoyance. Over the past several days, she had come to know the man well in many ways, and in not just physical ones. The cold commander she had always known was beginning to show cracks in his steely façade, cracks that were showing her he really did have some emotion in him. Perpetually quiet and serious, Kaspian St. Hèver actually had a bit of a personality, as she had seen. He was a man who had a wicked sense of humor and could show great annoyance if the situation called for it. Like now; she rather liked seeing this side of the man.

She liked the fire.

"I believe you," she said. "No need to become irate about it. I did not doubt you."

He frowned at her as she reclaimed her seat with the fruit. He sat across the table from her, watching her delicate features as she finished cutting the pears.

"I did not become irate," he said, more calmly now. "I simply do not need to be fussed over as you and Dolwyd seem to think is necessary. Truly, I am on the mend. I am fine."

She looked up from the fruit, offended by his words. "I do not fuss over you," she said. "I am simply doing what is necessary to ensure your health. Forgive me for showing too much concern. I shall try not to do so in the future."

She went back to cutting pears and his gaze lingered on her lowered head. That dark auburn hair with the red, glistening highlights had his attention, as did the rest of her. In the surcoat and apron she wore, he could see a hint of her delectable cleavage and he began to think about her delicious breasts upon his tongue. Thoughts such as that aroused him, as they had instantly as of late, so it was imperative to change those thoughts before he found himself in a very uncomfortable position.

"I do not mind if you show concern over me," he finally said, grumbling. "I suppose I would rather have it from you than from Dolwyd. What does he think I am going to do? Shatter into a thousand pieces right before his eyes?"

Madelayne didn't look up from her fruit. "I would not know for I have not asked him," she said, unwilling to forgive him quite so soon. "As I said, I will try not to show so much concern in the future if it upsets you so."

"I told you that I did not mind it coming from you."

"Your guts can pop out and you can explode like a pimple for all I care. I will not show you any concern at all."

Kaspian could sense something of a jest with her. She was toying with him and didn't want him to think she was. He bit his lip to keep from smiling.

"Then it will be a relief," he said. "I do not have time for anyone's concern, least of all yours."

She stopped peeling. "Is that so?" she looked at him, frowning. "It is well and good that you shall no longer have it."

"I know."

"So do I!"

He couldn't help the grin now, watching her as she scowled at him. "Are you really going to withhold your concern?"

Madelayne could see his grin and she lowered her head before he could see hers. "Ungrateful man," she said. "After everything I have done for you."

He let out a short. "Done for *me*?" he said. "What about everything I have done for *you*?"

She stopped peeling once again and looked at him, irate. "If you do not like me here, then send me back to my father. It is no difficult thing."

"Mayhap I will."

"Good!"

He didn't say anything for a moment, genuinely trying not to burst out laughing at her. "Would you really go back to your father?"

"I would!"

"What if I do not want you to?"

"Why not?"

"Because I would marry you instead of sending you back."

That cooled whatever Madelayne had building in her. She looked at him, all of the humor and outrage gone from her expression. Since he had asked her to marry him the first time, he'd not brought it up again. Until now. Looking into his handsome face, it began to occur to her that she wanted it more than anything. Marriage to St. Hèver would be nothing like marriage to Cairn. Was it even possible that people were married to those they could not stand to be without?

"I told you I would not marry you," she said quietly. "I told you why. I thought the matter was resolved."

Kaspian had a faint smile on his lips. "It is not," he said frankly. "I have tried to understand your reasons but I cannot. They are invalid. You are a widowed woman without any prospects and I am offering you an honorable proposal. You would be my wife and my chatelaine. I believe it is a perfect arrangement."

Madelayne kept her head down, focused on the fruit, because she knew if she looked at him, all would be lost. After a moment, she sighed with a hint of exasperation. "You say that it is perfect, but the truth is that it is not perfect at all," she said. "What will people think if

I agree to marry you so soon after Cairn's passing? It will be terribly scandalous."

"So you fear for your reputation?"

"And yours."

He frowned. "I do not care anything about my reputation," he said. "And if people think it is too soon for you to consider remarriage, they are fools. Do they think Cairn would want you to be a widow the rest of your life? Of course he would not. And he would know I have nothing but the utmost respect for you and that I would be a good husband. Is that not what he would want?"

Madelayne dared to look at him. "I... I suppose so."

"Then the matter is settled. You will marry me."

Madelayne's resistance to his proposal was wavering. *Remember that you cannot give the man sons!* She told herself. But it almost didn't matter any longer. So much in her heart had changed and it was on the tip of her tongue to agree. She felt such longing for the man, more than she had ever known she could feel. Cairn had never made such things blossom in her heart and soul as Kaspian had so effortlessly done. But she was torn, still in turmoil between Cairn and Kaspian, her heart and mind and soul leaning so close in Kaspian's direction but afraid to admit it. Afraid to say anything. Before she could open her mouth, however, voices were in the entry and people were appearing in the chamber.

"St. Hèver!" Nicholas greeted with Dolwyd following him. "I am told you were looking for me. I was just outside the keep when your physic found me. Great Gods, you are looking much better than you were the last time I saw you."

Attention torn from Madelayne's wide-eyed expression, there was no way Kaspian was going to show any weakness in front of Nicholas. He looked at the man and stood up as if he wasn't pained in the least, accepting Nicholas' hand in greeting.

"It was certainly a difficult situation the last time you saw me," he said evenly. "Thanks to excellent tending, I am as you see. I am on my way to recovery."

Nicholas looked him up and down. "I can see that," he said. Then, his attention inevitably moved to Madelayne, sitting on the other side of the table, and his expression immediately changed to one of great interest. "I have already been introduced to one lovely lady at Lavister. I see that there is a second."

Kaspian saw the shift in expression as clear as day and instantly, he could feel that primal jealousy rise within his chest, the type of jealousy that one man would have when protecting his mate from a predator. With Nicholas' expression taking on predatory characteristics, Kaspian went on the defensive. He'd never known anything like it but simply couldn't help it.

*Do not look at her like that, you bastard....*

"This is Lady l'Ebreux," he said, his voice oddly cold. "This is Cairn's widow. My lady, this is Sir Nicholas de Dalyn. He is here to help support our ranks for the time being."

Whether or not the lady was a widow made no difference to Nicholas but out of respect for the dead knight, the very man he had helped to kill, he subdued his manners towards her. As he watched the lady dip her lovely titian head in greeting, scenes from Cairn's death tumbled about in Nicholas' mind; the ambush, the man being pulled off his horse, and the man being set upon by men with knives. All of the things he could have prevented but didn't because he was more interested in gaining what l'Ebreux had – his position at Lavister. Now, that envy might very well extend to the man's widowed wife. She was stunning. But Nicholas' manners did not belie his thoughts.

"Lady l'Ebreux," he said politely. "It is a pleasure to meet you. Please accept my condolences on the passing of your husband. He was a fine knight."

Madelayne cocked her head, looking curiously to the handsome, blonde knight. "You knew my husband?"

Nicholas nodded, unsure how much he should tell the woman about his encounter with Cairn at Beeston, when Kaspian mercifully spoke.

"It was Nicholas who tried to save Cairn," Kaspian said quietly. "He was the one who brought Cairn back to us after he had fallen."

Madelayne was visibly moved by the information. "Is that so?" she asked, looking to Nicholas. "Were you there when he fell, then? Did you see what happened?"

*Careful,* Nicholas thought. "Alas, my lady, by the time I reached your husband, it was too late," he lied. "I am sorry I was not in time to help him. I hope you can forgive me for my failure."

Madelayne didn't particularly want to discuss Cairn's death. It was a sad subject and an uncomfortable one. *Failure.* It was an interesting choice of a word when discussing Cairn because that was exactly the way Madelayne felt – as if she had failed the man somehow by becoming attracted to Kaspian. Failing his memory. But she knew, in her heart, that Cairn would have wanted her to be happy. He was simply that way. So perhaps in a sense, she really hadn't failed him. Still, it was a subject she didn't wish to discuss.

"There is nothing to forgive," she said, putting her knife and fruit back into the bowl and picking everything up. "If you will excuse me, I will leave you men to your privacy. I am sure there is a good deal you need to discuss."

She was already moving away from the table when Kaspian spoke to her. "We shall see you returned for the evening meal, my lady?"

Madelayne was already in the chamber doorway when she paused and turned to look at the men standing at the table. She smiled weakly. "Aye," she said. "I will return for the meal. It should be within the hour, in fact."

With that, she left the chamber, leaving Nicholas and Kaspian still standing and both still looking at her. Dolwyd followed her out, leaving the two knights alone. Hearing the door to the keep close, Nicholas turned to Kaspian.

"A pity," he said. "She is very young and beautiful to be a widow. I had no idea Cairn had married so well."

There was that predatory expression again, setting Kaspian on edge. He sat down, ignoring Nicholas' statement. "I will not discuss Lady l'Ebreux with you," he said. "You and I have a good deal to discuss about Lavister."

Nicholas sensed he'd been cut short on the subject of Cairn's widow and it intrigued him. It also did nothing to deter his interest. But he did the polite thing and sat down, folding his hands on the tabletop expectantly. For now, at least, he would let St. Hèver think he was doing as he was told, but the truth was that he didn't like to be ordered around by anyone.

Especially the man he intended to replace.

"Indeed we do," Nicholas said. "In fact, there is something I must tell you. I stopped in Northwich for the night and came across several de Lara men. They told me that there is a Welsh buildup near Hawarden Castle, something of massive proportions."

Kaspian forgot all about his jealousy and listened seriously to Nicholas' news. "I am not entirely surprised to hear that," he said honestly. "Hawarden has always been at the center of any Welsh storm. How long ago did you hear this information?"

"Last night, in fact," Nicholas said. "The de Lara men were heading north to Carlisle to relay the information. They are seeking reinforcements for the trilateral castles because no one on the Marches has men to spare."

It sounded serious, indeed. "What of de Lohr?" Kaspian asked. "He has thousands of men."

Nicholas shook his head. "They are holding the entire southern portion of the Marches at this point," he said. "At least, that's what the de Lara men told me because I asked the same question. They are covering Hereford, for God's sake, and every castle in the de Lohr line is armed to the teeth – Shadowmoor, Dorstone, Cross Ash, and Clearwell. So I am positive that we cannot expect any reinforcement from the de Lohr stables. And de Lara has Trelystan, Hyssington, and Caradoc to worry about. Nay, my friend, the Marcher lords are dug in where they are, waiting to see what Dafydd ap Gruffydd is going to do."

Kaspian drew in a deep, thoughtful breath as he processed the information. He hadn't heard any of this and he was rather surprised. Usually, the flow of information in the north was good because all of the garrisons kept each other informed, but this news had come up from the south and it was rather shocking. Hawarden Castle was not far from Lavister and he felt somewhat blindsided by the information, as he should have been one of the first people to know of it. But he'd not heard a thing from any of his spies and he was sure that if Thomas had, the man would have told him. He leaned forward on the table, his big arms folded on the tabletop.

"Beeston is still in English hands, as is Lavister," he said. "So is Holt Castle, to the south of us. I will be honest when I say that I have heard nothing of this news and Hawarden is a two day's ride from Lavister. If what you say is true, we must seek our reinforcements from places other than the Marches. No one has resources to share. I would assume that Edward is aware of this situation?"

Nicholas nodded. "He is, indeed," he replied. "I sent him word of the victory at Beeston right after it happened and I am sure he has received word from other Marcher lords as well as to the situation with Hawarden. He has his eye on the Marches right now, have no doubt."

Kaspian was pensive. "I have family north at Pendragon Castle," he said. "I also have friends and allies at Aysgarth Castle and Exelby Castle in Yorkshire. I could send word to them and request reinforcements."

Nicholas was in agreement. "That would be wise," he said. "Lavister guards the road between Chester and Wrexham, which makes it strategic. If Dafydd manages to capture it, he can launch attacks on those towns and beyond. It could be catastrophic for the Welsh to gain control of Lavister."

Kaspian's gaze lingered on him a moment. "You sound concerned."

Nicholas eyed the man, a flash of something dark and threatening crossing his features, before breaking into a grin. It was all an act, however; Nicholas didn't like Kaspian's comment, as if he were afraid of the Welsh. No man would call him a coward. The grin, therefore, was to cover up the flash of murderous outrage in his heart. He didn't like the challenge to his manhood.

"I am not the least bit concerned, I assure you," he said. "I welcome any action the Welsh can bring. The skirmish at Beeston was the first one I'd seen in a very long time. I am more at home in a battle than most."

Kaspian cocked an eyebrow. "Let us hope it does not come to that," he said. "I would be perfectly happy if the Welsh would pass us by."

Nicholas regarded him. "Now *you* sound concerned."

Kaspian could have sworn there was a taunt in de Dalyn's tone. He could see the edginess in Nicholas' eyes no matter how hard the man tried to hide it. "To be concerned is to be prudent," he said steadily. "To be prudent is not to be caught off guard."

"Agreed."

"Good. Then let us share the evening meal and converse with the rest of Lavister's knights at the conclusion of the meal to discuss this situation. They will want to hear what de Lara's men told you as well."

Nicholas simply nodded his head, letting the conversation naturally shift away from the threat on the Marches and on to other things, but the entire time, he was thinking on how gratifying it would be when he was finally in command of Lavister. It was clear that St. Hèver was struggling with his recovery from the terrible injury and the man wasn't nearly as strong as he should be to command such an outpost. Aye, Nicholas had plans for Lavister that didn't involve Kaspian St. Hèver.

Another strategic missive to Edward might solve his problem, eventually.

If not, there were other ways of ridding himself of an obstacle.

The evening meal was held in Lavister's great hall, with its cold stone walls and sharply pitched roof. Since there were so many men at Lavister, and all of them needed to be fed on a regular basis, the great hall saw a good deal of use. It smelled like men and dogs, urine and smoke, and there were always men in the structure either eating or sleeping or playing games – sometimes all three. On this evening well after sunset, the hall was full of men as they crowded around the three big feasting tables, shoving each other aside for a spot to eat.

The hall could seat about five hundred men, and that was crammed to the rafters, so those who weren't fortunate enough to claim a seat in the hall were relegated to eating outside around the half-dozen fires that littered the bailey on any given night. Ioin, the old cook, was a master at stretching food stores to make sure the army had enough to eat and on this night, he'd boiled pork with beans and carrots, creating a thick and hearty stew to dip loaves of crusty brown bread into. The pears that Madelayne had spent her time cutting had been boiled up, too, with honey and spices to create a delicious compote that was reserved only for the knights and their guests.

It was a surprisingly mild evening with a clear, night sky overhead and a sickle-shaped moon high in the heavens. Madelayne had been busy all afternoon, helping the cook, making sure the servants fed the men in an orderly fashion, as was usually the case in the evenings. Such a large crowd of men needed to be fed in an organized way and Madelayne was very good at doing that, so she supervised the hall while Mavia made sure there was a separate section for the knights to eat their meal. They also had additional food that the rank and file of men didn't have, the compote being an example. Only the knights and other guests would have that. As soon as the knights entered the hall, however, the ladies went to the table to sit with them, leaving the servants to tend the soldiers.

Kaspian was moving slowly this night. After his meeting with Nicholas, he'd gone to lay in his bed to rest and ended up falling asleep. Dolwyd had been forced to shake him awake to attend the meal and Kaspian had struggled to get moving. He wasn't feeling well at all but he didn't want to show any weakness in front of Nicholas.

Kaspian had to admit that he was starting to regret Nicholas' arrival even though he'd told the other men that they were lucky to have de Dalyn. Perhaps they were; perhaps they weren't. All Kaspian knew was that there was something about Nicholas he didn't trust. He wasn't sure what it was yet, but the man bore watching and, like any good predator, Kaspian was sure the man would pounce on him if he knew how weak he was.

*Prey.*

Kaspian didn't want to fall prey to the man.

So he tried very hard not to appear weak or weary as he entered the hall with Thomas. Ewan and Reece were already there, as was Nicholas, who was sitting at the table in the company of Mavia. In fact, Mavia was sitting next to Nicholas, laughing at a story the man was evidently telling. Dressed in a lovely yellow brocade, she seemed most attentive to their newest knight. Kaspian scrutinized the man as he drew near the table where they were congregating.

But that scrutiny was momentary. The person he really wanted to see was Madelayne, and he did, over near the servant's entrance that led out to the kitchens behind the hall. She had a pitcher in her hand and was heading for the table with the knights, kicking the dogs out of the way and reaching the table about the time Kaspian arrived. Their eyes met and magic, like stardust, filled the air between them.

"Lady l'Ebreux, please sit," Kaspian told her, taking the pitcher from her hands and setting it down on the table. "Knowing you, you have been slaving away all afternoon. I do not know if I have ever seen you not busy."

Dressed in a linen surcoat with a soft, white shift beneath it, Madelayne looked quite radiant from her red-tinted cheeks. She had been running around most of the evening and was a wee bit weary as a result, but she smiled at Kaspian as he indicated the seat next to him. She finally sat, across from Nicholas, Mavia, and Ewan, as a male servant appeared to deliver their trenchers.

"There is much work to do," she said to Kaspian as Reece picked up the pitcher she had brought and began pouring sloppy cups of wine all around. "In fact, that is something I would like to speak with you about. There is too much work for Mavia and me to do and I would like to solicit more help from the neighboring villages, Rossett or even Grosford. We really do need the help, Kaspian. Would you allow taking on a few more women servants? Cairn once said that you did not like women at a military installation, but would you at least consider it?"

"Of course he will," Nicholas said before Kaspian could answer. He was focused intently on Madelayne. "In fact, Lady l'Ebreux, you should not be working at all. You are a fine and delicate lady and it is unseemly for you to be working so hard. You should be kept in your chamber with your fine sewing or painting, not working the kitchens like a common servant. St. Hèver should be ashamed that he permits you to do such lowly things."

It was a dig at Kaspian, who didn't react to the insult. Instead, he pretended as if Nicholas hadn't said anything at all. Ignoring him was better in this case because if he fired a barb at the man, the evening could turn ugly quite quickly. He found himself restrained in Madelayne's presence, not wanting to upset her.

"Of course," Kaspian said quietly to Madelayne. "We will discuss later what you have in mind and proceed accordingly. But I have known you for three years and this is the first time you have ever asked me for any assistance. I pray that you were not somehow reluctant to ask sooner."

Madelayne wasn't very happy with Nicholas, either, but Kaspian hadn't responded to the man so she didn't. It wasn't her place, after all. Instead, she was focused on Kaspian.

"I do not mind hard work, truly," she said. "But it has become a bit much as of late. Mayhap I am simply slowing down."

"Or mayhap you should not be doing it at all, as de Dalyn said."

She smiled weakly. "As I said, I do not mind, but it would be easier if there were more hands."

He smiled in return. "Then it shall be done," he said. Then, he turned to Nicholas, the smile gone from his face. "Do you have anything more to say about it?"

Nicholas, who was already on to his second cup of wine, lifted his big shoulders carelessly. "Me?" he asked. "Of course not. You are doing the right thing, St. Hèver. Good for you. All women need to be placed on their cushioned chairs and worshipped, not forced to work like slaves."

Before Kaspian could reply to yet another insult, Madelayne pointed a finger at him. "Sir Nicholas, that is the second time you have accused Sir Kaspian of the negligence of women in front of his men," she said sternly. "I do not think that was a polite thing for you to do. Sir Kaspian has never treated Lady Mavia or me poorly. In fact, he has always been considerate of us. We work because it must be done. You have only been here a matter of hours and do not yet know the ways of Lavister, so I suggest you take the time to observe before making any unsavory accusations."

Reece and Ewan snorted into their cups as Nicholas appeared genuinely apologetic. "Pray forgive, madam," he said sincerely. "I was only thinking of you and Lady Mavia, of course. Were you my wife, you would never know a day of work."

She cocked an eyebrow. "Then it is a good thing I am not your wife," she said. "I should not like to be told I must sit in a chair and sew all day. 'Tis a ridiculous notion to expect a woman to sit and do nothing. We are not made of glass, Sir Knight. We will not break."

Nicholas was amused by her fire; her speech was quite passionate. "My lady, I do believe you are close to a tantrum. Pray forgive me for provoking you so."

"It is Sir Kaspian you should be begging forgiveness from."

Nicholas' gaze trailed to Kaspian and there was a flash of defiance there, quickly gone. "My apologies, St. Hèver."

He didn't sound as if he meant a word of it and Madelayne's first impressions of Nicholas were not kind ones. She could already see an arrogant and imperious man, but she said nothing more and returned to her food. To her left, however, Kaspian was watching her.

Nicholas' apology meant nothing to him; he didn't even acknowledge it. He was more fascinated by Madelayne because the woman was being concerned for him again and it was something he was wholly unused to. He'd never had a woman defend him as she did or show interest in him as she did, so this was an entirely new experience for him. He couldn't even remember if she'd ever shown such concern for Cairn and he honestly couldn't, but the truth was that he'd never paid much attention to that kind of thing so it was possible that she did and he never noticed. In any case, she was a fearsome defender and it touched and flattered him. Rather than be put off by it, or emasculated, he rather liked the way she was willing to leap to his defense.

"Lady l'Ebreux and Lady Allington-More have been my chatelaines for several years now," Kaspian finally spoke, looking at Nicholas. "They do whatever work they feel necessary and have my support in any case. If they did not wish to do any work, I would support that as well. They do what they want to do."

Nicholas simply nodded, gulping at his wine, as a servant put a trencher in front of him filled with pork and beans and carrots. He smacked his lips and set the cup down, picking up his spoon.

"A very wise attitude, St. Hèver," he said as he scooped up beans with his spoon and shoved them his mouth. As he started to chew, his focus turned to Madelayne. "Tell me, Lady l'Ebreux; where were you born? What is your background?"

Madelayne picked up her spoon as well as her trencher was placed in front of her. "I was born in Wrexham," she said. "My father is a merchant."

Nicholas chewed, looking at her with interest. "Were you educated?"

"I was."

"I was born in Gloucester," Mavia said, interrupted the conversation. "My father is Lord Tiberton. I fostered at Sherborne Castle."

Madelayne couldn't help but notice that Mavia seemed a bit edgy, as if leaving her out of the conversation with Nicholas had upset her. She smiled at the woman. "Lady Allington-More's background is much more prestigious than mine," she said. "She has some very fine stories about her years at Sherborne."

Nicholas glanced at Mavia, who smiled rather eagerly at him. It was an odd gesture, really, one that didn't go unnoticed by Madelayne. It was almost as if she were quite eager for the man's attention, jealous that he has spoken to Madelayne. It was very strange.

"Lady Allington-More and I have spent the afternoon together, as she has been gracious enough to show me around Lavister," Nicholas said evenly before returning his attention to Madelayne. "But I have not had the chance yet to come to know you. Tell me more about yourself, Lady l'Ebreux."

"Let the woman eat her meal," Kaspian said, cleaving any further conversation. The tone of his voice suggested he wasn't pleased with the way Nicholas was pushing Madelayne for information. "She is not here to entertain you with conversation. You have four knights surrounding you who would be happy to regale you with stories. Ewan and Reece have many, in fact. They grew up in Wales in a rather horrible place called Netherworld Castle."

Reece heard him. The man was into his third cup of wine and feeling quite happy. "It is not as bad as all that, my lord," he said to Kaspian. "It is actually a very beautiful place in the summer. But it does come with a ghost."

Nicholas forgotten, Madelayne was grinning at Reece's somewhat drunken manner. He and his brother had backed off from flirting with her quite a bit as of late, as if someone had told them to. She suspected Kaspian might have told them that she was not interested in either of them, as unmarried knights, and she further suspected there might have been a threat or two thrown in. She tore apart her bread as she spoke.

"Do tell us about the ghost, Reece," she said. "Spirits have always interested me. There was one in my father's house because it was built on the foundations of an old Roman villa. The servants used to tell of things moving around in the kitchen or of footsteps in the hall. I heard the footsteps, once. It was thrilling."

Reece shoved bread into his mouth. "This ghost was *not* thrilling, I assure you, my lady," he said. "It would throw things around in the keep. It even pushed people. Some said it was the ghost of one of my ancestors, a very mean man who would harm people. Gryffyn was his name. He is still harming people in death as he did in life, and he is especially harmful to women."

Before Madelayne could respond, Nicholas snorted. "I do not believe in spirits or ghosts," he said. "Any man who does is foolish. Mayhap it was simply one of your servants, playing tricks on everyone."

Reece stopped chewing and looked at him. "Are you calling me a fool?"

The mood of the table suddenly plummeted with deadly hazard in Reece's tone. Kaspian was quite curious as to how it would all play out and, in particular, how Nicholas would handle it. If he was supposed to be in command of men, he could not be confrontational with them. If he was, then Kaspian was within his power to send Nicholas away. He was almost hoping the man snapped and gave him a reason. Therefore, he watched the situation very carefully.

Nicholas, however, didn't rise to the bait in Reece's tone. He didn't even look up from his food. "Of course I am not calling you a fool," he said. "I am simply saying that I do not believe in ghosts. They do not exist. It is more than likely a servant playing tricks."

That didn't soothe Reece in the least. His eyebrows lifted. "Have you ever seen a ghost, de Dalyn?"

"I have not."

"I have, so shut your trap!"

Nicholas looked up from his food, then. "I would be careful who I threaten, little man."

Mavia had the unfortunate position of sitting in between Reece and Nicholas. Reece moved in Nicholas' direction as if to throw a punch but ended up spilling his wine all over Mavia's yellow gown. The woman shrieked and leapt to her feet as the rest of the knights bolted to their feet because there was a fight to prevent, especially in front of women. Ewan grabbed his brother, literally pulling the man over the table to get him away from Nicholas as Thomas held out an arm to Nicholas to keep the man from charging.

"He has had too much to drink, de Dalyn," Thomas said calmly. "Let his brother take him away. He will probably not remember this come morning so I will apologize for him. He is young and spirited. You must take that into account."

Nicholas didn't say a word, his body coiled as he watched Ewan drag his brother from the hall. Meanwhile, Madelayne rushed to Mavia's aid. The woman's entire bodice was covered in purple wine.

"Let me help you," Madelayne offered, holding Mavia's right arm aloft because it was dripping with wine. "We must soak that stain immediately or the dress will be unsalvageable."

Mavia was very upset. "Reece is a fool!" she hissed. "When I see him next, I am going to box his silly ears!"

Madelayne was leading her away from the table. "Do not touch anything," she said. "Keep your hand aloft; aye, like that. You will drip onto your skirt if you do not."

They were moving past Nicholas, who had turned away from Reece and most definitely had his eye on Madelayne now.

"You are most kind to tend Lady Mavia," he said to her. "It was my fault, after all. Mayhap I should go with you both to make sure you reach your destination unmolested. I am sure Lavister, like any other place filled with men, can be quite dangerous to lone women."

Madelayne spoke before Mavia could. "That is not necessary, Sir Nicholas," she said. "Please stay and enjoy your meal. Mavia and I have control of the situation although we thank you for your offer."

Nicholas wouldn't be declined so easily. "My lady, please," he said, already starting to follow them. "It would be my privilege. Moreover, since you no longer have a husband, it is the duty of his colleagues to protect you where he cannot. I feel particularly responsible since it was I who was not in time to save him. Please allow me to help you, however small the gesture may be."

Madelayne looked at him, sharply. The reminder of Cairn's death was unnecessary, she thought, and the suggestion that he take Cairn's place where her protection was concerned was offensive. As if de Dalyn could ever take Cairn's place. As if she would ever want him to! As she prepared a not-so-kind reply, Kaspian spoke, quietly and most definitely with a hint of threat.

"You need not worry over Lady l'Ebreux," he rumbled. "She will indeed have a new husband, very soon. She is to be my wife so you will put her safety out of your mind, de Dalyn. You are not responsible for it."

Everyone who heard Kaspian looked at him with surprise and that included Madelayne. She couldn't recall actually consenting to their marriage but the moment he spoke of a betrothal between them, she honestly didn't mind. With everything that had transpired between them over the past few weeks, with the highs and lows and intimate situations, she realized that her resistance to the proposal was gone. They had spent time together and she was coming to feel things about the man that she had never felt for anyone else. To think of not spending her life with him was shattering, her silly reasons for resisting him be damned. Perhaps it was time to stand up and face her feelings rather than let her guilt about Cairn rule her.

Nay, she didn't feel strange about his announcement at all. In fact, she was rather proud.

It was Thomas who spoke first. "Kaspian, is this true?" he asked, trying to keep the shock out of his tone. "You are really to marry Lady l'Eb… I mean, Madelayne?"

Kaspian turned to the man, reading the astonishment in his face. "Aye," he replied steadily. "Do not look so shocked, all of you. I realize that Cairn has not been gone very long but it seems the right thing to do by marrying her. I imagine Cairn would want his wife taken care of, so why wait? It does not diminish the man's death or her grief over it, if she takes another husband who simply wishes to take care of her. Would you rather see her marry some other fool you do not know or would you rather have her marry a man whose character you trust?"

The way he put it made sense and the shock and even outrage over Kaspian marrying Cairn's widow so soon after Cairn's death quickly faded. In fact, it was probably the best of all worlds – Kaspian would respect Cairn's memory by taking care of Lady l'Ebreux through marriage. The woman would eventually need another husband, would she not? Was there truly much difference if she wanted one month or one year? More than likely, there wasn't much difference although for propriety's sake, waiting would have better. But it was of no matter. The woman deserved a bit of happiness and Kaspian seemed willing to provide it.

Nay, the marriage proposal didn't seem all that shocking upon reflection. Perhaps it really was the best for all involved, especially

Madelayne. She would be married to a man who would be good to her and, of course, that was what Cairn would have wanted most of all.

"I would rather see her happy and well-tended," Thomas said, looking between Kaspian and Madelayne. "That is what Cairn would have wanted, of course. You have my congratulations, Kaspian. As do you, my lady."

He went to Madelayne and kissed her politely on the cheek, even as Madelayne stood there and continued to hold Mavia's arm. Mavia, however, was still reeling with shock from the entire thing. She was looking at Madelayne with wide eyes.

"Truly, Madelayne?" she gasped. "Marriage so soon?"

Madelayne looked at Kaspian. Their eyes met and he smiled faintly at her, a reassuring gesture. It was one that gave Madelayne confidence. Looking at him, she very much liked the idea of becoming Lady St. Hèver.

"Aye," she said to Mavia, gently pulling the woman away from the table. "Kaspian and I have discussed it. A business arrangement of sorts. I believe Cairn would approve."

Mavia didn't say anything more; she wasn't so sure about all of this. Trapped in her miserable marriage with Thomas, she was envious that Madelayne should find happiness again so soon. She wanted such happiness, too. She had just spent a glorious afternoon with Lavister's newest knight and she was quite sure the man was smitten with her, which thrilled her. Perhaps there was hope for a thrill from an admirer, after all. As Madelayne led her away from the table, she looked to Nicholas, who was still standing next to the ladies. He had a bit of a startled expression on his face but Mavia didn't notice; she only noticed his pale blue eyes, eyes that could make her heart flutter wildly.

"Sir Nicholas," she said. "I would accept your offer to escort Madelayne and me to the keep. Surely this little incident will not dampen our evening, will it? You will tell me more of your adventures at Anchorsholme. That is what you were speaking of when the meal began, is it not? I am sure Madelayne would like to hear your stories, too. Your previous garrison sounds like a most fascinating place."

Nicholas was startled, indeed, by the marriage announcement. In truth, he was actually speechless about it. St. Hèver had made it plainly clear that Lady l'Ebreux belonged to him, for now the woman was to be his wife, but the truth was that marriage had never been much of a deterrent for Nicholas and a betrothal certainly wasn't. He had never viewed such things as a limitation to his wants. So he immediately looked at Mavia's request as an opportunity to charm Madelayne. Regardless of what St. Hèver said, he was going to take that opportunity and he knew that St. Hèver wouldn't dispute him or argue with him for fear of upsetting the women. With that in mind, he flashed a dimpled smile.

"It would be my pleasure to escort you both to the keep," he said, extending an elbow to Mavia, who immediately slipped her wine-stained hand into the crook of his elbow. He held out the other elbow for Madelayne. "My lady?"

Madelayne didn't want to accept the elbow and most especially in front of Kaspian. More and more, she was coming not to like Nicholas' bold manner.

"I am capable of walking on my own," she told him, pushing past both him and Mavia. "Come along; we must tend to that gown before it is ruined."

With that, she walked from the hall with Nicholas and Mavia in tow. Kaspian and Thomas watched the group leave before reclaiming their seats at the table, now vacated for the most part. It was just the two of them. Kaspian broke his bread apart and dipped it in his cooling stew.

"You have no qualms about Nicholas being so attentive to your wife?" Kaspian asked Thomas.

The knight seemed more interested in his food. "Mavia is easily flattered but it means nothing," he said. "She will pine over him for a while and she may even dream about it, but it is a passing fancy. I know my wife well enough to know that she isn't capable of anything more."

Kaspian grunted. "If Nicholas turned his attention on my wife the way he has turned his attention on yours, I would kill him."

"That must mean you have noticed the way he has looked at Lady l'Ebreux."

Kaspian shoved bread into his mouth. "I will not be as tolerant of him as you are."

Thomas didn't see the issue, to be truthful. Or perhaps, it was more that he really didn't much care. He and Mavia were married, and had been for almost ten years, and their existence these days was more companionship than anything else. There wasn't any real affection there and hadn't been for a very long time. Therefore, Mavia's passing flirtation with Nicholas didn't disturb him.

At least, it didn't disturb him until Ewan came to him later that night, when both were on guard, and mentioned that there was a rumor going about that Nicholas had been seen passionately kissing Mavia near the stables sometime before dinner, which meant Thomas had supped with a man who had taken advantage of his wife. More than having his feelings hurt, Thomas felt some humiliation if such a thing was true. Confronting Mavia when he went to bed later that night had only brought tears and a staunch denial.

As Thomas listened to his wife rage at the ridiculousness of such a rumor, he began to realize that it wasn't a rumor at all. He could see right through Mavia's hysteria.

Rumors usually had a seed of truth.

After that, he vowed to keep a close eye on the pair.

# CHAPTER NINE

The washerwoman couldn't seem to get the wine stain out of Mavia's yellow brocade gown. She had scrubbed and scrubbed until her hands were raw, but a faint stain remained. Madelayne had been in the kitchen conversing with the cook when she heard the washerwoman complain loudly about the stubborn spot. Strolling out into the kitchen yard, Madelayne took a try at removing the stain herself.

Since she wasn't one of those dainty, well-bred women who were afraid to touch anything suggestive of manual labor, she worked over the tub out in the muddy yard. The sky above was bluer than it had been in weeks. At least, it looked bluer. Perhaps it was just because she was happier than she had ever been in her life, since Kaspian had announced their betrothal. Whatever the case, life was a bit brighter, a bit happier this day.

But the stain on Mavia's gown was stubborn. After a good deal of scrubbing over the well-worn washing stones, Madelayne held it up, inspected it, and shook her head.

"'Tis not going to come clean," she said. "Perhaps we shall dye this dress another color to cover the stain. We'll have to ask Lady Mavia."

The old, toothless washerwoman agreed. "A lovely indigo."

"Indigo?"

"'Tis the only color dark enough to cover such a stain. I'll go ask her."

The woman waddled away and Madelayne put the gown back in the tub to give it one last try. Her long hair, gathered into a braid at the nape of her neck, fell over her shoulder and the ends splashed into the water. Exasperated, she grasped her hair with wet hands and tossed it back over her shoulder.

"Ouch!"

She had struck something with her wet hair. Turning sharply, she saw that Nicholas stood behind her, wiping his eye.

"Sir Nicholas!" she gasped. "Forgive me. I did not know you were behind me."

He blinked his blue eyes. "No harm done," he smiled, though his right eye stung terribly with soap. "I should not have snuck up on you as I did."

Madelayne didn't know what to say, so she shrugged her shoulders in a sort of forgiving gesture. "How may I assist you this day?" she asked.

He simply smiled at her, a dazzling gesture that had worked wonders with Mavia but Madelayne wasn't impressed by it. From what she had seen the previous night, the man was someone to be wary of. Moreover, he seemed to have a habit of looking at her as if she were a bit of juicy beef and that in and of itself made her vastly uncomfortable. Therefore, she purposely kept a safe distance.

If Nicholas noticed her standoffishness, he didn't let on. Instead, he pointed to the tub. "Do you always do the wash?" he asked.

Madelayne wiped a bit of hair from her face with the back of her hand. "Not always," she said. "But this is Lady Mavia's favorite gown and we cannot seem to rid it of the wine stain. I thought I would give it a try."

"From the unfortunate accident last night?"

"Aye."

Nicholas shook his head. "Meaning no disrespect, my lady, but does St. Hèver allow this? I cannot imagine for one moment that I would permit my intended to strain herself so over a wash tub. Lovely hands such as yours are best suited to needlework or painting."

She lifted an eyebrow at him. "Must I explain this again?" she said. "I am chatelaine here, Sir Nicholas. I would never have my servants do anything that I myself was not prepared to do. It's only a tub, for Heaven's sake; it's not as if I am plucking chickens or harvesting the fields."

He put up his hands in supplication. "As I said, I did not mean to offend." His clear blue eyes drifted over her, studying her long titian hair, angelic face, sweet lips. "I simply meant that a lady of such beauty and refinement should not worry over mundane things better left to servants. If you were my intended, I would make sure your feet never even touched the ground."

Madelayne was feeling vastly uncomfortable under his scrutiny. "Kaspian allows me a free hand in my duties to accomplish things however I see fit," she said. "Now, if there isn't anything else, I must be about my duties."

She turned her back on him, returning to the gown. Nicholas stood a respectful distance behind her, watching her delicious figure as she vigorously scrubbed the dress.

"I can see that you are very valuable to Kaspian," he said. "'Tis no wonder he has agreed to marry you. I applaud his foresight."

She didn't like the way he had worded his phrase. She peered at him over her shoulder. "Foresight?"

"Of course. Keeping you here at Lavister Crag before some other man could whisk you away."

"Who would want to whisk me away?"

Nicholas snorted. "Any man would. You are a beautiful woman, my lady. Or hadn't you realized that?"

Nicholas was trying to flatter her but Madelayne would have no part of it. She turned her back on him again and continued with the gown. "I have duties to attend to, my lord. Good day to you."

Nicholas nodded, a smile on his face. He would not push today, but another day would come when she might be more receptive to his flattery. He rather liked the fact that she wasn't falling all over herself to please him. "There is one thing, if you do not mind," he said. "I know it sounds strange, but I was wondering if you could have a tub brought up to my room. I'm a bit strange in that I like to bathe on occasion, at least once a week. Otherwise I smell like something that has been dead for a few days. Could you see to it?"

She nodded. "As you wish, my lord. I'll have it brought up today."

He walked up behind her, slowly, coming to rest beside the wash tub as she continued to rub away at the stain. He watched her red hands and laughed softly. "You know, I'll need help bathing. Never could do my hair or my back without assistance. You seem so good at washing things that I was wondering if…."

That was as far as he got before Madelayne flared. Outraged and incensed over what he was surely about to say, she shoved him hard enough to topple him into the wash tub. The entire contraption crashed to the ground, knight, suds and all, and Nicholas found himself wallowing in soapy mud. She stood over him, as furious as a wet cat.

"That is all the washing you'll get from me, Nicholas de Dalyn," she seethed. "I would advise that from now on you keep your distance, else this is only a foretaste of my wrath to come. Is that clear?"

He was having trouble keeping a straight face. "Ever so, my lady."

She spun on her heel and stormed off, as angry as she had ever been and frankly fearful of what Kaspian's reaction would be to Nicholas' near-suggestion. She knew such a thing would get back to him. But Nicholas clearly wasn't worried. As she entered the kitchen, she heard the distinct sounds of his laughter.

Madelayne stormed through the kitchen and into the great hall, kicking at the dogs because they were in her way. By the time she crossed the bailey and headed into the keep, her cheeks were red with fury, something that did not go unnoticed by Mavia who was just quitting the keep.

"Madelayne!" Mavia exclaimed. "What's the matter?"

Before she could consider that discretion was the better option at this point, in her anger she spilled out everything. Mavia paled with jealousy at the story, but Madelayne didn't notice. She needed time to cool her fury so she marched past Mavia, up the stairs, and into the chamber she and Kaspian had shared for the better part of several weeks. He wasn't there, as she had suspected, for he had been spending most afternoons with Dolwyd trying to regain some strength in his torso. The muscles had been badly damaged and the old man had worked out a regime for Kaspian to begin strengthening them.

It was quiet and still, the sounds of the ward far below drifting in through the lancet windows. The noise drew her and she leaned against the windowsill, gazing to the green horizon that disappeared into Wales. It was clear and cool on this day, the beauty of the land and the stillness of the chamber soothing her anger. She breathed deeply, drawing in the tranquil air. She still could not believe Sir Nicholas' boldness and her furious reaction had been just in her opinion. Now, she needed time to regain her composure.

Time passed and she forced herself to cool. Pulling out a piece of sewing she had been working on, she sat near the window and steadily notched the tiny stitches that formed a graceful hummingbird in what would soon be a lovely shawl. It was a pretty piece she had originally meant for the baby, but now it was just something she struggled to finish. With her anger finally under control, she was actually enjoying a tranquil moment when the chamber door flew open and Kaspian, larger than life, stood in the doorway.

Madelayne's tranquility took flight when she saw his expression. He glared at her, the posture of his body indicating everything she needed to know before he even said it.

"What did he say to you?"

His voice rolled like thunder. Dolwyd was standing behind him, wrought with distress, and Madelayne struggled to keep her newly-gained calm.

"Nothing that would warrant his death," she said steadily. "I believe I dealt with him quite efficiently. Now he will know where I stand on the subject."

Kaspian was as angry as she had ever seen him and she had known the man many years. He had always been the paragon of cool. Now he looked like an enraged bull, his body thinner than it had been before his injury, but nonetheless strung with powerful muscles. He could very easily destroy. And the fact that he stood a foot and a half taller than she did only added to his aura of intimidation.

"Subject of what?" he demanded. "Madelayne, I want you to tell me exactly what happened."

Madelayne knew that Mavia had gone right to her husband with what she had been told and Thomas had rightly passed the information on to Kaspian. There was no telling what had been lost in translation. Swishing her hand at Dolwyd in a vacating motion, the old man obediently quit the chamber and shut the door. Madelayne put her hands on Kaspian's chest and attempted to push him toward the bed.

"Please, sit down," she instructed. "You look as if you are ready to explode."

He grasped the hands on his chest and refused to move. "Tell me now, Madelayne. No more delays. What did de Dalyn say to you that caused you to throw a tub at him?"

She sighed. "I did not throw a tub at him. I pushed him into it."

"Why?"

"Because he asked me to help him bathe."

Kaspian stared at her. In the next moment, he was moving for the door like a man possessed and Madelayne threw her arms around his neck, dragging on him like an anchor.

"Nay!" she pleaded. "Kaspian, you are not strong enough to take him on yet and I'll not bury another husband!"

His jaw was grinding. "I'm strong enough and you'll not bury me any time soon." He was at the door with her draped down his body. "Let go, Madelayne. I must teach Nicholas a lesson he'll not soon forget."

"You do not need to," she refused to let go and he wasn't pulling her away, not yet. "I won't let you fight him, Kaspian. I swear I'll jump into the middle of it and you'll not be able to make a good go at him."

He glared down at her. "You would protect him?"

"I would protect *you*." Tears glistened in her eyes as she looked at him. "Please do not, Kaspian. I'm sure Nicholas won't do anything so bold again. He was simply testing me, I fear, to see what I am made of."

Kaspian's blood was boiling. But gazing into her magnificent eyes, he felt himself relent. "And he found out, no doubt."

A smile tugged at her lips. "He accused me of a tantrum last night," she said. "I fear I gave him an example of the real thing."

He took a deep breath, struggling for calm. "I cannot let this go unanswered. You know that."

She nodded patiently. "I know," she said softly. "But perhaps you can simply have a word with him, not gut him. If it happens again after that, I'll not stop you from what needs to be done."

His jaw twitched and she could see that he was seriously considering her request. She pulled herself up and kissed him, very gently, on his stubbled cheek. "Please, Kaspian."

It was the first time she had voluntarily kissed him and Kaspian yielded like a weakling. "Very well. I'll speak with him. But if it happens again…."

"You have my permission."

He eyed her, still flushed with outrage. Madelayne could think of only one thing to calm him.

"Come," she let go of his neck and took his hand. Pulling him toward the bed, she smiled. "You've had a trying afternoon. You must regain your strength."

He eyed the bed. "What did you have in mind?"

Madelayne began to fumble with her bodice. "I've been full to bursting. Relieve me of this load before I explode."

He didn't argue and, as she knew, his anger was quickly forgotten with the anticipation of her delicious breasts. Kaspian lay on his back, expecting her to lay beside him, but instead she surprised him by straddling him and sitting on his abdomen, very carefully to avoid putting any strain on his injury. Sliding her gown off her shoulders, she lay forward, depositing a rosy nipple directly into his mouth.

It was utterly erotic, on a higher level than they had ever dared broach. One hand slid down Madelayne's torso to her round buttocks as she straddled him, and he cupped one cheek in a huge palm. The other hand held the breast in his mouth, pulling and kneading as he suckled. All thoughts of Nicholas flew from his mind. Madelayne belonged to him now and he had never felt more contentment.

Madelayne stroked his blonde hair, kissing his forehead gently as he moved from one breast to the other. She was trembling with an excitement she had never allowed herself to feel, giving in to the pull between them. Kaspian's hand moved from her buttocks, snaking underneath her gown and stroking her silky thigh. He never moved high enough to touch her woman's center, yet his exploration of her was apparent. Madelayne enjoyed every stroke, every caress.

Although he tried to make it last, she was soon dry on both breasts. Knowing that his prolonged suckling tended to make her sore and chaffed, he reluctantly removed himself from her nipples and gently dried them off with a corner of the bed linen. Madelayne watched him, his delicate movements, seeing a whole new side to Kaspian St. Hèver that she had never before realized. He was taking on a new dimension before her very eyes. Kaspian glanced up, noticed she was staring at him, and choked off a laugh.

"You were saying something, dearest?"

She wasn't sure where his sudden joviality came from. "I haven't said a word."

He shifted, turning so that she was cradled beside him on the bed. His powerful arms went around her, truly holding her for the first time in an intimate embrace. "Aye, you did, several minutes ago. Something about not killing Nicholas. You seem to have convinced me not to do it."

She smiled, relishing his heat, the strength of his body against her. "Have I some power over you, do you suggest?"

"You have something, that is clear. To cause me to forget my anger is no easy feat."

Her smile faded. "I was not attempting to manipulate you. I am only concerned for your welfare."

"I know."

"What are you going to say to him?"

"I'm not sure yet. But it will come to me."

Madelayne lingered on that a moment. The sun was dimming through the lancet window, reminding her that she had a meal to oversee. She sighed, not wanting to leave him, not wanting to spoil the moment.

"I should go to the kitchen and supervise the evening meal," she said. "What will you do now?"

She was gazing up at him and he stroked an errant hair from her cheek. He found himself running a finger over her soft skin, admiring the shape of her face. "Christ, you are a lovely creature. I always knew that, but I suppose I never let myself explore just how beautiful you truly were."

Pink touched her cheeks. "Why not?"

"Because you were married to Cairn, of course."

She propped herself up on an elbow. Impulsively, she kissed his nose and giggled, and he pulled her back down to him and kissed her deeply. With each successive kiss, they were coming to crave each other more and more, like an insatiable hunger that only mounted with each bite.

Kaspian finally pulled away with a groan. He was engorged and uncomfortable. "Go downstairs, then. If you stay here any longer I am afraid of what I might do to you."

She smirked but dutifully rose from the bed. She felt flustered, lightheaded and wonderful. "You cannot do anything to me until we are married."

He cocked an eyebrow at her. "I was fondling your breasts not five minutes ago. According to the church, we should not even be doing that."

She matched his raised eyebrow. "Then I suppose, according to the church, I should not have nursed you when you were wounded. It could be considered a sin."

"Not true. You were saving a dying man."

She held up a finger. "Ah, but you touched me during those times in a manner that was not consistent with healing of any kind."

"I did not."

"Aye, you did. Or did I imagine those caresses and kisses?"

"You did."

She yelped in outrage, although it was good natured. Before she could reach the door, however, Kaspian was up, blocking her path. When they gazed at each other, eyes smoldering, there were smiles on their lips.

"Why did you stop me?" she demanded softly. "I was about to throw another temper tantrum."

The corner of his mouth twitched. "I will save you the trouble. You did not, in fact, imagine my kisses or caresses. They were meant that you should notice them."

"Truthfully, I wasn't sure."

He leaned down and kissed her, very tenderly, on the lips. Lifting the latch, he opened the door for her. "From now on I shall be more obvious."

CR

Smoke lay against the ceiling of the great hall like a ghostly bank of clouds. The fire spit as much haze into the room as up the chimney, the sharp smell mingling with those of roast mutton and dogs and sweat. The knights and several senior soldiers lingered around the long scrubbed table, while the rest of the room was cluttered with lesser fighting men enjoying their meal.

Madelayne, not one to sit and leisurely enjoy the meal while there was work to be done, poured wine for Kaspian and Nicholas, making sure to stay between them in case something should erupt. It wasn't that she didn't trust Kaspian; she didn't trust Nicholas not to bring up the events in the yard that afternoon and provoke Kaspian beyond reason. And then she could not stop the consequences.

Kaspian, however, had barely acknowledged Nicholas in any manner, his mood growing darker as Nicholas seemed to pay an overly generous amount of attention to Madelayne. But the knight was sly; he hadn't said more than a word or two to her, but his looks had positively sizzled. She ignored him soundly, much to Kaspian's approval, but Nicholas was persistent. If he could make eye contact with her, he would, but he stopped short of touching her in any fashion. Even for him, that would have been an overt, dangerous maneuver.

It was a cool, hazardous game being played. But there was something else Kaspian had noticed throughout the course of the meal, and that was the way Lady Mavia was staring at Nicholas, as if she were admiring something lustful and marvelous. He didn't give it much thought, however, being more concerned with how Nicholas was dealing with Madelayne.

But Thomas noticed. After what Ewan had told him last night and after his confrontation with Mavia about the rumor of her being kissed by Nicholas, he made it his particular mission to watch the interaction between Nicholas and his wife on this night. The more he watched, the more he could see that the rumor of their intimate encounter was not a rumor at all. Mavia was looking at Nicholas with such adoration that it was enough to make Thomas' blood boil. He remembered seeing that look in her eyes long ago when they were first married and it was admiration in its purest form. Now she had that same look towards Nicholas. What had once been Thomas' disinterest towards de Dalyn was now turning into something else.

*Humiliation.* Thomas had been most supportive of Nicholas' arrival at Lavister, but that was apparently no longer. Not when his wife gazed so dreamily at the man and it was rumored that Nicholas had taken advantage of her. Drink filled Thomas' veins and the sting of dishonor stirred within him. He wondered what kind of a man would so brazenly molest the wife of another man without care to consequences. When Mavia laughed at something witty Nicholas said, the hammer finally came down.

Thomas' big fists slammed against the table. He was on his feet, glaring at Nicholas with seething fury.

"I've had enough of you," he growled. "Your pretty words, your fine manners. You are like a serpent, attempting to seduce every woman at Lavister. You are here to fight, de Dalyn, not to rut like a bull!"

Nicholas was very cool, gazing at Thomas as if surprised by his statement. "Thomas," he said. "What have I done? I would apologize immediately for…."

Thomas cut him off, drunk and angry. "You cannot possibly apologize for your seduction of my wife, or for the blatant disrespect to Lady Madelayne. I've always heard you to be manipulative, but never against those who supported you. Never against men you fight with."

Nicholas stood up, his blue eyes glittering. "I do not know what you mean."

Thomas snorted. "Certainly you do. It goes on right here, right before my eyes. Everyone can see you for the snake you are."

For a second night in a row, the ambiance of the room darkened. Wide eyed, Madelayne moved close to Kaspian, afraid that swords were going to be drawn at any moment. Kaspian, watching the confrontation carefully, felt her bump in to him and looked up, noting her fearful expression. Gently, he put his arm around her waist and pulled her aside, well out of the range of any swords should violence break out.

"Nicholas, Thomas," he said in a low tone. "You are frightening the women. Sit down, the both of you, and let no more be said. Deal with your differences at another time. I would enjoy my meal in peace."

Thomas looked at him. "Is that all you have to say for the grievous insult he dealt Lady Madelayne this afternoon?"

The attention was back on Kaspian. Thomas had voiced what everyone was thinking but were too fearful to express. Thanks to Mavia, the entire castle knew what had happened to varying degrees. Some tales actually had Nicholas ravaging Madelayne. Everyone waited with baited breath as Thomas' question sank deep, but Kaspian, true to form, remained inherently calm.

"Nicholas knows what he did was in appropriate at the very least," he finally said. "But I believe Lady Madelayne dealt with him appropriately. I trust nothing like that will ever happen again, lest he be forced then to answer to me."

Nicholas lifted an eyebrow. "What, pray, did I do?"

Kaspian looked at him, unable to keep the expression of disbelief off his face. He was having difficulty understanding why the man would deny it. "Is it truly necessary for me to explain, considering it was and continues to be a private matter?" he asked.

Nicholas continued to appear innocent. "I did nothing more than ask that a bathtub be brought to my room."

Kaspian was left with no choice. "You asked that Lady Madelayne bathe you."

A collective gasp could be heard in the crowd, but Nicholas simply shook his head. "I did nothing of the kind, Kaspian. She never let me finish my sentence before she was flying into a rage."

Madelayne was shocked at his outright fabrication. She couldn't help but jump into the conversation. "You stated, sir, quite plainly, that since I was so good at washing things, would I be so kind as to wash you."

"I never asked you to wash me."

"You did!"

"Did you hear those exact words come out of my mouth?"

She opened her mouth, but stopped a moment to think; no, she hadn't heard him say that exactly. But that was what he was going to say, wasn't it? "You... well, you certainly intimated it. Your words were most leading. What else was I to think?"

Nicholas smiled, a gesture that thoroughly enraged her. "What I was going to ask is if you could recommend someone to help me, since you yourself were so good at washing things. I thought you would be the correct person to ask. But you never let me finish. Before I knew it, I was sitting in a tub of wash."

He was right. She hadn't let him finish. She was so sure of what he was going to say that she had reacted prematurely. Aghast, she looked at Kaspian, a thousand silent apologies filling her eyes, but he wasn't listening. He knew Nicholas far too well and the man was a master at manipulating the truth.

"Be that as it may, I would prefer that any such requests for Lady Madelayne come through me directly," he said. "Is this in any way unclear, Nicholas?"

Nicholas shook his head, very unruffled, very much unoffended by the entire conversation. "Of course, my lord. I apologize for any misunderstanding I might have caused." He looked at Madelayne. "And to you, my lady, I apologize. I understand now why you saw fit to manhandle me."

He was far too collected, making Madelayne look like a fool. But she knew without a doubt that the tone of their conversation in the yard had been suggestive and leading. It couldn't have been as innocent as he said; she simply wasn't that naïve. Now that the entire castle thought she was causing trouble between Kaspian and Nicholas with her assumptions, she was embarrassed and turned away without acknowledging his apology.

She should have stayed in the great hall to show that she wasn't the least bit concerned about public opinion, but she couldn't. Slipping out through a small door that led into the kitchens outside, she needed a moment to clear her head.

She could see, ominously, that Sir Nicholas De Dalyn had the potential for a great deal of trouble.

# CHAPTER TEN

Madelayne made her way out into the ward where the soldiers were clustered around a scattering of bonfires that littered the yard. The sky above was black as pitch, littered with stars that gleamed brightly. It wasn't particularly cold this night, surprisingly, and she was comfortable in her light woolen gown. Her feet seemed to have a mind of their own, taking her to the wall as she distractedly pondered Nicholas.

She also found herself thinking of Cairn and how her life had changed since his death. Mounting the narrow spiral stairs that led to the battlements of the eastern wall, she realized her heart still ached somewhat from missing her husband but she wasn't regretful of the direction her life had taken. She was very lucky that Kaspian had decided to marry her. She felt as if she were embarking on an entirely new life.

The stars were brighter upon the wall where the wind blew softly and the trees in the distance rattled their dead leaves. She leaned against the stones, gazing at the countryside below, her thoughts turning from Cairn to Nicholas once again. Perhaps she should apologize for acting so abruptly, but she would not apologize for misunderstanding him. She knew she hadn't, no matter how logical he made it all sound. And she, too, had noticed how Mavia had stared at him all evening and she was at a loss to understand why.

The world was growing more complicated by the moment.

"It's a beautiful evening," came a soft voice.

Madelayne started, whirling to Kaspian as he stood behind her. She patted her chest to calm her racing heart. "You startled me."

He smiled and moved up beside her, leaning on the wall as she had been. "This was Cairn's favorite spot. The man could stand here for hours, gazing out into the distance as if he could see things none of us could. How did you know to come here?"

"I didn't. It's simply a beautiful view."

"Cairn thought it was the best view in all of Lavister."

Madelayne studied his strong features in the moonlight. "You miss him."

"Of course I do. He was my friend and a fine knight. Were he alive, de Dalyn would not be here and things would be considerably calmer."

"But you and I would not be betrothed."

"True enough," he said. "But I cannot be glad for a man's death, no matter how badly I want his wife."

She shrugged, attempting levity. "You could have fought him for me, you know."

"As a chivalrous knight, I would do no such thing."

"I suppose I'm not worth it, then."

"You are worth that and more. But honor is important and must be placed in each situation accordingly. 'Twould not have been honorable to battle my friend for your favor."

"I would have thought less of you if you had."

He looked at her and they smiled at one another. "I am pleased to hear you say that," he said. "You are also, as I knew, a woman of honor."

She leaned back against the wall, brushing against his massive arm and feeling bolts of excitement race through her. The sounds of the night were all around them, soothing the anxiety left by the dinner conversation. But Madelayne felt the need to clear the air.

"I am sorry about Nicholas," she finally said. "Although it is true and he never actually spoke the words, I swear to you that the conversation was leading to what I believed would be an inappropriate suggestion. I never meant to make assumptions about it or lie."

"I know," he said. "Nicholas is very clever. I have no doubt that he was about to say exactly what you thought. Do not ever think for one moment that I doubted you."

"I just did not want you to think…."

"I did not."

She smiled. Impulsively, she leaned over and kissed him on the cheek. "Thank you," she said softly.

Her lips were an invitation. Unable to control himself, he pulled her to him and kissed her deeply. She was terribly sweet and soft, and he forgot that they were in a public place for all to see. Pulling away, he helped her stand upright for a moment, for her wits seemed to have left her. She giggled uncontrollably, struggling with her balance, and he was compelled to laugh with her. He was coming to enjoy her tremendously in more ways than just one.

He had no intention of leaving the wall at this moment, a private place to spend time with her. But a glint on the dark horizon caught his eye and his warrior's instincts took over. He tracked the glint until it came into focus, a single rider on a horse that was riding for hell. Concern filled him.

Kaspian bellowed to the sentries, who also began to track the figure and called for the men below to open the gates. The rider began the long trek up the hill leading for Lavister and Kaspian took hold of Madelayne, helping her down from the wall. He intended to meet the rider, but he had no intention of letting her out of his sight in a ward full of soldiers and, undoubtedly, Nicholas when he was summoned.

He did not hold her hand or any other part of her while they stood in the ward, but he made sure she was within arm's reach. The steed and rider came pounding through the open gates, kicking up clumps of earth. The horse was exhausted to the point of collapse. Several soldiers reached up to halt the frothing animal and the rider slid from the saddle, struggling to stand before Kaspian.

Nicholas was suddenly at his liege's side, his face taut with concern. He reached out to steady the man, an English messenger, bearing the colors of Edward.

"You are in the presence of Kaspian St. Hèver, commander of Lavister," Nicholas snapped. "What news do you bring?"

The messenger was close to swooning but he made a valiant effort to maintain his composure. "Hawarden Castle, my lord," he gasped. "Dafydd ap Gruffydd attacked at dawn."

"By the Devil's Beard!" Nicholas cursed softly. He glanced at Kaspian, trying to read the man's reaction. "Who is in charge of Hawarden?"

"Unless I am mistaken, it is Sir Denys le Bec," Kaspian replied. He looked at the messenger. "What is Gruffydd's force?"

"Five hundred perhaps, mostly untrained, but skilled knights," the man replied. "Sir Denys sent messengers to Lavister Crag Castle, Beeston Castle, and Holt Castle asking for reinforcements. Lavister is the closest. I've only been a day's ride."

"Were they digging in for a siege when you left or was it simply a melee?"

"Gruffydd was building a siege tower and his men were digging in, my lord."

Nicholas began shouting orders before Kaspian could react. After sending several men on the run, the blonde knight turned back to Kaspian, his manner laced with excitement. "Dafydd is a fool. Hawarden is well fortified; he'll never take her. Why in the hell would he even try?"

Kaspian shook his head. "I do not know. I can only think that he believes the castle vulnerable because it has been going through rebuilding phases for the better part of a year and is not up to full strength." He paused thoughtfully. "However, Hawarden is operational enough to guard the major road from Chester to Bangor and I'm sure Dafydd's intention is to do as much harm as he can before retreating. Or...."

"Or what?"

"It *could* be a diversion."

Nicholas cocked an eyebrow, following his train of thought. "To pull the English troops along the Marches into a skirmish while he takes a lesser castle, one he knows he can capture?"

"Exactly. Dafydd has a few thousand rebels at his command. We saw evidence of that at Beeston. So... where are the rest while some are harrying Hawarden?"

Nicholas shook his head. "I do not know. But I must agree with your logic, Kaspian. Do you think Dafydd would be foolish enough to attempt to take an English castle on the Marches?"

Kaspian shrugged. "It would certainly be a thorn in the king's side if he did." He suddenly turned on his heel, marching for the keep, but not before he grasped Madelayne by the hand and pulled her with him. "We send four hundred men to Hawarden and leave the rest here. If Dafydd is indeed eyeing a border castle, we could very well be the target. Send men to Beeston and Holt to tell them of our presumptions. Get the army moving now, Nicholas. There is no time to waste for any of this."

Nicholas cocked an eyebrow. "You will not have the army wait until morning to depart?"

Kaspian shook his head. "I will not," he replied. "Hawarden is less than ten miles from here. If you leave now, you will be there at dawn. That will be a nasty surprise for the Welsh."

Nicholas was on the move. It was obvious, even with his injury, that Kaspian was still very much in charge of the fortress in spite of Nicholas' presence. It brought a sense of comfort to them all in this uncertain time. As Nicholas carried out Kaspian's orders, bellowing to the men, Kaspian entered the keep with Madelayne trotting after him and mounted the stairs to the upper chambers. Once inside the room that he and Madelayne unofficially shared, he collected his sword from its place against the wall. Madelayne's eyes widened when she realized what he was up to.

"What do you mean to do?" she demanded suspiciously.

"Defend Lavister, of course," he said evenly. "I do not trust the Welsh."

"But you cannot," she exclaimed softly. "You are healing from a grievous wound. You cannot strain yourself so!"

"I will not strain myself at all. I will simply observe and direct. That is not strain."

Madelayne's surprise quickly turned to fury. "You cannot do this, Kaspian. You must listen to me!"

"I am listening to you, dearest. I hear every word you say. But are you listening to *me*?"

She was infuriated and frightened. "I'm listening to a stubborn creature who continues to defy both God and me by doing what he damn well pleases, and to the Devil with what the rest of us think!"

She had quickly reached a tantrum state. Kaspian suspected that he had to calm her; otherwise, she might very well throw herself down in front of him to prevent him from going about his duties. It was an odd situation, for he had never in his life had to deal with anyone opposed to his will or tasks. But in that awareness, he realized that he wanted very much to appease her.

"I swear to you that I will not strain myself in any way," he said soothingly. "Should anything arise that requires physical exertion, I will have the others take care of it. Is that satisfactory?"

Madelayne eyed him, halfway mollified, half not. "You shouldn't be doing this at all."

"I know. But I would feel better if I could observe the situation first hand." He smiled at her and reached out, gently, to touch her fingers. "Moreover, I must help Nicholas prepare the men to depart for Hawarden. It is the warrior in me, Madelayne. I cannot help it. 'Tis my duty."

In spite of herself, she responded to his touch and soon their fingers were intertwining. He gently tugged her toward him, kissing her hand when she came within range.

"You are a child, Kaspian St. Hèver," she scolded softly, watching his lips drift across her fingers. "A spoiled, obstinate child."

He grinned. "I've been called worse."

She tried to resist his smile but could not. "Observe and direct, that's all?"

"Observe and direct."

"Promise?"

"On my oath as a knight."

There was nothing more she could say. He had the better of her and they both knew it. "Go, then," she said. "And be mindful that you keep your promise or I'll let you suffer the consequences without lifting a finger to help you."

"You are a cruel woman," he said softly.

He kissed her once, twice, deeply the third time and quit the chamber. Long after he was gone, his taste lingered on Madelayne's lips. She licked them repeatedly.

From the chamber window nearly two hours later, Madelayne watched Nicholas and four hundred men depart for Hawarden Castle beneath a half-moon. It was a very short time to prepare a departing army but there was a sense of urgency in the air that drove the men to their duties faster. The weather was mild and the sky clear, making for decent traveling conditions even at night. Once Nicholas and the army left, however, she fell asleep after a time, awaking hours later and realizing Kaspian had not returned.

Wrapped in a heavy woolen robe, she went in search of him, thinking that she did not want him standing on the wall all night in the cold, irritating his healing scar. Surely he could not have gone further than the wall in his promise to observe and direct. But the only senior knight she saw, from her perch on the steps of the keep, was Thomas as he paced his rounds. It had never occurred to her that Kaspian had intended to ride with the army. The thought had never entered her mind because he was still so very weak. And that was what Nicholas was here for, was he not?

Her anxiety took flight. Too timid to approach the soldiers and ask where Kaspian was, she went to the last place she could think of, a small room on the first floor of the keep that the knights sometimes used to gather in, the one that used to be the guard's room. A faint glow radiated from the small window cut into the old door. Gingerly, she opened the ancient panel.

Kaspian's blonde head was bent over the table in the middle of the room, a table so large that they had literally built the room around it. It was strong enough to support several men sitting atop it. He was clad in his mail, looking for all the world as if he were fully prepared to go to war. Hearing the door creak open, he had lifted his eyes, not surprised to see who stood in the dim light. In fact, he smiled.

"Why aren't you sleeping?"

She stepped into the room, feeling a bit guilty, as if she should not have come. But there were no words she could find to describe the relief she felt upon seeing him.

"I... I couldn't sleep," she lied softly. "I've gotten so used to your snoring that I can't sleep without it."

He went to her, pulling the woolen cloak more tightly about her in the chill of the room. "A gracious fabrication, madam," he said. "But I happen to know that I keep you awake with it. I've seen you fall asleep in mid-afternoon because you've been up most of the night."

She tried not to look sheepish. "Not because your snoring keeps me awake," she said. "If I have been up in the night, it has been tending you, my lord."

He snorted. "Again, your tact is astonishing." He gazed down at her a moment, taking in the beauty of her face, and felt himself warming inside. "You really should go back to bed. This is no place for you."

She shrugged. "I was worried about you. The cold will aggravate your wound." She looked around him, at the vellum on the table. "What is keeping you so occupied that you must spend the night in this Godforsaken room?"

He put his arm around her shoulders and led her to the table. "A map," he said, gesturing to the dark lines on the tanned hide. "This is the border of England and Wales. The red marks you see are the castles. Lavister is here," he thumped the map, "and Hawarden is here."

Madelayne could read but the map looked like a bunch of squiggles to her. "I saw Nicholas and the army leave," she said. "What has you so worried about Hawarden, Kaspian?"

He shrugged, his blue eyes riveted to the map. "I'm trying to see if there is any pattern to Dafydd's attacks," he said. "He may be planning something I'm just not seeing. Having been ill for these past weeks, I'm afraid my mind hasn't been as sharp as it usually is."

"Do you see a pattern?"

"Not yet. But he's up to something; I can feel it."

Her eyes moved from the map to his face, studying his strong profile in the light of the taper. It was quiet and peaceful, and she realized as she gazed at him that the only reason she had come to find him was because she couldn't stand to be away from him, not even for a couple of hours. He was coming to fill her whole world like some great flowing energy, filling the holes that used to exist, creating a complete person with his aura. He caught her staring at him and he smiled.

"What is it?" he asked softly.

Her cheeks flushed. How could she say what she was feeling without sounding like a silly woman? Shaking her head, she looked away. "Nothing," she whispered. "I should return and leave you to your work."

He grasped her chin gently, forcing her to look at him. "I asked you a question, madam. Why were you gazing at me so?"

She tried to pull away but he wouldn't let her. He put his arms around her, trapping her, when she pulled harder. "Why?" he asked again.

She tried to avoid his eyes but they inevitably met. He was smiling at her and softly, in resignation, she laughed. "Because I wanted to," she said with feigned irritation. "Is that so difficult to understand?"

"No," he said. "Provided you let me stare at you as well without thinking me a fool."

"I would never think that."

They stared at each other a moment longer, laughing awkwardly when there was nothing more to be said. Kaspian thought that he would take the opportunity to kiss her again but the door to the room suddenly burst open and Thomas loomed in the archway.

"My lord," he said, the tension in his voice evident. "Our patrols have captured a spy. You had better come."

Kaspian was on the move, Madelayne in hand. Without a word, he quickly escorted her to the steps of the keep, leaving her standing to watch him walk away. He and Thomas disappeared into the gatehouse and instead of letting them go about their business alone, Madelayne decided to following. She was wildly curious about what was transpiring, for spies were intrigue and mystery that piqued the imagination. She knew very well she should retreat to her chamber, but she somehow felt the need to know of the danger Kaspian, and Lavister, was facing. As if the spy would somehow cause Kaspian to jump into action and she must be there to stop him.

The gatehouse of Lavister Crag, as massive as it was, also contained the vault. There were two sublevels, one beneath the other, and

Madelayne could hear voices as she entered. She knew they were down below her in the innards of the structure and, silently, she slipped down the spiral stairs, staying well out of sight. It was dank and musty, and more than once she struggled to keep from sneezing. Slipping into an alcove on the stairwell that was meant to store weapons, she felt like a spy herself as she listened to the voices below.

The light from two torches filled the room, causing shadows to dance on the wall. Thomas and Kaspian were muttering between them in tones she could not discern, hisses resonating off the walls. Kaspian's voice sounded like echoes of thunder.

"You might as well tell us what we wish to know," Thomas could finally be understood. "Your life is forfeit if you do not. Speak and we may spare you."

The alleged spy was small and thin, and had been caught by a patrol lingering at the base of the hill that led to Lavister. His black eyes glared up at his captors, unafraid.

"I do not know anything. I am a farmer."

"Farmers do not carry weapons."

"I told those idiots who captured me that I was hunting. I'm not a warrior."

"A farmer who hunts at night with a Welsh crossbow?" Thomas shook his head. "You cannot honestly expect us to believe that."

"Believe what you will. That's the truth."

"Somehow I doubt that. Let me see your left hand."

The man's calm facade wavered. "Why?"

Thomas gestured to a pair of soldiers standing beside the prisoner, who immediately wrestled the man's bound hands into view. Thomas inspected the middle finger on the left hand, running an experienced eye over the area.

"Your finger is bent at the topmost joint and heavily calloused as well. This is the hand of an archer." His stare was hard on the man. "How does a farmer explain that?"

The man didn't say anything for quite some time. Kaspian, observing, never intervened in an interrogation unless nothing else could be done to obtain the information sought. Thomas was usually quite brilliant at such things and Kaspian simply sat back, as most good commanders do, and observed while his second in command waged the confrontation.

"So you are planning to do away with me, then," the man finally muttered. "The longer I do not tell you what you want to know, the longer I'll live."

"Untrue," Thomas countered. "If you do not speak, we will simply do away with you and be no worse off than we were before. You may want to consider that."

Uncertainty flickered in the prisoner's eyes. "Then, in truth, I will tell you that I am only an observer. I know nothing of any value. I cannot help you."

"What battles have you seen with Dafydd?"

The man sighed in resignation; there was no use in going through the ruse of denial any longer. He wasn't particularly strong and thought perhaps his cooperation would save his life. The words came quickly. "Many," he said. "Most recently, Hawarden."

"So it was Dafydd," Thomas confirmed, casting a long look at Kaspian, who was back in the shadows. "We had heard as much. You realize that we have an army heading to Hawarden as we speak."

"I know."

"I suspect that is why you are here, is it not? To report back to Dafydd on the movement from Lavister?"

The man hesitated a brief moment before answering. "Aye," he said. "But it will not matter what you do or how many men you send. Hawarden will fall."

"You are confident."

The man's dark eyes glittered. "I know Dafydd," he said. "The siege of Hawarden has been going on for days. From the beginning Dafydd was determined to slaughter. I saw him personally swing a flail at an English knight and hit him in the head. Knocked him clean off his mount. I… I heard the knight pray, softly, because he was so badly injured. But Dafydd had no mercy. He killed him."

An ominous sense of disgust arose in Kaspian as the man continued. "The knight lay in the mud and called for his wife and unborn child. He didn't weep, mind you, but more a prayer for their safety. He asked God to watch over his family. But Dafydd stood over him with a look of death in his eye. He was determined to have the first kill of the battle and he did. He bashed the knight's brains to mush. He had to set an example to the rest of us."

Thomas looked at Kaspian and they both thought the same thing: *Cairn.* It was the same thing that had happened to Cairn, that brutal savagery of the Welsh towards the English that was meant to send a message to all of England. And send a message, it had. They were all prepared for the worst.

"Dafydd means to destroy everything his brother has worked so hard to secure," Thomas said after a moment. "Doesn't he realize he is only going to destroy himself and Wales in the process? Edward will never relent and we have far more men and resources than you do."

The man shrugged his shoulders wearily. "We must try. If it were Dafydd invading England, would you not try to stop him?"

Kaspian's voice came from the shadows. "We are warriors, not politicians. We fight where and when we are told and our opinions have little bearing." He stepped closer, into the light, his focus on the spy. "Dafydd cannot possibly imagine that he will take Hawarden."

"It was quite a battle the last I saw. He will try."

Kaspian gazed at the man a moment, his blue eyes hard. "He would have to be insane to try, which leads me to believe that Hawarden is not his true objective."

The man lowered his eyes. "I cannot read his mind. I would not know."

Madelayne crouched in the alcove, listening to the confession with interest. Much was said that she didn't understand but much was said that was frightening. Still, after a few minutes, she grew bored. There wasn't anything particularly telling of excitement happening and she considered leaving. But the moment she moved to do so, footsteps reverberated down the spiral stairs. She shrank back into the alcove as a soldier came rushing past her.

"My lords!" the soldier called. "We've movement on the horizon, heading this way. An army!"

Kaspian looked at the prisoner; the man's face was unreadable. Thomas raced back up the stairs with the soldier who had brought the message, leaving orders to put the spy in the dungeon. Madelayne pressed herself flat against the wall as Kaspian mounted the steps past her with another soldier behind him. When the pair had cleared the top of the stairs, Madelayne's attention was drawn to the room below where she could hear more voices and footsteps.

Suddenly, the tone changed and a great bang echoed against the walls. The sounds of a struggle were unmistakable and she fearfully peered from her alcove, watching the shadows of a two-man dance across the walls. There was a fight going on, that much was certain. Startled, she stood there in disbelief until the sounds of a struggle stopped. When footfalls quickly approached her, she spun around to race up the steps but lost her footing. Before she could recover, a hand was biting into her arm.

"Ah!" It was a man she didn't recognize and assumed him to be the spy. "I need you, wench. Show me the way from this place!"

Madelayne was terrified. "Let me go!"

The prisoner was small but strong. He yanked at her, bruising her arm. "Show me the way out or I'll kill you where you stand!"

Madelayne didn't know what to do. The spy had already killed the soldier below, she was sure, and therefore he would have no qualms about killing her as well. Stumbling up the steps into the floor level of the gatehouse, the ward beyond was a chaos of men. Not wanting to be seen, the spy pulled her behind various barriers to shield them. He had her hand twisted painfully behind her back and, on more than one occasion, she yelped with pain, but fearing for her life, she led him back toward the kitchens were a passage led down into a series of caves beneath the castle.

They were small caves used as dovecotes for the castle food supply as well as for storage. There was, however, a crack that led out onto the hillside that could be used to slip free. It was a secret escape for Lavister as well as a secret entrance The hillside was so steep, however, that the opening had never been breached. Also, it would have been easy to pick off one man at a time, as the opening was barely wide enough for single file. Frightened, Madelayne led the man into the wall and consequently to the stairs that led down to the dark, narrow passage. She had no sooner reached the first step when the spy suddenly grunted and released her. Startled, she whirled about to see Kaspian standing behind her with the hilt of his sword held aloft like a hammer.

The spy lay at their feet in a crumpled pile. She opened her mouth to speak to Kaspian, an apology or thanks or anything else that came to mind, but the only thing she could manage was a choked sob. Kaspian immediately sheathed the sword and picked her up into his arms. It was safe and warm and comforting there.

"Hush now," he crooned softly. "You are safe. Did he injure you?"

Madelayne's face was buried in his mailed neck, her arms tightly around his head and shoulders. "I'm fine," she gasped. She didn't want to tell him that the spy captured her because she was eavesdropping. "How did you find me?"

"I heard what sounded strangely like a dog yelping and then I caught a glimpse of your captor entering the western wall." He glanced down at the spy, out cold from the knock on his head. "Bastard. He deserves worse than I gave him. How in the hell did he capture you?"

"I... I'm not sure," she lied. "I turned around and there he was. He wanted me to help him escape, else he said he would kill me."

"I wonder how he escaped in the first place."

Madelayne didn't say anything more lest she confess she was in the wrong place at the wrong time. She was fortunate that the man hadn't raped or killed her. Kaspian returned her to the keep, making sure to send enough soldiers to take the unconscious, yet wily, prisoner back to the pit.

He carried her until he reached his chamber, and even then he continued to hold her, for just a moment. But the sounds of activity in the bailey were growing louder by the moment and Kaspian kissed her gently on the forehead before setting her down.

"I need you to stay here, where I know you are safe," he said. "We could be in for a siege and I do not want to worry over your safety."

Madelayne had been through sieges before. She knew what was expected of her, even though she now had the added trouble of worrying over Kaspian's health. "Is it Dafydd?"

"I do not know. I was distracted by your near abduction before I could find out." He moved for the door, adjusting a strap on his breastplate that rubbed against his healing wound. "Stay in the keep unless I tell you differently. I want no one, servant or woman, out in the ward. Is that understood?"

She nodded obediently. "Kaspian?"

"Aye?"

"Observe and direct only?"

He paused in the doorway, his blue eyes softening. "I cannot promise, dearest. If Lavister is sieged, I must fight."

She sighed, knowing he had no choice. The man was a warrior. Quickly, she went to him, wrapping her arms around his massive neck and pulling herself up to his cheek. "Be safe, then," she murmured as she kissed him.

His eyes glittered. Unable to think of a suitable reply, he took her face in his two hands and kissed her until she gasped for air. "I shall endeavor to do my best," he said huskily, pecking her on the lips once more for good measure.

Giddy, and apprehensive, Madelayne turned away from him as he walked through the door. She expected to hear it close behind her. Instead, she heard Kaspian's voice from where he had paused outside.

"By the way," he said. "I would prefer you not eavesdrop again. If you wish to know something, simply ask me. If it is appropriate, I shall tell you. As it was, you got a good scare and I would wager to say you'll not do anything so foolish again."

She felt like an idiot. Pursing her lips, she shook her head. "You knew?"

"Let's just say that I let it go far enough to teach you a lesson."

"*Kaspian!*"

He grinned, giving her a saucy wink before he disappeared. Madelayne heard him laugh, once or twice, as he descended the narrow stairs.

# CHAPTER ELEVEN

"**M**y God," Mavia whispered fervently. "Is it ever going to end?"

Madelayne shook her head wearily. "Not any time soon, it appears."

The bloody mess at their feet had been the fourteenth soldier to die that morning. Since the Welsh lay siege at dawn the day before, there had been nothing but death and destruction. The great hall of Lavister Crag had been converted into a hospital with wounded lying all over the floor, with Madelayne and Mavia and a host of servants trying to keep up with the volume.

Dolwyd had ridden with Nicholas and the army to Hawarden. There hadn't been any word from the army at the front, which had Kaspian worried. He didn't know if they made it or if they had been intercepted by a horde of Welsh. He had been well over a day without sleep, he and Thomas directing the remaining troops to defend Lavister against what was surely a thousand Welsh insurgents. But what worried him even more was that since mid-day yesterday, the attackers had been building a siege tower at the base of the hill. While the majority of the Welsh went about the standard war tactics, projectiles and ladders in an attempt to mount the wall, the real threat was at the base of the hill, nearing completion.

Now, they were on their second day of a gruesome siege. It was sometime in the early afternoon and Madelayne was sick of watching men die, men she could do little more than comfort as they bled to death. The floor of the hall literally ran red and the smell of the blood was making her nauseous. She was exhausted but determined to work as long as she was needed. Great pots of water boiled on the hearth for washing away the dirt of the wounds for stitching; every once in a while a servant would throw buckets of the scalding liquid on the floor to wash away the stench. To make matters worse, it had started to rain outside, turning the whole of Lavister into a miserable quagmire of muddy death.

From the dreary, sloppy ward outside, Kaspian entered the hall with a lackluster attitude that was unlike him. He was horribly exhausted, his weakness and wound draining him. When he still should have been resting, recovering from his injury, he found himself fighting off a Welsh attack and cursed himself that his hunch of a ruse had been correct.

There had been pockets of fighting as ladders reached the top of the wall, but nothing the men of Lavister couldn't ward off. Projectiles, however, had been another matter; flaming balls of tar and wood had sailed over the walls, killing men and destroying property. The rain has lessened the severity of those attacks, however. More still, there were legions of Welsh archers shooting arrows over the walls in a deadly rain. The Welsh were more than determined to take Lavister and the siege was as brutal as any he had ever seen.

Dirty, exhausted, and wet, once inside the great hall his eyes searched for Madelayne. There was almost a desperate panic to find her among the sea of wounded, something in his soul crying out for soothing. He finally located her bent over a soldier, sewing a gash to the man's arm in her small, careful stitches.

Kaspian watched her a moment, thinking in the midst of this hellish destruction that he had never in his life seen a more beautiful woman. Dressed in a durable wool gown, her hair pulled away from her face, she was pale and exhausted, too, but working fervently. Her fortitude and bravery were impressive. He made his way through the field of injured men, standing over her as she finished her final stitch.

"Madelayne," he said softly. "I must speak with you."

She looked up, startled by his voice. Her face was instantly alight to see him. "Of course, my lord," she said. "With pleasure."

He helped her stand, pulling her into a corner where they could converse privately. Madelayne was the first to speak.

"Kaspian, you are exhausted," she murmured. "Please take a rest, just for a short time."

He shook his head. "I cannot," he said. "I need you and Mavia to come with me now."

"Come with you?" she repeated. "Why?"

He sighed. Reaching out, he took her hands and pulled them to his lips. "The Welsh have built a siege tower," he said quietly. "As we speak, they are pulling it up the hill towards the gates. Once in place, they'll breach the castle with ease. I cannot stop them. I need to put you and Mavia in a safe place."

Madelayne tried to be brave but terror overwhelmed her. "Kaspian," she whispered, blinking back tears. "I'm so afraid for you. Please, come with us. We'll escape through the caverns!"

He kissed her warm hands. "I cannot go with you, dearest. But it is my priority and my duty to make sure you are safe above all. I want you to collect all of the women you can and prepare to go with me immediately. We must get you away from this place."

She gripped him tightly. "There are only me and Mavia and two other serving women," she said. "But I will not leave you, Kaspian. My place is with you."

He was touched by her words, so much so that he actually considered relenting, but he knew he could not. The only hope for her safety would be in his strength to do what he knew he must.

"Although I appreciate your loyalty, you've no choice in the matter," he said. "Find Mavia and the others."

Madelayne did not like to be refuted. "Who is going to take care of all these wounded, then?" she demanded. "And you; you are not nearly well enough to fight. Who is going to tend you should you overexert yourself, or worse, become wounded again?"

He touched her cheek to calm her. "Madelayne, listen to yourself," he admonished quietly. "I am a knight. This is my life and the risks are a part of that. My concern now is for your safety and I will not stand here and argue with you about this. Go now; collect Mavia and the other women. We must get you to safety."

He thought she might refuse him again. She had a very stubborn look in her eye. But she lowered her head after a moment and blinked back the tears. "Please, Kaspian," she said softly. "I couldn't bear it if anything happened to you. Not when you have taken me from the depths of despair and given me more happiness than I've ever known to exist. You mean so much to me that I can hardly express it."

He stared at her. Not knowing what to say, he simply pulled her into his arms, listening to her soft sobs. "Madelayne," he murmured. "I was kind to you in your moment of need, a companion when you needed one. It is only natural that there is some attachment."

She yanked away from him, catching her hair in the joints of his armor and ripping out several strands. He was surprised by the brutality of the movement and even more surprised at the look of outrage in her eyes. Long auburn hair hung, disjointedly, from the chinks of mail on his left arm.

"How dare you suggest that what I feel for you is something less than what it is," she hissed, her lower lip trembling. "I'm a grown woman and know my own heart. I would not say it if it wasn't true."

He had never even dared to hope and was extremely sorry he had dealt with her admission so badly. Truthfully, she had caught him off guard. "I did not mean to imply that," he said quietly. "It's just that I never imagined in my wildest dreams that you would feel for me as I do for you."

It was her turn to stare at him. "You... you feel for me, too?"

"Of course I do. Why do you think I insisted on marrying you?"

"Because it made a sensible arrangement."

He cocked an eyebrow. "I couldn't stand the thought of anyone else having you."

The look of outrage on Madelayne's face was replaced by one of joy. Kaspian smiled in return, a show of sincerity, and extended a hand to her. After a moment, she put her fingers in his open palm and he pulled her to him, kissing her hand tenderly.

"Please, Madelayne, no more arguments," he said, a twinkle in his eye. "I would have you obey me like a good, obedient girl."

"But...!"

"Please."

She sighed heavily. "Very well. But I do not want to leave the fortress. We'll be just as vulnerable to the wilds outside as we will be to the rebels inside. I would stay near you, Kaspian. *Please.*"

He shook his head and kissed her hand again. "Silly wench, who said anything about going outside the fortress? I'm simply going to put you and the other women someplace safe, someplace that only I can get you in and out of."

She was puzzled. "Where is that?"

"Find the other women and I shall show you."

☙

There was no longer the luxury of time to hide the women. Kaspian escorted four women from the keep, the only females at Lavister, and took them to the gatehouse currently under siege. The great siege tower was at the threshold and high above, men were battling as the wooden arm meant to bridge the gap between the tower and the wall came down. Projectiles were still hurling over the walls, making for a horribly frightening scene.

Smoke and death were everywhere as the small group scurried across the ward and into the depths of the gatehouse. Kaspian took them down the narrow stairs, so recently the sight of Madelayne's folly with the Welsh spy, and into the sublevel that held the two locked cells and a hole in the floor for the pit dungeon. With a huge iron key, Kaspian unlocked one of the cells.

"Get in, quickly."

The women didn't hesitate, except for Madelayne. Her eyes went between the dark, frightening cell and Kaspian.

"You would put us in... *that?*" she demanded.

He took her by the arm and gently tried to pull her in. "It's perfectly safe. The rebels cannot get in without a key, which you will have. Unless you give it to them, they won't be able to reach you."

"But you are locking us up!"

"I'm locking you *in*."

She wasn't convinced. "But what if they occupy the castle? They can keep us here and starve us! We cannot escape!"

"Madelayne, I do not have time for this. Please get in." He gave her a quick shove and she stumbled into the cell. Slamming the heavy iron grate, he locked it with the ungainly key. Madelayne was standing against the bars, panic on her face, and he leaned forward and kissed her tenderly. "Do not worry, dearest. Everything will be fine."

He deposited the key in her hand. She looked at it as if it confused her somehow. Kaspian turned on his heels and marched for the stairs, sending a surge of terror through her. It wasn't so much he was leaving her alone in this terrible place; it was the fact that he was going to where men were dying.

"*Kaspian!*" she cried.

He paused at the base of the stairs, the impression of her frightened face forever etched in his memory. But he had a battle to direct topside and he could not afford to be distracted any longer than necessary. Madelayne was safe and he was content. He mounted the stairs without another word.

It was cold and dark in the vault. They had one torch between them, and when that was gone, they would be pitched into blackness. The women looked at each other, fearfully, until Mavia finally took charge. Madelayne still hung against the bars where Kaspian had left her and it was apparent that she was in no position to take the lead.

"We've enough dry straw here to make a decent bed," she said crisply. "Let's pile it against this back wall, well away from the door. We've nothing to do now but sleep and wait this out."

The women eyed Madelayne as they worked. She hadn't moved. When the straw was piled and the washer woman and the other female servant were seated on it in a huddle, Mavia went to her.

"Why do not you sit down and rest?" she said gently. "You've been on your feet since yesterday."

Madelayne shook her head. "I cannot rest," she whispered. "Not when the castle is being overrun and Kaspian is in the midst of it. Not when he could be...."

Mavia quieted her. "You'll not think like that. He and Thomas have been fighting battles for many years together. They'll survive."

Madelayne turned to the woman. "You've not seen Thomas since yesterday. He didn't even come down here to say farewell when Kaspian locked us up. Why not?"

Mavia's brave smile vanished and she lowered her gaze. "He's not speaking to me."

"Why not?"

"Because... well, suffice it to say that he is not."

"Because of Nicholas?"

A look of extreme guilt crossed Mavia's face. "It would seem so."

Madelayne's attention was momentarily diverted from Kaspian and their predicament. "Mavia, you haven't...?"

She wouldn't answer directly. "Thomas has been so cold to me for most of our marriage," she said. "Now, suddenly, he is wildly jealous. Sometimes I feel as if I cannot breathe the way he clings and spies."

Madelayne was quiet a moment, trying to think of something tactful to say. "You *have* paid quite a bit of attention to Nicholas."

"It is my duty."

"It is my duty as well but Kaspian bade me stay away from him."

Mavia grew flustered. "Therefore, I must make up for the attention you have denied him. He is our guest, after all."

Madelayne could see that she was defensive and decided to let the subject drop. Moreover, the servants in the corner had big ears. Her attention inevitably turned back to Kaspian and the battle above.

Leaning against the bars, as if that somehow would bring her closer to Kaspian, the sounds of shouting and scuffling could be heard up above. The noise grew louder and the women in the cell grew increasingly fearful. Suddenly, great bangs could be heard and the women started, one of them beginning to cry. Though terrified, Madelayne tried hard to be brave.

"Kaspian won't let anything happen to us," she said confidently. "He's the greatest warrior on the border. He'll chase off those Welsh in no time at all."

Before anyone could reply, a great clamor was heard at the top of the stairs. Bodies were suddenly racing down the steps, whooping and yelling, looking for anything to burn or steal or destroy. Madelayne fell back, away from the bars, as the women in the cell cowered in terror. It took little time for the Welsh rebels to the see the women behind bars.

They slowed in their chaos, men who were apparently peasants with some form of weaponry. They were dirty and coarse, and they eyed the women with something of surprise and a good amount of glee. The first man walked up and rattled the locked door, thwarted to find it secured. A second man came to help him and then a third. Finally, all five of them were rattling the bars as if to pull the gate from the stone itself. Mavia screamed in terror and closed her eyes, but Madelayne watched them closely. The stone mortar that held the iron didn't look close to breaking, but she did not want to take the chance. Empowered with the need for self-preservation, she grabbed the torch from one of the other women and thrust it at the men's hands.

"Get back!" she hissed. "Go away or I'll burn your hands off!"

She had already burned a couple of them seriously enough so that they quit the vault in search of more easily obtained booty. But three of the men stayed behind, leering at her, smirking. "Why would ye do that, luv?" the first man asked. "We're only tryin' tae free ye. Why would ye hurt us?"

"We do not want to be freed," Madelayne snapped. "Go away this instant!"

The first man meandered near the bars, his eyes drifting over Madelayne in the most seductive way. It was apparent that he was thinking of all the wicked things he could do to her. "What's yer name, luv?"

"My name is for those I choose to associate with. Not for the likes of you."

The men laughed at her. The first man moved closer to the bars. "Spitfire lass. Do not ye want tae come out o'there?"

Her answer was to thrust the torch at him again and light his beard ablaze. The man yelped and, with help from his companions, put the fire out. His happy demeanor had vanished with the whiskers on the left side of his face.

"Stupid wench," he snarled. "What'd ye do that for?"

Madelayne would not back down. The iron bars between them fed her courage. "I told you to go away," she hissed. "I meant it. Come any closer and I'll burn you again."

The man leapt at the bars, rattling them terribly. Mavia screamed, as did the other women, but Madelayne merely thrust the torch at him again as promised. But in their deadly game of thrust and parry, she came too close and he reached between the bars and grabbed the torch, unable to pull it through but able to knock it out of her hands. Pulled forward by the momentum, Madelayne fell against the bars and the man grabbed her around the neck.

"Now, wench," he spat in her ear, "ye'll pay for the blow ye dealt me!"

It was apparent he meant to snap her neck. Madelayne struggled and fought, but he was too strong and had the advantage through the bars. He hit her repeatedly in the head, trying to subdue her, and her pretty face was turning shades of red. It was apparent she couldn't last much longer. Mavia, seized with panic, picked up the torch from where it had rolled against the wall and shoved it into the man's face, lighting the rest of his beard afire and part of his hair. Screaming, the man fell back and dropped Madelayne. Mavia dragged her unconscious form well away from the bars as the man, once again, put out the fire on his face.

"Bitches!" he screamed. "Ye'll all die now, do ye hear? *Ye'll die!*"

Unable to claim the women as spoils of war, the men were now determined to destroy them. They had ceased to be viewed as chattel and were now the enemy. The man and his two remaining companions collected whatever they could find in the vault that was flammable, which wasn't much; a couple of stools and some old, urine-soaked hay. Putting it into a pile near the cell, they lit it afire. Slowly, an orange flame appeared and puffs of smoke began to pour out. Mavia and the other women watched the growing blaze with terror.

The rebels left the vault without another word. The fire continued to grow and the ladies knew that the flame wouldn't kill them, but the smoke would. Panicked, Mavia struggled to revive Madelayne. When that didn't work, she went searching her gown for the key to the cell and was stricken to realize that it was nowhere on her person. As the smoke in the vault increased, she and the serving women fell to their hands and knees, searching for the key that they knew Madelayne had possessed. Suddenly, one of the servants cried out and pointed to the floor just outside the cell. There, almost hidden beneath the burning straw and stools, glittered the old iron key.

"My God," Mavia gasped as she stared at the key. "It must have fallen off her during the struggle. I cannot believe those ruffians didn't see or hear it. Can anyone reach it?"

The three women strained to grasp the key, obviously several inches from their reach, but none would admit it. The smoke was now reaching annoying proportions and they began coughing, trying to devise ways to pull the key to them. Mavia removed an iron hairpin and tied it to a strip of cloth she tore from her dress, hoping to hook the key. But the pin had no effect against the iron. They grabbed thick pieces of straw, hoping to budge it. All they succeeded in doing was pushing it further away.

The straw and wood was smoking heavily now. The women had to lay on the ground, under the smoke, but the black air was filling their lungs, threatening to choke them. Mavia tried again to rouse Madelayne, but she was out cold. Her forehead was turning shades of purple where the man had hit her and Mavia reasoned that if she had to die, then at least she was unconscious and there would be no pain about it. The other two women were already incapacitated by the smoke, but Mavia would not give up. Looping the strip of cloth that had once held the hairpin, she struggled to catch the loop around the end of the key and pull it toward her.

Time was running out.

## ⋘

Kaspian couldn't remember seeing such rain. It literally poured down in sheets, making it difficult to see just a few feet in front of him. There were Welsh everywhere, looting the interior of the keep, killing his men, and generally wreaking havoc. His thoughts began to turn toward abandoning Lavister, simply to regroup and reclaim; he hadn't enough men to fight off the onslaught and he knew it. He needed the rest of his army back if he was going to do anything of measure. At the moment, it was a losing battle.

His thoughts turned to the women in the cell down below and his need to free them upon relinquishing the castle. Fighting off one man who suddenly jumped out at him from the mist, he strained his torso badly with the final deadly swing of his broadsword and he had to make a conscious effort not to hold his side, as had become something of a habit.

Stomping through the mud on his way to the gatehouse, he swung his sword at anything that came close to him, including a couple of his own men that he barely missed. Thomas was nowhere to be found and he seriously wondered for the man's health, but he could not be concerned about that at the moment. His greater concern was to free the women and take them to safety. Confiscating several Lavister soldiers to aid him, and sending yet others to spread the word that they were abandoning the fortress, he was within a mere few feet of the gatehouse before he saw it; dark smoke billowing from the opening.

Kaspian stared at it a moment as if he could not believe his eyes. Then, with a surge of terror, he thundered through the opening, choking on the black smoke, calling Madelayne's name in a tone that bordered on panic. The smoke was so thick he could hardly see and at the bottom of the stairs, he and the soldiers that had followed him fell to their hands and knees, crawling through the blackness towards the cells. It brought great relief to him to hear coughing and he could see the supine outline of several figures in the distant chamber. Mavia's panicked face greeted him through the gloom.

"My lord!" she cried. "The key is in the fire!"

Kaspian rounded the burning mound, searching desperately in the area Mavia was pointing. Locating the key, he picked it up with his mailed glove, feeling the heat burn through the mail and leather. His eyes watering to the point of blindness, he fumbled with the lock until the door swung open. While the soldiers helped the servants out, Kaspian fell to his knees beside Madelayne's limp form.

"What in the hell happened to her?" he demanded.

Mavia coughed and sputtered. "Some Welshmen came down here and tried to break into the cell. Madelayne bravely fought them off until one of them caught her through the bars and tried to choke her." Mavia touched the bruised forehead. "He smacked her soundly, my lord."

His expression was beyond grim. "Did they start the fire?"

"To kill us when we wouldn't come out."

Without another word, Kaspian collected Madelayne into one arm while crawling across the floor beneath the smoke. When they hit the top of the stairs leading from the gatehouse, he collected her into both arms and headed for the staircase that led to the caverns below. With the gatehouse so compromised, it was the only safe way to take the women. Somewhere across the wet bailey, Thomas joined them but refused to speak to or even assist his wife. Devastated, Mavia clung to Kaspian and the exodus proceeded down into the bowels of the mountain that supported the castle.

As the stream of Welsh poured in, raising the blue and white flag of Dafydd ap Gruffydd, a line of English poured out, single file, from the southern side of the mountain.

# CHAPTER TWELVE

**D**aybreak saw the ragtag army from Lavister Crag Castle at the gates of Kirk Castle, about fifteen miles south of Lavister. They were an Edwardian supporter and the closest ally that wasn't under attack. Several of the Lavister men were on horseback, inferior mounts stolen from the Welsh rebels.

Kaspian rode astride a great, gray, draft horse with Madelayne cradled carefully against him. She hadn't woken yet, but the color was coming back to her cheeks and he was sure she was merely sleeping at this point. Kirk Castle loomed in the distance, manned by a huge combined force of Welsh and English, loyal to Edward at the moment. In this terrible weather, Kaspian felt it was their nearest option for safety.

Owain, or Lord de Kirk as he was known, was the Lord of Kirk Castle and also the heir to the princes of Powys, rivals of Llywelyn and Dafydd. Kirk was a massive fortress and Kaspian felt considerably better when his troops were welcomed and given shelter. Owain's wife, Hawys, was kind enough to prepare rooms in the enormous keep for Kaspian and Madelayne, and the embattled couple of Thomas and Mavia. The woman went on the assumption that Madelayne was Kaspian's wife, and Kaspian was not in any mood or condition to explain the situation. When the woman finally left them alone and bustled off to tend to other duties, Kaspian closed the chamber door and lay Madelayne on the bed in their cramped, borrowed room.

She was so very still as he examined the bruising around her neck where the rebel had attempted to strangle her. He felt so much disgust and remorse for what had happened. Carefully, he stripped off her wet clothing, admiring her completely nude body for the first time before covering her up with the heavy linens. He then removed his hauberk and unstrapped his broadsword, placing both on a chair along with the rest of his mail. The damp padded tunic came off and ended up somewhere near the fire.

After that, all he could smell was smoke and his own bad scent. But they were alive, no matter how bad the situation was, and that was all that mattered. He had to get word to Nicholas immediately as to the situation, else the man would be returning home to a fortress full of Welsh, but he had a feeling that Thomas had already taken care of that. Last he saw of the man, he was ignoring his wife completely and disbanding the army.

Kaspian sat on the edge of the bed, holding Madelayne's hand and staring at her sleeping face. He kissed her hand a couple of times, interrupted by a knock on the door. An older couple respectfully entered, carrying hot water and food. When they left, Kaspian took a moment to wash himself with borrowed soap and a rag, and took a few bites of the meal, wanting to save the majority for Madelayne when she awoke. Exhausted himself, he could no longer stay on his feet and stripped off the rest of his clothing, climbing into bed beside her and carefully taking her in his arms.

Her breasts brushed against his chest and he could feel the moisture from her nipples. He knew, as she had so often put it, that she was full to bursting and the thought of suckling her brought instant peace to him, and instant arousal.

Reckoning that he could not let her become so completely uncomfortable, he slid down in the bed and took a nipple in his mouth, drawing from her the rich, sweet fluid that seemed to content him like nothing else he had ever known. She was warm and delicious and naked against him and, feeling like a cad, he allowed himself the stolen pleasure of touching every inch of her body. His exploring fingers parted the delicate curls between her legs and to realize she was drenched with moisture hardened him like a rock.

"You would take advantage of me, then?" she whispered.

His head came up from her breasts and he felt rather like that cat caught with the mouse. "Madelayne," he murmured. "You are awake."

Her eyes opened and she smiled at him. "Of course," she said. "How could I stay asleep during all of your attention?"

He looked rather sheepish, propping himself up on one elbow so he was looming over her. "I could not help myself," he said. "I hope you will forgive me."

She reached up, touching his stubbled cheek. "There is nothing to forgive. We are betrothed and I am your property. It is your right to inspect me."

"You make it sound as if I'm purchasing a mare," he said, a tinge of irony in his tone. His gaze fell on the lump on her forehead and he touched it gently. "Speaking of my property, how do you feel?"

Her fingers flitted over the lump. "I've a headache," she said. "Otherwise, I do not feel overly terrible. But what's all that smell of smoke? And where are we?"

"We're at Kirk Castle," he said. "Lavister was overrun and we were forced to abandon it. As for the smell of smoke, that occurred when the rebels who had tried to kill you decided to finish the job by lighting the vault afire. Thank God I got you out in time."

She was quiet a moment, letting the ominous news sink in. "Will Edward punish you now that Lavister is lost?"

Kaspian shook his head. "Of course not," he said. "We were simply outnumbered and there is no shame in a retreat under those circumstances. But I've got to get word to Nicholas that Lavister is now under Dafydd's control and discuss the alternatives therein."

"He doesn't know?"

"Officially, he does not, but I suspect word has already been sent to him by Thomas or Lord de Kirk."

"What do we do now?"

Kaspian lifted his big shoulders. "Amass an army to take the fortress back," he said as if it were the most obvious thing in the world. "I am going to head south to Shrewsbury Castle because there is a big contingent of Edward's troop there. I must converse with the garrison commander. I'll need his help."

"Can I go with you?"

He shook his head. "I would feel better if you would stay here. You'll be safe."

She didn't want to stay in this strange place. She had heard of Kirk, but wasn't exactly sure where it was. Everything was alien and foreign to her except for Kaspian and now he wanted to leave her. Her head began to throb and she rolled onto her side, away from him, lest he see her grim expression.

He had seen it nonetheless. "Do not turn away from me," he commanded softly. "What is the matter?"

She curled onto her side. "I'm just... tired," she said. It wasn't like her to complain, especially when he had greater things on his mind. "Do not worry about me."

Kaspian knew exactly what the problem was. Her soft, creamy back was to him and he reached out, stroking a finger along her spine. "I shan't be long," he said. "But this I must do. My fortress is in the hands of a madman."

"I know." She trembled as his fingers moved across her back. "But I… I shall miss you."

"And I shall miss you."

She could hear his breathing growing heavy behind her as his hand moved across her shoulders and down one arm. When he reached her elbow, it was inevitable that his hand found its way to her breast. Madelayne shuddered as he cupped her breast, giving it a gentle squeeze and spraying a stream of milk onto the linens. They laughed together, softly, as she rolled onto her back, rivets of milk running down her torso.

Kaspian didn't say a word as he swooped upon her to lap up the milk, covering her with his big body, his hands on both breasts, squeezing the nourishing liquid out until it ran all over her in erotic streams for him to drink up. He licked and suckled, listening to her moan with pleasure, feeling his swollen member throb with the desperate desire to make love to her.

Madelayne instinctively spread her legs, allowing him to lay between them, feeling the weight and strength of his body with the greatest of joy. It was inherent for them to want to join their bodies in a meld of desire, forgetting the fact that Madelayne had given birth a mere few weeks before and should have given more time to the healing process. But she wanted to feel Kaspian inside her in the worst way, and he had never known a stronger urge to bury himself deep within a woman's flesh. The more he licked and suckled, the more fevered their desire became.

Their passion was at a frenzy. Kaspian lifted himself up, sliding his great member into her with an ease that suggested she was made to accommodate him and him alone. He seated himself to the hilt with comfort and grace, enough to bring tears to his eyes. Madelayne emitted a soft cry, clinging to him as he drove into her, wrapping her legs around him as if to never let him go. His sheer size was smothering her in a most wonderful way, but somewhere in their passion he rolled onto his side, her left leg pulled up over his hip as he made love to her with ardent fervor. He put his mouth over hers, his tongue licking her sweet depths, continuing to kiss her even as he released his seed deep into her body.

Madelayne felt him tremble and she, too, joined him in his pleasure-filled tremors, finally experiencing a climax with him that she didn't have to hide. When it was over, they hardly knew what had overcome them, only that the experience had been beyond powerful.

Kaspian kissed her eyes, her nose, her jaw line, his hands in her hair. It was an exquisitely tender moment. Madelayne sighed raggedly, relishing every touch.

"I should apologize, but I cannot," he confessed. "I've wanted to take you for the longest time. It was sweeter than I could have imagined. Did I injure you?"

She pressed against him, his arms around her tightly. The warmth of his body made her feel safe, cherished, whole. "Of course not. It was more than wonderful."

"My feelings precisely."

"Promise me something, Kaspian."

"Anything."

"Promise that you will never leave me."

"I promise."

"I would die if you did."

"Then you will die a very old woman. I will never leave your side."

She believed him without question. Kaspian St. Hèver never said anything he did not mean and his word was as good as gold. They continued to lay together in warm, wonderful silence as the day progressed. Kaspian eventually fell asleep and it was tremendously comforting to Madelayne to listen to his deep, steady breathing. She wished they could stay just as they were forever. It was the happiest she had ever been in her life, the culmination of everything she could have ever hoped for.

But forever came too soon. A knock on the door rattled the chamber just before sundown and Kaspian was instantly awake. While Madelayne struggled to awaken from a long nap, he was sliding his heavy woolen hose on and answering the door.

Thomas was standing at the door, looking horribly gray. "Kaspian," he said hoarsely. "I... I need your help."

"What's wrong?"

"It's Mavia...."

Hearing the name, Madelayne was immediately alert. Wrapping herself in the coverlet, she stumbled to the door. "What did you do to her?" she said accusingly.

Thomas looked stricken. "What did *I* do to her?"

Madelayne was furious at him, though she wasn't sure why. Hadn't Mavia said that Thomas refused to speak to her, that he had been insanely jealous over Nicholas? Now something was apparently wrong and Madelayne was certain that Thomas was to blame.

"She said that you hadn't spoken to her because of a foolish jealousy," she snapped. "Where is she? What did you say to upset her so?"

Thomas' pale cheeks darkened. "So she lied to you, too. You have no idea what has happened!"

"You mistrust your own wife? How horrible of you!"

Kaspian would not allow them to bicker. He put his hands on Madelayne's shoulders and turned her around. "Madelayne, get dressed please." When she did as she was told, hissing like an angry cat all the way, he turned back to Thomas. "What about Mavia? Where is she?"

Thomas leaned against the wall as if it were the only thing to sustain him. "In the ward. She jumped to her death not a half hour ago."

Behind him, Kaspian heard Madelayne scream.

# CHAPTER THIRTEEN

The rain hadn't stopped for days. It was dreary and cold, soaking man and beast. High in the keep of Kirk Castle, however, Madelayne had managed to stay comfortably dry with Kaspian to tend to her every need. He'd said nothing about riding for Shrewsbury Castle, though he had mentioned that Hawarden Castle had been successfully defended and Lavister's troops were now heading to Kirk. Since the entire happenstance had been a ruse, he hadn't been surprised that Hawarden remained intact in spite of what the Welsh spy had said. Other than that remark, he had been completely focused on her and had not allowed anything to enter their world.

It was more than attention. It was as if he simply couldn't get enough of her, as if he had to spend every waking moment by her side, talking to her, laughing with her, making sure she wasn't too cold or hot or anything else. In truth, Madelayne found the attention wonderful. It helped ease the ache of Mavia's death and the upheaval of Lavister in general. Pleading exhaustion, they hadn't even joined the rest of the castle for the evening meal in the great hall. They had stayed to their room, just the two of them, sharing a quiet meal.

A priest had been summoned for Mavia's funeral and arrived on the morning of the third day since their arrival at Kirk. In one of Lady Hawys' borrowed gowns, since she hadn't any of her own, Madelayne was determined to greet the priest on behalf of her friend and help him prepare a proper mass. Thomas had made himself scarce since his wife's passing and it was rumored he was holed up somewhere in the castle drinking himself to death. Kaspian had tried to find him, more than once, but the knight remained elusive. With the loss of Cairn and now, temporarily, Thomas, there were many concerns on Kaspian's mind that he had not yet voiced. Even though his world with Madelayne was solid, professionally, his command seemed to be falling apart.

But the main line of focus was Mavia's burial mass on this day and not the fragility of Kaspian's command structure. The priest, Father Rothas, was from Shrewsbury. He was a small man with thin gray hair and enormous brown eyes. He had been told only that a lady of noble breeding had died and required mass, but nothing more. A servant with a sizable pouch of money had come for him and he would not refuse.

Madelayne greeted the priest in the bailey along with Lady Hawys and the two of them escorted him to the lord's lavish solar. Kaspian went off to find Thomas, concerned that the man needed to be present when discussing the burial details of his own wife. In the meanwhile, the priest made himself comfortable as Lady Hawys, in her high-pitched voice, explained the situation.

When she came to the part of the circumstances of death, the priest visibly balked. "You say she leapt to her death?" he asked.

Madelayne nodded. She was having difficulty getting a word in with Lady Hawys' chatter and took the opportunity. "She was distraught over failings in her marriage. But she was a good lady, kind to the poor, and…."

The priest shook his head vehemently. "It does not matter, my lady. You know very well the church frowns upon suicide. She cannot be buried in consecrated ground, nor can I say mass for her. She is damned, I'm afraid."

Madelayne's reaction was instant. "That is not true!" she exclaimed. "You can say mass to plead with God not to condemn her soul eternally, but to allow her penance in the levels of Purgatory until she is able to ascend. She was a very good woman, with a good heart, and I cannot believe God will condemn her without thought."

The priest wasn't trying to be cruel, merely factual. "My dear lady, I must insist that I can do no such thing. There is a designated hell for those of suicide, those foolish enough to waste God's gift of life. The upper levels of Purgatory are for those such as unbaptized babies or good souls who were ignorant of God, or…."

"But we can do penance for her, can we not?" Madelayne was rapidly working herself up into a state. "We can pray for her and make donations to the church on her behalf. Surely there is something that we, as her family and friends, can do for her?"

Father Rothas shook his head. "This is not a case of simple sin, my lady. What Lady Mavia did was a cardinal offense. Most things can be forgiven in the eyes of God, but this cannot. There is nothing to be done. She is condemned to everlasting damnation."

Madelayne was shocked by his lack of concern. Out of that shock grew anger. "Sins do not have varied degrees of severity," she hissed. "All sins are an offense to God, whether I bed another woman's husband or throw myself from the battlements. Are you telling me that to bear false witness against my neighbor has less value in the eyes of God than murdering my brother? Both are part of the Ten Commandments. Since when is suicide more critical than any of God's sacred commandments, the only unforgivable sin to be committed? I have never heard of this being listed as Man's most evil sin, one unworthy of forgiveness."

The priest was not intimidated by her. "I do not make the rules, my lady, I merely follow them. If Lady Mavia committed suicide, then I cannot say mass for her."

Madelayne let out a bark of frustration. "You hide behind the technicalities of this religion when a woman's soul is at stake. Aren't you, as a priest, supposed to do everything possible to *save* souls?"

Kaspian chose that moment to enter the room. He had heard Madelayne from the moment he entered the keep, her tone telling him that she was seriously agitated. He wondered what the priest had said to upset her so, but upon catching the gist of the conversation, he realized what had happened.

"My lady," he greeted both Hawys and Madelayne. He eyed the priest. "I am Kaspian St. Hèver, commander of Lavister Crag Castle and servant of his majesty King Edward. What goes on here?"

The priest cast a long glance at the slovenly, drunken knight who stumbled to a halt next to Kaspian. "We were simply discussing the details of Lady Mavia's death. 'Twould seem that I was not entirely informed of the circumstances." He looked closely at Kaspian. "Lord St. Hèver, I fail to understand your association here."

Kaspian indicated Thomas. "This is Lady Mavia's husband, Sir Thomas Allington-More. We are guests of Lord de Kirk."

Rothas nodded in understanding, more interested in Thomas now. "My lord," he said. "Perhaps you can tell me the circumstances of your wife's death. These fine ladies may have been misinformed."

Thomas was drunk, so drunk that he could barely stand. He reeked of liquor and vomit, and Madelayne was frankly shocked to see him in such condition. Thomas was usually the epitome of proper decorum in any circumstance. Aside from that, however, she realized that the priest was attempting to give them another chance to lie about Lady Mavia's death. Perhaps she had misjudged the man. But Thomas was unaware of the preceding conversation.

"She killed herself," he said flatly. "Her shame was so great that she could do nothing more than take the dishonorable path to death so she leapt, like an idiot, from the battlements."

Madelayne could have slapped the man. She tried hard to think of something to say. "She could have slipped," she said weakly. "No one actually saw her throw herself off the ledge. We do not know that it wasn't an accident."

Thomas pursed his lips, emitting a long, foul sound indicative of his contention. "Nicholas de Dalyn took her to his bed mere hours after his arrival to Lavister," he snarled. "When I first heard the rumors about it, I confronted her but she denied it. Then, I came across them in a passionate embrace and saw it with my own eyes. I cursed myself for being foolish enough to believe her lies. Two days ago she told me she believed herself pregnant. I told her I was going to kill de Dalyn and she threatened to kill herself if I harmed him. It seems that she carried out her threat."

Madelayne went pale. "Oh, Thomas... it cannot be. You must be mistaken."

"I wish I was."

"But it is too soon for her to know if she was with child! Nicholas has not been with us that long!"

Thomas shrugged. "That is what she has told me."

Madelayne sighed heavily. "But the child...it could be yours, of course."

He smiled ruefully. "I had an accident many years ago in a tournament. Mavia and I have never been able to have children. Did you not wonder why we never had children after being married for so long? Did Mavia never tell you?"

Shocked, Madelayne shook her head. "We never discussed it."

"Now you know."

Madelayne felt as if she had been hit in the stomach; all of her breath left her. "Then why didn't you say something to me?" she begged softly. "Mayhap I could have spoken to her."

He shook his head. "It would not have done any good. De Dalyn bewitched her, that much is clear. Only you were strong enough to resist him. I wish Mavia would not have been so blind. She's not an evil woman, just... weak."

Madelayne looked at Kaspian helplessly, but his expression was neutral. She didn't know what else to say on her friend's behalf, only that she wished the woman had been honest with her. Now she felt as if she had been betrayed, too. Thomas had kept to himself and she had known nothing of the true story and now she felt like a fool.

Father Rothas didn't seem overly surprised or overly sympathetic. In fact, he looked at Madelayne pointedly.

"An adulteress as well," he said quietly. "I cannot do any more for her. I am truly sorry."

Lady Hawys was overcome by the entire circumstance and excused herself. Madelayne could only imagine what the woman was thinking of these mad, immoral people from Lavister she had allowed into her home. Father Rothas quietly collected his cloak and the bag he had brought with him.

"Perhaps you can direct me to my escort, Sir Kaspian," he said. "It would seem that there is no work for me here."

Kaspian didn't move to aid the man. Instead, he looked at Madelayne. "I believe there is, indeed, work for you, priest," he said. "There is a marriage for you to perform."

Madelayne looked sharply at Kaspian, her face suddenly alight when she realized what he meant.

Father Rothas looked confused. "What marriage?"

Kaspian answered, "Mine and the lady's."

Father Rothas frowned. "What's this you say? I cannot simply perform a marriage with no background, no…."

"One hundred silver marks shall be yours. The lady is widowed and I have never been married. We are from noble families and wish to be wed. That is all you need to know."

Rothas looked as if he were debating what to do. "What of her dowry?"

"I shall supply it."

"Familial consent?"

"She has no family."

There was no reason not to perform what he had asked. In a borrowed gown, with a drunken Thomas as witness, Madelayne l'Ebreux became Lady St. Hèver.

CB

Kaspian's first task as Madelayne's husband was to decide what was to be done with Lady Mavia. Dampening the thrill of becoming Kaspian's wife, Madelayne was devastated that the woman would not have a proper burial and insisted that she and Kaspian had to think of something appropriate. Thomas was useless in his drunken state and offered nothing by way of opinion or aid. Lord de Kirk and his wife were making themselves scarce, so the burden fell on Kaspian and Madelayne alone.

Kaspian finally decided to pay one of the castle's carpenters to construct a casket for Mavia and, with Lord de Kirk's permission, store her in an unused section of Kirk's vault until they could return her to Lavister. It was the best they could do and in spite of what the priest said, Madelayne spent an entire afternoon praying over Mavia's body, hoping God would be merciful. Kaspian had stood beside her, offering whatever silent support he could.

By sundown, however, the situation at Kirk markedly changed when the sentries on the battlements sighted Lavister's incoming army. There was anticipation in the air, and some concern, as Kaspian waited for them in the ward, a cavernous area three times the size of Lavister's bailey.

Kaspian was anxious to speak to Nicholas, to find out what had transpired at Hawarden, and to devise a plan to regain his fortress. There was still the matter of going to Shrewsbury to solicit aid, something he had put off because of Mavia's death and his need to be near Madelayne. He forced himself to focus on regaining his fortress, though thoughts of his new wife were constant. It was difficult to shake her, even though he tried.

But not hard enough. Like a gentle fog, she lingered.

The soldiers of Kirk began to light the torches on the wall, illuminating the dreary dusk as the Lavister army began to filter in through the open gate. Kaspian was joined by Lord de Kirk and the two men stood side by side, watching the army trickle in, waiting for the appearance of the senior knights. Owain was a short man with black hair and sharp black eyes. Kaspian had only met him once before, at a tourney on the Marches, and so far this visit had provided little time to know him better. Much as his wife had, Kaspian could only imagine what Owain thought of this dramatic group from Lavister. So far, they'd proven little else.

As Kaspian and Owain watched and waited, Nicholas finally charged through the open gates astride his dappled horse, looking for all the world like a knight from tales of old. Laden with weapons, he showed little of the fatigue that his men were displaying. He spied Kaspian immediately and went to him, the charger kicking up mud and spraying both Kaspian and Owain.

"Kaspian!" Nicholas exclaimed. "Are you well, man?"

Kaspian pretended not to notice Owain wiping mud from his face. "Well enough," he said. "We were informed that Hawarden was saved."

"It was," Nicholas replied. "We were informed that Lavister fell."

"It did," Kaspian replied without missing a beat. "What is the army's status?"

Nicholas flipped up his visor and dismounted his weary beast. "We lost twenty-two men, including Ewan."

Kaspian sighed. "God's Bones," he groaned. "How did it happen?"

That answer was simple, although Kaspian would never know the truth. Ewan had been cut down when he and Nicholas had been fighting side by side and Nicholas had drawn back to let Ewan suffer the brunt of the attack. *Another knight from Lavister down….*

"One moment he was mounted, the next he was down with an arrow through his neck," Nicholas replied emotionlessly. "He suffered more than a day before finally succumbing."

Kaspian was sickened to hear that. "How's Reece?"

"Devastated, but functional." Nicholas removed his helm and peeled back his mail hood, his blonde hair damp and dirty. "What happened to Lavister?"

Kaspian was grim. "It was a ruse, as we suspected. They overcame us with over a thousand men, as near as I can guess. We lost a total over two hundred men, either to death or desertion. It is hard to know. I took a head count when we arrived here and out of the six hundred I had, I only have three hundred and ninety-eight. Therefore, it is my intention that we ride for Shrewsbury and seek reinforcements from the garrison immediately. I want my fortress back."

Nicholas nodded. "As soon as I rest my horse and have something to eat, we can leave." Ever the diplomat, he turned to Lord de Kirk. "My lord, I am Sir Nicholas de Dalyn. I know that St. Hèver has thanked you for your generosity in allowing Lavister refuge, but may I add my personal thanks for your graciousness as well. We are forever in your debt."

Lord de Kirk studied the knight with his intense black eyes. "You are de Dalyn?"

Nicholas had no idea that the man had heard terrible things about him from Lady Hawys. He smiled as if to find humor that perhaps his mighty reputation had preceded him. "Aye, my lord, at your service."

De Kirk didn't reply, but he cast Kaspian a long look before turning away. Nicholas was perceptive enough to understand that de Kirk wanted nothing more to do with him and looked at Kaspian curiously. Kaspian had to tell him something.

"Much has happened since you've been at Hawarden," he said. "To begin with, Madelayne and I have been married and I will take this opportunity to make myself very, very clear to you. She is my wife now, and my property, and if I find you so much as looking in her direction without my permission, you'll rue the day you were born. Do I make myself perfectly clear, Nicholas?"

Nicholas was his usual cool self. "Of course, Kaspian. You needn't say as much. I would never...."

Kaspian held up a sharp hand. "Lies do not become you. Do not forget that I have known you a long time, Nicholas."

"What is that supposed to mean?"

"I know what you are capable of."

Nicholas didn't say anything for a moment. Then, he smiled humorlessly. "If I didn't know you better, I might have been insulted by that remark. As it is, I will ask you to clarify it."

"I shall do better than that," Kaspian said. "I will tell you that Lady Mavia, pregnant with your child, jumped to her death three days ago. Thomas is in ruins. Shall I continue?"

Nicholas, ever cool, struggled not to react. "I am truly sorry to hear that," he said. "But if you think I had something to do with...."

"Thomas told us that he found you in a compromised position with Mavia." When Nicholas continued to look at him, stone-faced, Kaspian took a step toward him, his nose an inch from the man's face. "Therefore, I will tell you again. You are a fine knight, Nicholas, and I am grateful for your assistance with Lavister. But you've disrupted the lives of my people since you've been with us. If I find you anywhere near my wife, I will kill you without hesitation. Is this in any way indistinct?"

Nicholas would not show his intimidation, but their relationship somehow changed at that point. It grew darker, a shadow cast between them. Everything was spelled out clearly between them now so there would be no mistake. A mistake could be deadly.

"I understand perfectly, Kaspian," Nicholas said quietly. "You needn't worry in the least."

Above them, the rain poured down and the thunder rolled as if to emphasize the storm now brewing between them. They stared at each other a moment longer before Kaspian finally turned away. But he had to look into Nicholas' eyes long enough to emphasize how serious he was. This was no game he was playing. He wasn't sure if Nicholas understood that or not.

It was a situation about to go from bad to worse. Through the rain, Kaspian caught a glimpse of something swift and metal-clad. Behind him, Nicholas suddenly went down into the mud and Kaspian turned to see Thomas hanging over the supine knight, his broadsword in his hand and a look of murder in his eye.

"Get up!" Thomas bellowed at Nicholas. "Stand up and take your punishment, you bastard!"

Kaspian froze, his gaze moving between Nicholas, who was rapidly bounding to his feet, and Thomas' twisted face. Whatever happened, he could not intervene. It was a matter of honor for Thomas, and a matter of life and death for Nicholas. They would have to settle their own differences and one of them would have to lose. He found himself hoping it wasn't Thomas.

The men in the ward rapidly caught on that a battle was about to take place, perhaps greater than those fought at Lavister and Hawarden. They fell back into a large circle, surrounding the two combatants who were now circling each other like a pair of rabid dogs. The last of Lavister's army entered the bailey to a spectacle and men began vying for prime positions. Even Dolwyd, one of the last to enter with his old surgeon's cart, found a place by which to watch the ensuing battle. He, too, had known this moment would be coming. Having seen how Nicholas had taken to Lady Mavia the day he arrived at Lavister, the old physic knew it was only a matter of time.

He found himself wishing that Thomas would be the victor, too.

Lord de Kirk resumed his position next to Kaspian, evaluating the situation before them. "De Dalyn has twenty pounds and several inches on Allington-More," he commented.

Kaspian watched the two of them carefully as they continued to circle one another, each one waiting for the other to throw the first strike. "Thomas is as fast as a cat, but Nicholas has a good deal of power," he said. "Both of them are exhausted, however; Nicholas from his march and Thomas from his drinking. I can't say either has the advantage right now."

"Who will win?"

"I cannot predict that."

"But you are going to allow them to fight?"

"I must, my lord."

De Kirk nodded in understanding, his eyes on Thomas. "I'd do the same to any man who bedded my wife."

Their words were cut off by Thomas casting the first blow. Nicholas responded strongly, charging him with several heavy thrusts and throwing him off balance. When Thomas stumbled, Nicholas cut into his left arm in a gap between the mail and his glove, drawing a flow of bright red blood. Thomas didn't flinch, however; he came back strongly, undercutting Nicholas with a series of swift swings that sent the knight back-stepping several feet. The last thrust hit Nicholas on the thigh, grating against the mail.

Men were clamoring to see the fight. They lined the ward and the battlements above. To see two senior knights battle to the death was an exciting event. Thomas charged Nicholas again and again, viciously swinging his sword in controlled bursts, making contact with Nicholas' weapon. Had it not been raining, sparks would have undoubtedly flown.

Men were placing wagers as the knights continued to battle. It was apparent that Thomas was fighting with his emotions, whereas Nicholas was not. Thomas began cursing Nicholas as he landed blow after blow, only to be firmly and silently answered by Nicholas' return thrusts. At one point, Thomas fell and then tripped Nicholas in his struggle to get up. His broadsword caught the blonde knight on the back of the neck and blood seeped beneath the mail. He also clipped him on the ear, cutting the tip of it. Blood streamed down the side of Nicholas' head and served to throw a measure of anger into his swing. Fists, as well as the swords, were now flying.

They were beating each other to death now, throwing punches when they could get close enough. The fight continued for some time without anyone gaining ground. With the last series of thrusts and parries, both knights stumbled to their knees, too exhausted to do any more fighting. Thomas actually seemed to be crying, too much exhaustion and alcohol rendering him unable to kill for his wife's honor. Nicholas was unable to stand any longer. Kaspian stood there longer than he should have, waiting to see if either one of them would make a final attempt. Finally sensing a stalemate, he stepped forward and stood between the two.

"I declare this bout over," he said softly but firmly. "Since there is no decisive victor, I will call a draw and command that there be no more battles between either of you."

Thomas sat on his arse, in the rain, and wept. He was so very discouraged. Nicholas, exhausted to the point of collapse, somehow made it to his feet and staggered away. With a glance around the ward that sent the men scattering, Kaspian looked down at Thomas.

"Would you allow me to help you to stand?" he asked quietly.

Thomas shook his head. Collecting himself, he pushed himself up on his sword. "It doesn't matter anyway," he muttered. "De Dalyn will be dead by dawn."

Kaspian's brow furrowed. "What do you mean?"

Dolwyd wandered up, having heard Thomas' words. He looked at Kaspian with concern, but Kaspian was focused on the knight. Thomas had stopped crying, now snorting ironically.

"My blade was bathed in poison," he said. "The cuts I gave him should be enough to kill him. You see, I knew I wouldn't have the strength to mortally wound him. So I had to do it another way."

Kaspian tried not to appear shocked. "Where did you come by this poison?"

"Mavia had it. I think she meant to kill me with it. So I turned it on her lover instead."

Kaspian was outraged now. "You are mad. Where would she have gotten this poison?"

Thomas shrugged. "The castle physic, a serving wench, who is to say? But I found it in our chamber and used it on de Dalyn."

Kaspian could hardly believe his ears. He raked his fingers through his wet hair, a gesture of disbelief and agitation. When he spoke, it was to the physic. "The rain probably washed it away," he said. "I doubt much was left on the sword by the time Thomas cut him."

Dolwyd was grim. "We'll know soon enough."

The old man turned away, off to find de Dalyn and see just how deeply the poison had offended him. Kaspian looked back to his knight, disgust in his tone. "Thomas, when did you become so dishonorable?"

"When de Dalyn beds your wife, see if you do not become the same way."

Kaspian sighed faintly. "It is not as if you loved the woman," he muttered so only Thomas could hear. "I realize it is a matter of honor to avenge Mavia, but using poison on your sword...."

He couldn't finish. Thomas simply looked at him, absolutely no regret in his expression. "Love has nothing to do with it," he said quietly. "Nicholas humiliated me. It is my own honor I'm avenging, not my wife's. She clearly had none."

It was a brutal thing to say and Kaspian didn't reply to it. He was still lingering on Thomas' previous statement of de Dalyn bedding Madelayne. Kaspian had already told Nicholas that he would kill him if he came near Madelayne. And not too long ago, he had wanted to kill the man for the bathing request. There was no telling what would happen the next time Nicholas made a play for Madelayne, if there indeed was one.

Turning on his heel, he made haste for the keep.

# CHAPTER FOURTEEN

*The next day*

"**I** cannot put off Shrewsbury any longer," Kaspian said. "I should have gone days ago. The longer Lavister stays in the hands of the Welsh, the harder she will be to regain."

It was mid-morning on a blustery, sunny day. In yet another borrowed gown from Lady Hawys, Madelayne sat by the window of their bower with a half-finished dress in her hand, for Lady Hawys had given her the material to sew a garment of her own. It had been a pleasant morning until Kaspian started talking of Shrewsbury. Now, her stomach twisted in knots and she could no longer work on the colorful bit of cloth.

"I know," she murmured. "When will you leave?"

"This afternoon, most likely. I am taking Thomas and Reece with me."

"Can I come too?"

"Nay, dearest. I told you I would be happier if you stayed here."

"Then why aren't you taking Nicholas if you are leaving me here?"

Madelayne knew about the fight the previous evening. But she did not know that Thomas had poisoned his sword. True to his prediction, Nicholas had become sick and sicker still as the night progressed. Dolwyd tended him, assuring Kaspian that the knight was ill enough that he could do no damage until he returned from Shrewsbury.

"He's exhausted and ill," he said without elaborating. "I do not expect that you will see or hear from him the entire time I am gone."

"How long do you expect to be gone?"

He looked at her a moment. Then, crouching beside her chair, he took her hand in his and brought it to his lips. "I would suspect that we will ride directly from Shrewsbury to Lavister."

She tried not to look too upset. "But you'll have to come back for the army."

He shook his head. "I'll send word to have them sent on to Lavister. We'll merge the Shrewsbury and Lavister forces and lay siege. There's truly no telling how long this will take."

No matter how badly she wanted to make a fuss, she would not. She had selfishly had him to herself for several days now while he had neglected his duties. Now, he needed to focus on his responsibilities to Edward. Quietly, she set her sewing aside and wrapped her arms around his neck, squeezing him tightly. He stood up, lifting her, holding her close against him. Neither one of them said a word for some time, relishing the feel of each other for the times to come when there would be no comfort, no warmth.

"You will return to me," she whispered.

"On my honor as a knight, I swear it."

"I do not want to be without you, Kaspian, not for a minute, not for a day. But I know you must do as you must."

He was silent a moment. "For the first time in my life, I find that my attention is not where is should be. When I should be determined to regain my fortress, I'm content to stay in another man's castle and languish away the hours with you. I cannot go a minute without thinking of you, as if you consume my entire being. I do not want the responsibility any longer of manning a border garrison for the king. I simply want to be your husband and live my life by your side. It's mad, truly."

She pulled her face from the crook of his neck to look at him. "Not as mad as me wanting to tag along with you everywhere you go, into battle or otherwise. I know that I cannot go with you to Shrewsbury, but that doesn't stop me from wanting to. It's not a matter of you going anywhere without me; 'tis a matter of me being *without* you. Does that make any sense?"

He smiled at her, drinking in her beautiful face, thinking at that moment that he was the most fortunate man on the face of the earth. "Madelayne," he said slowly, "I think we are in love with each other."

"You *think*? Kaspian, I *know*."

He couldn't think of any response other than to kiss her. He'd never been so happy and it was difficult to know how to manage it. Lavister was gone, his knights were in turmoil, but he wasn't the least bit guilty that he felt so elated. Nothing else seemed quite as important. He whirled Madelayne around and around until she screamed, listening to her delighted giggles. When he finally set her down, she was blushing furiously.

"Thank you, Madelayne," he said softly.

"For what?"

He shrugged his shoulders, not at all sure how to put anything into words. He had never been any good at verbalizing his emotions. "For marrying me," he said simply.

They ate the nooning meal in the privacy of their room, enjoying quiet conversation of what their life would be like once they return to Lavister. The first thing Kaspian was determined to do was rid themselves of Nicholas, confident he was feeling well enough to lead his troops once again. He had always had faith in the man, as a comrade, but Nicholas' introduction to Lavister made Kaspian realize that the man's negative attributes outweighed any benefits he might bring. Nicholas had only brought chaos with him from the moment he set foot inside Lavister's gatehouse and Kaspian would be relieved to be rid of him. He didn't relay his ideas to Madelayne, however; she was bubbling on about something else and he did not want to dampen her mood.

"Where are your thoughts, husband?"

Madelayne's voice was soft and sweet, and Kaspian realized that he had been daydreaming of vanquishing Nicholas so much so that he hadn't heard a word she'd said. He smiled at her sheepishly, reaching out and pulling her from her chair onto his lap. She slid onto his massive thighs easily, curling up like a cat.

"I was thinking about taking a trip into Shrewsbury to shop," he gently lied.

"Shop? For what?"

"A wedding ring."

She smiled with veiled excitement. "For me? I've never had one, you know."

"I know," he said. "I fancy buying you an obscenely large gold and garnet ring. What do you think?"

She thought a moment. "I rather like diamonds. They shine so prettily in the sun."

"Fine. An obscenely large diamond, then."

"What about you? Will you wear a wedding ring?"

His brow furrowed. "Men do not wear wedding rings." She simply smiled, as if to graciously accept his refusal, and he abruptly changed his mind. "But if you want me to wear one, I will. I've never had one either."

Her expression brightened. "Gold, I should think. I know pewter or silver is more popular, but I like the way gold shines."

"Gold it shall be. But no diamonds for me. I must draw the line somewhere. Besides, the church frowns on anything garish."

She giggled in agreement. Then she sobered, absently stroking the back of his neck. "Thank you, Kaspian."

He found himself watching the way her lips moved when she talked. "For what?"

"For marrying me."

His response to her, as it had been so often as of late, was to kiss her. It wasn't long before Lady Hawys' gown was a pile on the floor, with Kaspian's clothes right beside it. His first instinct was to suckle her breasts, as usual, but she stopped him. He looked at her questioningly.

"I... I am thinking to let them dry up," she said, almost apologetically. "You are well enough now that there is really no reason to keep my milk flowing. It can be most painful sometimes."

He ran a finger down her cheek. "I will be gone for several days, maybe weeks. That will be time enough for you to dry up. But for now... as selfish as it sounds, I find it most comforting."

Her reply was to push his mouth down on her nipple, and he drank deeply, sucking her so hard that the pleasure-pain of it made it almost too difficult to bear. Kaspian's hands were on her shoulder blades, holding her fast to him, feeling more wild passion than he had ever known possible. When she was dry on both breasts, his mouth trailed down her torso, tasting her natural sweetness, suckling her hips, her thighs, her feet.

When he finally covered her small body with his large one, he did it with such gentleness that there was no weight involved at all, only an intimate closeness that covered her from head to toe. She welcomed him deep inside her, feeling her healed body stretch to accommodate him, savoring the sensation of his hardness. He thrust slowly but firmly at first, gaining in speed and power until Madelayne stopped him. Pushing him over onto his back, she slid atop him, riding him until an explosion of stars filled her eyes and delicious tremors overtook her body. Buried deep within her, Kaspian took his release with the greatest of pleasure.

He didn't know how long they lay in each other's arms, touching, feeling, exploring and caressing. All he knew was that he never wanted to leave her. The afternoon was cool and dreamy, perfect for languishing away the hours in the wonderful world of discovery. When a knock finally came at the door, however, he knew their stolen hours were over.

It was Reece. Since Ewan's death, the young man had been lost. But with Thomas emotionally disabled and Nicholas on his death bed, Kaspian put the junior knight in charge of the preparation and restoration of Lavister's remaining army and the activity seemed to help him a great deal. The death of his brother and the new responsibilities had matured him.

Kaspian answered the door fully clothed. Madelayne sat in the chair where her embroidery was laid, looking fully clothed but, in fact, the stays down the back of her dress remained undone from the hasty dressing. She smiled at Reece, who looked somewhat uncomfortable to have disturbed his liege.

"My lord," he said. "Everything is prepared as ordered. We can be at Shrewsbury in a few hours."

Kaspian nodded shortly. "I shall join you in a moment."

Reece quit the room with a stiff bow in Madelayne's direction. When he was gone, she laughed softly. "I think he is angry at you for marrying me. He can no longer flirt with me without incurring your wrath."

Kaspian simply lifted an eyebrow in agreement as he sat down on the bed to pull on his heavy leather boots. His mail was down in the armory, having been cared for by the tradesmen of Kirk until it was almost new-looking. Madelayne went to stand beside him, waiting until he was done with his boots before motioning to the stays on her back. Before fastening each successive stay, he kissed the flesh on her back that it would cover until there were no more stays left. Then he playfully bit her neck and she yelped in delight.

"Now, I must go down to join Reece and don my armor," he said. "I shall see you before I depart, have no fear."

She had hold of his hand, firmly. "What of Thomas?" she asked. "Will he be going with you?"

Kaspian shook his head, sadly. "He will not," he said. "Thomas has not been sober since Mavia's death. I will have to depend on Reece, who is, so far, doing an excellent job."

Madelayne was saddened about Thomas' state, too. He was a great knight, now sucked into the quagmire of grief and alcohol in the turmoil of Mavia and Nicholas. "I will watch over him while you are away," she said. "For now, however, I want to go with you to the armory."

"That is no place for you."

"Neither was the vault of Lavister, but I was there."

He pursed his lips irritably. "Cheeky wench."

She grinned. He didn't want her around the dirt and earthiness of the soldiers in the armory, but he couldn't resist a chance to squeeze in a last few stolen moments with her. Her hand in the crook of his elbow, Madelayne escorted her husband down to Kirk's armory to spend a final few moments with the man before he departed.

The moments were precious and swift and, before she realized it, he was beyond Kirk's big gates, heading off to the south and Shrewsbury.

〇3

Kaspian had only been gone a matter of hours and already Madelayne felt as if he'd been gone for years. The evening meal was finished for the most part, the only meal she had actually eaten in the great hall since her arrival to Kirk. Lady Hawys had been gracious and had seemingly forgotten about the turmoil the disruptive people from Lavister had caused the first few days of their arrival. In fact, Madelayne was enjoying tremendous respect and status as the wife of Kaspian St. Hèver. She'd never realized until now how highly the vassals of Edward thought of him until Lady Hawys began treating her as an equal. It was an elevation in social ranking she had never imagined.

But Lady Hawys' socialization did not extend beyond the cursory. With Mavia gone, Madelayne's closest companion was now Dolwyd. The old man looked older than he had only weeks earlier, his gray hair grayer and his walk more stooped. Mavia's death had upset him, as had Ewan's, and the situation between Thomas and Nicholas was still an explosion waiting to happen. Thomas had not gone with Kaspian, reluctantly, and Nicholas still lay in the knight's quarters, ill with a poison that refused to leave him. As Dolwyd had said, the inhabitants of Lavister Crag had all gone stark raving mad and life wasn't what it should be.

But he was a comfort to Madelayne nonetheless. He had spent most of his time with Nicholas, coaxing the knight from the brink of death, but tonight he had taken the time to sit with Madelayne at sup because Kaspian had asked him to. He didn't want his wife to be alone in this strange place. Kaspian, in fact, had gone to visit Nicholas directly before he departed Kirk and had been greeted with a man gray and weak. In truth, he only wanted to convince himself that Nicholas was still too ill to wreak havoc with Madelayne while he was away. Satisfied of the man's perilous condition, he went along his way.

Madelayne was enjoying the last of her mead, a drink that Kaspian and even Cairn had found most foul. They preferred the hard knocks of their ale and wine to the soft, honeyed drink more suited to women. The hall of Kirk had quieted somewhat, some people finding a place in the corner to sleep off too much wine and the dogs going about looking for scraps. Lord and Lady de Kirk had long since retired, leaving few people still enjoying the evening and conversation. But Madelayne wasn't conversing with anyone other than Dolwyd; she didn't particularly want to return to the chamber she shared with Kaspian and face it alone. She missed him so badly that it hurt.

"Greetings, Lady St. Hèver."

A voice from behind startled her. Looking up, she found herself gazing into healthy-looking blue eyes. Nicholas smiled back, looking nothing like the man she had been led to believe was dying. Shocked, Madelayne's jaw dropped.

"Nicholas!" she exclaimed in surprise. "What are you doing out of bed?"

He presumptuously took the seat next to her, demanding a trencher from the nearest serving wench. "I'm feeling much better, actually," he said, his eyes drifting over her. "You, however, look marvelous. Marriage agrees with you."

Dolwyd was up, his old body moving faster than it should have. "De Dalyn, you are a madman! Your wound is festering with poison!"

Nicholas waved the old man off. "It is doing no such thing. I feel much better, truly."

Dolwyd eyed him with a great deal of suspicion. He knew immediately what he was up to. "I would wager to guess that this feeling of abundant health came over you the moment St. Hèver left the gates."

Nicholas shrugged carelessly. "I wouldn't know when, exactly, he left in order to correctly answer your assessment."

"You pretended to be ill when he came to see you just before he left!"

"I have pretended nothing."

"You wanted him to leave his wife here without protection, vulnerable to your advances!"

"You are imagining things, Dolwyd."

The old man wasn't fooled for a moment. "Whether or not I am, I'll tell you what Kaspian told you; if you value your life, you'll leave Lady Madelayne alone."

Nicholas was quite innocent. "Dolwyd, your mind is running away with you. Have some more wine and calm yourself."

The physic batted at the pitcher in Nicholas' outstretched hand. "I'll do no such thing!" He reached down and practically yanked Madelayne to her feet. "My lady, we will retreat to your chamber immediately."

Nicholas watched the pair over the rim of his goblet. "By the Devil's Beard, Dolwyd, I won't bite. Sit and finish your drink, both of you."

Dolwyd pulled Madelayne away, so she was lodged behind him. "Take your meal and return to bed, de Dalyn. You are not a well man."

"I'm fine."

"Then you should be on the road with St. Hèver and not lollygagging around here."

Nicholas merely cocked an eyebrow at him, watching the old man practically yank Madelayne from the hall. Things hadn't gone exactly as he had planned, but there was plenty of time now that Kaspian was away on a quest to regain his fortress. The thought occurred to him that Dolwyd might send word to Kaspian of Nicholas' miraculous recovery, but he doubted the old man had the courage to do it. Still, something told him to be alert.

His instincts were correct; Nicholas captured the messenger the moment the man left the gates and tied him, exposed to the elements, to a tree on the outskirts of the castle. To be certain, it was necessary, as he had a plan to finally gain his wishes once and for all, a plan that involved separating Lady St. Hèver from her new husband.

Kaspian St Hèver stood in the way of all Nicholas wanted and he was tired of waiting. He had to rid himself of the man. Being very clever, and ambitiously evil, Nicholas knew what he had to do. He knew what would make the lady turn against her husband.

And Kaspian would not be here to defend himself.

*Or her.*

# CHAPTER FIFTEEN

*The next day*

"**I** won't take you, I say!" Dolwyd shouted. "You are mad! Kaspian will have my head if I allow you to do this... this *folly*!"

Madelayne was patient in the face of his tantrum. "It is not a folly," she said patiently. "I merely wish to go into town and purchase a wedding band for him as a surprise. We talked about it right before he left. He said he would wear one and I intend to purchase one for him. You may escort me into town or you may stay here. It makes no difference to me."

Dolwyd was about to have a stroke. His face was red and his veins bulged. "You'll not go alone!" he croaked. "De Kirk will send an army with you if you go into town!"

"So be it."

"And how do you intend to pay for these gains? You have no money!"

"I will promise that my husband will send them the money. Kaspian St. Hèver's name should be good enough."

Madelayne watched Dolwyd grumble and stomp. Clad in an emerald brocade gown that swished along the floor as she walked, she turned to the too-big slippers courtesy of her hostess. "And I must have some gowns made as well, considering we do not know how long we will be at Kirk and I have imposed on my hostess far too much already."

"Not to mention she is taller and fatter than you are."

"Dolwyd, how cruel."

The physic knew there was no talking her out of her trip. It was a bright spring morning, and somewhat warm, which was rare in these parts, and Madelayne had awoken full of vinegar and fire. Perhaps it was the fact that her husband was gone and her anxiety was shadowing her manner, but Dolwyd thought perhaps she was unsteady from the knowledge that de Dalyn was up and about. Only last night they had seen him, but already, the tension was palpable. It seemed that Madelayne was determined to put distance between herself and the castle where Nicholas stalked.

Not that he could blame her. Sighing, the old man threw up his hands in resignation. "I'll tell de Kirk, then. We'll have an escort for you within the hour if you are determined to do this foolish thing."

Madelayne smiled prettily for him, but he would have no part of it. He waved his hands at her as he headed for the door.

"Do not use your charms on me, Lady St. Hèver," he scolded. "Your husband may succumb like a weakling to you, but I do not."

She continued to smile at him, mocking him. "Thank you, Dolwyd, ever so much."

He growled at her as he left the chamber. In precisely an hour, Madelayne was in the bailey, greeted by a twenty-man escort bearing the colors of Edward. All were Lavister men who had assumed their duty to their liege's new wife. Lord de Kirk didn't say much to her even though he was in the ward; she was coming to think that the man thought she and the people from Lavister were a load of trouble. He was right. She was almost embarrassed to look him in the eye for all of the nuisance they had caused. Mounting a small, gray palfrey, she took her place amongst the escort and followed them from the great ward.

The landscape outside of the castle walls was starting to come to life with various shades of green. The rain that had pounded the area for the past several weeks had ended and now the land was beginning to show signs of growth. The day was bright and the sun gave off a slight amount of warmth, making travel pleasant.

Dolwyd plodded along behind her on his old horse, a beast that she was sure was as old as Dolwyd himself. She could feel his angry stare on her back but she ignored him soundly; the old man hated any inconvenience, any stir from the routine of the ordinary, and she would not indulge his displeasure. Truth be told, she was eager to pass the time in any way possible until Kaspian's return. And Nicholas' presence at Kirk was as good a reason as any for her to put distance between her and the castle.

The town of Kirk was rather large, butting up against the castle and filled with streets and structures. But it was a dirty town with dirty streets, too many people wandering about their business. As the sun warmed the air, the gutters stank and homeless dogs huddled under wagons and in doorways.

Oddly enough, the bright day only seemed to emphasize the dreariness of the town. As the troop from the castle entered the berg, the peasants looked at them as if they were straight from the bowels of hell. It was like a town full of ignorants and Madelayne was the slightest bit uncomfortable. She could hear Dolwyd behind her, cursing her stubbornness.

Deeper into town was a wider street with several merchant shops. These people seemed friendlier and Madelayne immediately found a shop with bolts of fabric from France and beyond. With pleasure, she examined the satins and brocades, and the yards of damask that were both heavy and fragile at the same time. The man who ran the shop had a wife who sewed and, after much haggling, Madelayne commissioned the woman to make her four gowns, promising her a more than fair price should she deliver the gowns within the next couple of days.

Proceeding to the rear of the shop, the woman and her daughter-in-law took Madelayne's measurements and made a great fuss over her beautiful figure. But it was painful for her when they measure her bust line, engorged and bound in an attempt to dry up her milk. Standing there with her arms raised as they worked was a surreal experience; Madelayne thought that her dead child and life with Cairn seemed like it had happened a lifetime ago. This new life she was experiencing was something overwhelming and fantastic, but something wonderful and rich with a man she loved as opposed to a comfortable life with a man she was simply fond of. Love, she discovered, made all of the difference in the world.

Perhaps the queen of the lost stars, and lost souls, wasn't so lost anymore.

Perhaps she had finally found her way, after all.

When the measurements were finished and the deal made, Madelayne thanked the merchant and moved on. There were several farmers selling early spring produce, a baker with great loaves of brown currant bread, and a woman selling dried flowers. Cruising the entire street with her escort in tow, she was disappointed to realize there was no jeweler, only a metalworker. Upon discussions with the man, however, she discovered that he could work steel into a thick, lovely band for Kaspian and add semi-precious stones to it. But Madelayne didn't think stones suited him at all, so she asked the man to work two rings, identical, one for her and one for him. She wanted something for her husband, even if it was a steel ring, to announce to the world their bond of marriage. She began to think it was rather like branding him.

The thought made her giggle. In fact, they *were* branding each other.

With her shopping done, so was the day. Already the sun was passing into the early afternoon and it was time to return home. The soldiers were eager to return, of course, bored silly with having escorted St. Hèver's wife on a shopping trip. Madelayne was preparing to mount her palfrey even as the soldiers were moving out. Everyone was so focused on the road ahead and making it home before the evening meal that they failed to notice, out of twenty-one men, that Lady St. Hèver neglected to mount her horse as expected. Instead, something caught her attention and she immediately wandered off.

It was a small hovel next to the metalworker's shed. The words above the door were worn and barely legible, but the symbol was big and recognizable. A star, it was, indicating fortunes and she grinned at the thought of a fortune teller. Perhaps to divine her future with Kaspian? She was more than intrigued. Madelayne ducked into the doorway, entering a dark room that stank with an herb that set her to sneezing.

Her sneezing brought a quick response. From a crouched position beside the smoking hearth, a wild gray head snapped up.

"Bones, bones!" the old woman cackled.

Madelayne came to an uncertain halt. She eyed the woman, barely visible in the dark light. "Pardon?" she asked.

The woman struggled up from her knees, an old stick in her hand from poking at the embers. "Ye come for the bones, missy!"

Madelayne suddenly felt very foolish and perhaps the least bit intimidated. She had always been far too level headed for this nonsense, now wondering why she had even come. "Nay," she said softly, backing for the door. "I... I have changed my mind."

The old woman grasped her arm with bony fingers. "Ye came for the bones, missy. I can see it in yer eyes. Ye want tae know!"

Madelayne found herself gazing into one milky eye, one good one. The face was as old as time. The old crone yanked at her, pulling her deeper into the room. "Come along, come along. I'll tell ye what ye've come tae know!"

Madelayne weakly tried to pull away. "Truly, I do not wish to know anything. I already...."

The woman pulled hard on her, forcing her to the ground before the hearth. "Sit!" she commanded. Hobbling to a bag hanging on the wall against numerous other divining implements, she yanked it off the wall, opened the strings, and sank to her knees across from Madelayne. She stared at Madelayne closely as she dug into the bag for its contents.

"Give me yer finger," she croaked.

Madelayne hesitated before gingerly holding out her right hand. The old woman snatched it, pricking her index finger with something from the bag. Madelayne yelped as the woman squeezed drops of blood onto the dirt before them. Then, she spit into the mix.

"Ah," the old crone said as she stirred the dirt and spit and blood with a dirty fingernail. "I can see ye now. Ye're the queen of loss, lady. Ye've had much loss in yer life. I see many lost souls around ye, like stars in the heavens. But ye've held yerself strong. Ye've learned tae endure."

Madelayne looked at the old woman with a mixture of fear and awe. God's Bones, wasn't that what her mother had said once? That the lost souls were the stars in the heavens? Madelayne began to feel very uncomfortable that this woman should immediately pick up on such a thing with her. Was it so obvious? Was she truly the queen of all that was lost? Frightened, she stood up.

"I should not have come," she said, turning for the door. "You cannot tell me what I do not already know. I do not want to…."

The old woman cut her off. "Ye love him now," she said before Madelayne could escape. "Ye love him now and ye feel guilty. Never feel the guilt; ye've earned what ye have. Ye've endured enough."

Madelayne paused by the door, turning to look at the old woman, who was still on her knees in the dirt, fingers swirling in the spit and blood. It was so very odd what the woman had said and leadingly prophetic. It set Madelayne to pondering her very urge to enter the hovel; if this woman could see so much, perhaps there was reason for her to be there. Perhaps the fates were trying to tell her something. As foolish as it seemed, perhaps there was something the old woman could tell her, something she didn't already know.

For certain, her curiosity was piqued now with the old witch. Since she'd never had much faith in God, perhaps having faith in a mystic would tell her what she wanted to know. Reluctantly, she headed back into the room.

"Sons," she said finally. "Will there be sons for us?"

The old woman turned back to the mixture of blood and spit in the dirt. She took something out of the bag by her side and sprinkled it into the mixture as Madelayne watched with great interest. After a moment, she nodded.

"Aye," she said. "There will be sons. But yer tribulations are not over, lass. Ye're a survivor and ye're an avenger. Some that are lost... they cry for justice."

The answer both pleased and frightened Madelayne. She wasn't sure she wanted to hear anything more but morbid curiosity made her ask. "Who wants justice?"

The old woman continued to stare at her disgusting mixture in the dirt. "They call for vengeance."

"*Who?*"

"Those who were betrayed."

"But that makes no sense – who was betrayed?"

"Ye shall know soon enough."

Madelayne had no idea what the old woman meant and the more puzzled she became, the more fearful she became. What on earth could the old crone possibly mean? Confused and edgy, she turned for the door once more.

"I will send you coin," she said. "I have none with me. My name is Lady St. Hèver. My husband is a great knight. You can be assured I will send you the money."

She didn't wait for a reply, bolting from the door and hearing it slam behind her as she headed back to her escort. Just as she reached the collection of soldiers and horses, men who had begun searching the area for Lady St. Hèver caught sight of her and rushed to her side, demanding to know if she had been abducted. Madelayne assured them that she was well and she apologized for wandering off. Calmed, the group returned to their mounts as one of the soldiers helped Madelayne onto her palfrey. Just as she was settled, Dolwyd reined his ancient beast next to her.

"Did you find out what you wanted to know?" he asked.

Madelayne glanced at him as she gathered her reins. "What do you mean?"

Dolwyd looked off in the direction where Madelayne had come from, seeing the alleyway between buildings and the small hovel shoved back in the shadows. He, too, could see the carved sign even from the distance – a symbol of a star. He knew what it meant.

"I asked if you were told your future," he said, glancing at her. "I don't discount the mystics. There are things in this world that we cannot explain and things we don't understand."

Madelayne looked at him with mild surprise. "Then you believe in mystics and witches? Dolwyd, I'm shocked."

The old physic shook his head. "I didn't say I believed in them," he said. "But I don't discount anything, either."

It was a noncommittal answer that made her grin. The escort began to move out and Madelayne didn't say any more about the mystic or anything else. As they headed back to the castle, she kept thinking on the old crone's words – *those who were betrayed*. The implication alone was horrifying but Madelayne couldn't make any sense of it. *Who* was betrayed? She thought on everyone who had passed away in her life, those lost stars that lingered above her – her mother, her babies, Cairn... the old crone must have been referring to one of those souls but the only one the reference made any sense for would have been Cairn. He was the only one who could have been betrayed because her lost children certainly weren't. Neither was her mother.

Did Cairn need vengeance for a betrayal?

... *dear God*... could the old crone have meant the betrayal of affections, perhaps her loving Kaspian?

She wondered.

CƷ

**2.**     *Kirk Castle*

It was well after noon by the time Madelayne and her escort returned to Kirk Castle and the place was bustling with the coming of the mid-day meal. Lord and Lady de Kirk made a big production of every meal, including the smaller ones, so there were servants hurrying about in preparation for the event.

Dismounting her palfrey in the bailey, Madelayne headed for the keep as the escort disbanded. Dolwyd followed behind her, shuffling through the dirt, thinking on telling the woman that she needed to rest after her busy morning but, then again, she never listened to him so he wouldn't waste his breath. Much as her husband did, she would only do what she wanted to do.

And she did. Having no intention of resting, Madelayne retired to her chamber to remove her borrowed cloak and brush off her borrowed dress of the dust from traveling. Since the nooning meal was upon them, Madelayne thought she might attend in the great hall and try to be social. She'd spent so much of her stay at Kirk being hidden away with Kaspian that she thought that being more social while the man was away was a show of good manners. She didn't want to leave Kirk with Lady de Kirk still thinking terrible things of the Lavister inhabitants considering all of the chaos they'd brought with them.

So she washed her face with rosewater and brushed her hair, braiding it and then wrapping that braid into a bun at the nape of her neck. The hairpins she had were Mavia's, borrowed from the woman, and as she shoved them into her hair, she inevitably thought of the woman and about the scandal with Nicholas. She could still hardly believe it. She only wished that Mavia had confided in her about what was going on. Perhaps she could have helped; perhaps not. In any case, now she would never know and that realization saddened her a great deal. She still hurt for her friend, yet another lost star.

Washed and combed, she left her chamber and made her way down to the entry level of the keep. There was a soldier guarding the entry, as there always was, and she passed the man and on into the bailey as she headed for the great hall. She wondered where Dolwyd was because the old physic was never far away from her these days but she assumed he would meet her in the hall. He was probably off sulking because she had insisted on the trip to town and he hadn't wanted her to go. She smiled about that, hoping to soothe the old man so he would not tell Kaspian what she had done. Lost in thought as she neared the hall, a figure suddenly slipped up beside her.

"Greetings, Lady St. Hèver," he said.

Startled, Madelayne found herself looking up at Nicholas. Immediately, she put distance between them. "I do not wish to speak to you," she said. "Please respect my wishes and go away."

Nicholas wasn't deterred in the least. In fact, he had been waiting all morning for Madelayne to return from the town so he could put his wicked plan into action. He'd been watching from his window for that long, waiting for the right moment to confront her, and he saw it a few minutes ago when the woman quit the keep and headed towards the great hall, alone. He'd run all the way from his quarters to intercept her.

Now, he had her.

"I am pleased to find you without your shadow," Nicholas said, referring to Dolwyd. "My lady, there is something very serious I must speak with you about, privately. The old physic must not hear this for if he did, your life would be in danger. For your own safety, I must tell you what I know."

Madelayne was quickly losing patience. "I do not want to hear anything from you," she said. "Please leave me alone."

"It has to do with Cairn."

Now, her patience was gone and she came to a halt just shy of the great hall entry, facing Nicholas beneath the bright sun. "You will *not* speak of him, do you hear?" she hissed. "I do not want to hear anything from you, Nicholas de Dalyn. I am not sure how much plainer I can be."

As she turned for the entry, he spoke quickly. "His death was not an accident."

Madelayne almost kept walking. She really did. But there was something that made her stop, something annoying and abrasive, something just irritating enough to cause her to come to a halt and turn to Nicholas once more. There was nothing but contempt in her expression.

"I told you not to speak of him," she said. "If I must tell you again, I will go straight to Lord de Kirk and have him banish you from Kirk. Do you understand me? I will not allow you to harass me and I will not permit you to use Cairn to do it."

Nicholas held up his hands in supplication, his expression quite serious. "Please my lady," he begged softly. "I ask for two minutes of your time. Only two. After that, if you do not believe me, I will never bother you again. I swear it."

Madelayne knew he was lying. Frustrated and upset, she growled as she turned away from him yet again. "I will not hear you."

"St. Hèver killed Cairn because of you!"

Madelayne froze. Her brittle mind digested the words and she turned for Nicholas, retracing her steps in his direction, and when she finally came upon him, she lashed out a hand and slapped him across the face. Nicholas' head snapped from the blow.

"You lying, vicious bastard," she seethed. "How dare you say that! It is not true and you know it!"

Nicholas' jaw was ticking as he looked at her, furious that she should strike him. But he had to keep his composure; it was imperative if he had any hope of destroying hers. He wanted her to feel unsteady and upset. Reaching out, he grabbed her by the arms and held her fast.

"It is not a lie," he hissed. "I was at Beeston. I saw St. Hèver order Cairn into an impossible situation where he was overrun by Welsh. He did it because he wanted you, do you understand? He wanted to marry you and the only way to do that was to rid himself of Cairn. By the time he ordered me to help the man, it was too late. St. Hèver ordered Cairn to his death and if you do not watch yourself, he will see that you meet your death as well!"

He was hissing in her face, spraying spittle on her, and she jerked her arms out of his grip, slapping at him again. This time, he blocked her hands, holding on to them as she wrestled to pull free.

"You are a liar!" she said, finally kicking him in the shin to force him to let her go. "How dare you say such things! I am going to tell Kaspian and he will make sure you leave Kirk, and Lavister, for good! Everything was well and good until you came along and now your poison has destroyed good people. You have destroyed my friends! I will not let you destroy me, do you hear? Leave me alone!"

With that, she yanked herself away from him and started running, running towards the keep. Her first thought was to lock herself inside her chamber but she was fearful of what would happen if Nicholas tried to break in. She would be cornered, unable to get away. Not wanting to be cornered by the man, it was best to hide from him so she ran around the side of Kirk's keep, heading for the stables on the east side.

The structure of Kirk was very new as far as castles went, only built during the last part of the previous century, so the big walls actually had rooms built into them and the keep was part of the wall. The stables were built up into the north side of the structure, big stone buildings, and she ran to them. At this time of day, the stables were busy with horses being tended and men moving about, so she lost herself in the collection of grooms and soldiers that happened to be around, disappearing into one of the two stable structures and hoping she could evade Nicholas.

Time passed and he didn't show himself. It was quiet and cool in the stable, smelling strongly of hay and urine and horses, but Madelayne didn't care. She felt somewhat safe there, relieved that Nicholas hadn't followed her. She still wasn't over his attempt to upset her, to turn her against Kaspian, and she had already determined that she was going to ask Lord de Kirk to send a message to Kaspian in Shrewsbury. She wanted the man to return for she felt very vulnerable with Nicholas on the prowl, and she was quite certain that Kaspian would want to know that Nicholas was not as ill as he had led everyone to believe. Just another one of his lies in a long string of fabrications.

In the dimness of the stable, she was able to calm herself. Even though it was clear Nicholas hadn't followed her, she knew at some point she would run into him again and she thought she should probably arm herself in case she had to beat him away.

Against the wall near the door, several barn implements were leaning. There were a couple of shovels, a pitch fork, and a few large sticks that were probably used for prodding the animals. She rushed to the collection of implements and grabbed one of the big, heavy sticks. She had no reservation about using it and, somehow, she didn't feel quite so vulnerable anymore now that she was armed. At least she had something to defend herself with if Nicholas tried to grab her again.

Armed or not, she wasn't ready to leave the shelter of the stables yet. She felt safe here. Therefore, she wandered back to the stalls where some of the riding horses were stabled. They were gentle creatures for the most part and she recognized the palfrey she had ridden into town. She had her big stick in one hand as she reached out to pet the little, gray mare. She was rubbing the animal's velvety nose when a shadow fell across the entry.

Startled, and fearful, she wielded her stick, expecting to see Nicholas but instead seeing one of Lavister's senior soldiers. She recognized the man; tall and dark-haired with a round face, he was a sergeant that had been with Lavister a very long time. He was a fixture in the army and trusted by the knights. Relieved at the sight of him, she lowered the stick and he smiled hesitantly at her.

"I am sorry to disturb you, my lady," he said. "I saw you run in here and came to see if everything was well. Is there anything I can do for you?"

Madelayne didn't hesitate in her response. "Aye," she said. "I need for you to send word to my husband and tell him that Nicholas de Dalyn is threatening me. Kaspian is in Shrewsbury but he must come back immediately."

The smile faded from the sergeant's face. "May I ask what de Dalyn has done?" he said. "Of course I will send word to Lord St. Hèver, but what has that knight done?"

*That knight.* It was clear from the way he said it that he didn't have much love for de Dalyn, either. Madelayne was coming to feel a good deal better with the sergeant's presence. At last, someone who could help her!

"He has been spewing lies," she said. "He harasses me and will not leave me alone. I have this stick now because if he tries to harass me again, I will beat him."

The sergeant saw the big stick in her hand. "No doubt he deserves it, my lady," he muttered. "I will send word to your husband right away. May... may I ask what de Dalyn has said to you? Is there something I can do?"

Madelayne looked at the man; since he had been with Lavister's army a long time, he had been under Cairn's command. She was fairly certain he had been at the battle of Beeston, as well. Nicholas' words came tumbling down on her and try as she might to resist them, they still upset her. *St. Hèver killed Cairn because of you!* Nicholas was the epitome of a lying bastard, a dishonorable rake as far as Madelayne was concerned. She was furious and hurt by his attempts to upset her. But there was something in his words that had planted a seed of curiosity, and perhaps confusion, in her mind. She wanted to know the truth.

"I am not sure if you can do anything," she said. "But may I ask you a question?"

He nodded. "Of course, my lady."

"Were you at Beeston?"

Again, he nodded. "I was indeed, my lady," he said. Then, he appeared somewhat hesitant. "If it is not appropriate for me to speak on the subject, then I apologize, but I would like to say that I am very sorry for your loss of Sir Cairn. He was a good man. Sir Kaspian is also a good man and greatly respected. My best wishes for your marriage to him, my lady."

Madelayne simply nodded. "Thank you," she said, still eyeing the man. "It *is* about Kaspian, in fact. Did you... while you were at the battle at Beeston, did you hear... did anyone ever say... that Kaspian was responsible for Cairn's death? I insist you tell me the truth, sergeant. I must know if you heard anything to that regard."

The sergeant appeared rather uncomfortable. He scratched his head and averted his gaze, eventually shaking his head. "Nay, Lady St. Hèver," he said. "I heard nothing of the sort and if you have been told that, it is not the truth. Sir Kaspian would have sacrificed himself if it would have saved Cairn. You must believe that."

Madelayne felt a wave of relief wash over her, confirming what she already knew. *Damn Nicholas and his lies!* "I know," she said. "But I was told... that is to say, I heard that Kaspian sent Cairn to his death."

The sergeant continued to shake his head, the wagging more pronounced now. "Never, my lady," he said firmly. "He would not do that, at least not knowingly."

"That is good."

"But...."

He suddenly stopped and she peered at him curious. "But *what*?" she said. "Go on, man. If you have heard something else, you must tell me. I must know."

The sergeant was quite reluctant. "I do not want to fill your head with soldiers' rumors."

"Tell me!"

He grunted unhappily before continuing. "If you insist," he said. "But Sir Kaspian will probably have my head for telling you such gossip."

"I will not tell him that you told me. *Please*, sergeant. What more did you hear?"

He lifted his eyebrows with resignation, knowing he had no choice. Oddly enough, he was rather glad to be telling her. Perhaps if she knew, then something could be done about it.

Done about *him*.

"Sir Cairn was fighting the Welsh with several Lavister men by his side," he said quietly. "You must understand... I heard this from men who saw Sir Cairn's death. They have said that Sir Nicholas had the chance to save him and did not. As Sir Cairn begged for help, Sir Nicholas did nothing to fight off the Welsh that were attacking Sir Cairn. The men have said that Sir Nicholas stood by and did nothing while Sir Cairn was killed, and then he rode in and collected the man's body, telling everyone he was too late to save him. That is what I have been told, my lady, by men I trust."

Madelayne stared at him in horror. She could never have imagined that the man would tell her such a thing and the impact of the words was like a punch to the stomach. She could hardly breathe.

"My... God!" she gasped. "Is this true?"

The sergeant lowered his head in sorrow. "I believe that it is."

"Do you really?"

He sighed heavily. "I do, my lady," he said firmly. "There have always been rumors about de Dalyn and his ambitions, how he would sacrifice men in order to achieve his posts. Soldiers talk, my lady. We face a good deal of life and death together, and we talk. We see things and we hear things. I do not doubt that Sir Nicholas is capable of doing what my men said he did."

Madelayne realized she had no doubt, either. With what happened to Mavia and with the behavior she had witnessed from the man, she was fully willing to believe the sergeant's truth. She was seized with utter distress.

"But what of Sir Ewan?" she wanted to know. "Have you heard that de Dalyn had anything to do with his death as well?"

The sergeant cast her a long glance. "He was under Sir Nicholas' command at the time," he said. "Although I did not see his death, the men said that Sir Nicholas put Sir Ewan in an indefensible situation and the man took an arrow to the neck for it."

It was all so horrifying to hear that Madelayne actually grabbed hold of the stall next to her, holding on to the wood frame to steady herself.

"Why have you not told Kaspian any of this?" she demanded. "He will want to know."

The sergeant shook his head. "What good would it do, my lady?" he said. "Sir Nicholas would only deny it. The men who saw him refuse to save Cairn could take an oath of truth and swear they saw his actions, but they are only fighting men. They would not be believed over a knight with a reputation like Sir Nicholas'. It is said that de Dalyn is a favorite of Edward, in fact. Do you truly believe lowly fighting men would be believed?"

He was right. God help them all, he was right. Madelayne stared at the man, her horror turning into something deeper and darker, more indefinable in the sense that it was more than pure shock that she felt. It was far more than that. And then she suddenly remembered what the old crone had said earlier in the day as she stirred the dirt and blood and spit together.

*Those who were betrayed.*

Dear God, those words that made no sense at the time suddenly made a good deal of sense now that she'd heard the sergeant's tales. Never for one moment did she doubt what the man was saying, for she knew that fighting men sometimes saw more, and knew more, than the rest of them did. They saw the worst of life at times and, in this case, they had seen the betrayal of good knights by one they were supposed to be allied with. But it was clear that the only side Nicholas was on was his own. Whatever his goals, whatever his aspirations, he was killing men to get it. First Cairn, then Ewan. He'd already tried to get to

Thomas through Mavia. Madelayne was coming to think that Kaspian would be next on Nicholas' list and that thought scared her to death.

She couldn't bury another husband and especially not the man she loved with all her heart.

"My God," she breathed, sagging against the wall of the stall. "You are correct; you are absolutely correct that fighting men would not be believed over an honorable knight but in this case, I believe what you tell me because I have seen what Nicholas is capable of. He came to Lavister and has nearly destroyed our little world with his evil. But for what? Why would he do such a thing?"

The sergeant could see how shaken she was. "Who is to say, my lady?" he said. "It is possible he wants command of Lavister and control of her wealth. That would be my guess."

Madelayne looked at him, greatly distressed. "But killing knights to do it?" she said. "Why would he kill Cairn and Ewan? And if he has killed them, surely he will not stop. Kaspian and Thomas will be next."

The sergeant nodded his head faintly. "I would surmise that as well, my lady."

Madelayne pondered the situation for a few moments longer before realizing she had to do something about it. She couldn't stand by idly while Nicholas killed everyone she loved or was fond of. Cairn and Ewan were already gone. So was Mavia. But, God help her, that was where it would end. If, for no other reason, the old crone had been right – the dead needed to be avenged. Cairn and Ewan and Mavia needed to be avenged.

Especially Cairn. As he was her former husband, it was her duty to seek justice. For a man who had protected her and tried so hard to make her love him, perhaps after death, she would show him just how much she had appreciated him. Nay, she didn't love him and never would, but he had meant a great deal to her. Through him, she had met the love of her life in the form of Kaspian.

As odd as it seemed in that sense, there was a great deal to be thankful to Cairn for and she would not let Nicholas de Dalyn's treachery go unanswered. For Cairn, she would do this. It was her duty as much as her right. But she had another stake in it as well; as much as the dead needed to be avenged, the living needed to be protected.

*Kaspian.*

Rage filled her, the likes of which she had never experienced before. She was so angry that she could hardly breathe. She turned to the sergeant, who was watching her somewhat anxiously.

"What is your name?" she asked him.

"Bouse, my lady," he said. "I am known as Bouse."

Madelayne reached out and grasped his arm, squeezing it in a gesture of gratitude. "You have my thanks, Bouse," she said. "Go now and send the missive to Kaspian. And tell no one what you told me; when Kaspian returns, you will tell him personally, do you hear?"

Bouse nodded faintly. "Aye, my lady."

"Good."

She started to move out of the stable but he followed her. "Allow me to escort you to the keep, my lady," he said. "If Sir Nicholas is about, you will need protection."

Madelayne looked the man in the eye as she lifted the stick in her hand. Strangely, she felt no more fear of Nicholas, not in the least. She had been fearful of the man when she had entered the stable but upon exiting the stable, there was no fear at all. In fact, she very much hoped she ran into him.

*A killer of men.*

"It is he who will need protection from *me*," she said quietly.

Bouse didn't doubt her for a moment. But the moment she went into the keep, he went in search of Thomas. Something told him that Lady St. Hèver might need help.

Or saving.

# CHAPTER SIXTEEN

He would be back to Kirk in an hour.

Thundering up the road from Shrewsbury, Kaspian and about twenty men were riding at breakneck speed back to Kirk Castle to solicit assistance from Lord de Kirk. Shrewsbury's garrison was already preparing to march on Lavister and Kaspian had left the small Lavister force he'd taken to Shrewsbury, including Reece, to assimilate with the Shrewsbury troops, but the garrison commander of Shrewsbury was convinced they also needed Kirk's help. The larger the force, the easier it would go for them in regaining Lavister, so Kaspian was headed back to Kirk to ask Owain for his assistance.

Owain had, indeed, offered manpower at one point and Kaspian had tentatively accepted, but he was more concerned with soliciting Edward's troops at Shrewsbury because he hadn't wanted to take de Kirk's men away from Kirk Castle with Dafydd so close. He'd already put de Kirk out enough. However, the truth was that it was better if they all banded together to drive Dafydd away. A united front, and more men, would do that.

So, with Lavister men integrating with Shrewsbury men, Kaspian was on his way back to ask Lord de Kirk for a couple hundred more men. Then, they would all converge on Lavister in two days to drive out the Welsh. At least, that was the plan. Kaspian wasn't looking forward to battle so soon again, and especially in light of his injury which wasn't fully healed, but he had little choice. He wanted his fortress back.

But he had another reason for returning to Kirk Castle – he wanted to see Madelayne before he went to battle again. He had told her that he would probably go straight to Lavister from Shrewsbury and he could have very well sent a messenger back to Kirk to request men from Lord de Kirk, but the reality was that he wanted to see his wife one last time. He couldn't stand to be away from her, not even for an hour, so he pushed his men and the horses hard, hoping to make it back to Kirk Castle before sunset. The more time spent at Kirk, the more time spent with Madelayne. From the consummate knight who, for most of his life, had breathed and slept and ate war, the introduction of a wife he was mad about was something he was wholly unaccustomed to.

But it was something that consumed his entire being… and he didn't care in the least.

Still, there was more to his desire to see her than simple emotion. There was concern as well. Even though he knew de Dalyn was very ill and unable to move about, there was still an inherent distrust of the man. He knew, if Nicholas was able, that he'd drag himself out of his deathbed if it meant he could get close to Madelayne without Kaspian hanging about. Kaspian didn't want to admit that very reason was predominantly why he was racing to Kirk at breakneck speed.

The truth was that he didn't trust Nicholas in the least.

So the party raced down the road, avoiding the ruts from the recent rains and, on more than one occasion, found themselves up on the grassy shoulders of the road, running along the grass rather than the uneven road. Kaspian was still experiencing pain and fatigue as the result of his wound but he ignored it, pushing through it, because he felt such a sense of urgency to return to Kirk. Even if someone had asked him why he was so determined to return, he couldn't have really explained it. All he knew was that the sense of urgency was clawing at him and he had to make it back to Kirk quickly, to see Madelayne and to make sure she was well. More than that, he was seriously considering asking Lord de Kirk to lock Nicholas up in the vault for the duration of his absence from Kirk. He knew he would only relax if the man was imprisoned.

In fact, it became the only option as far as he was concerned. He would seek out Lord de Kirk and ask him to put a guard on Nicholas' room. But that thought vanished when he finally entered the bailey of Kirk to face a scene he never thought he would ever see. It was something so confusing, and startling, that once he envisioned it, all else seemed to fade from his mind. All he could think of was fury, fear, and death as he had never embraced it in his life.

Nicholas, Thomas, and Madelayne were grouped near one another and it was clear that something terrible had happened. He saw weapons and blood. Then he heard his wife's voice; she was crying his name. Bailing from his steed, his broadsword was out before his feet even hit the ground.

Kaspian St. Hèver, in all of his deadly forms, was released. The reckoning, for all of them, had finally come.

# CHAPTER SEVENTEEN

After leaving the sergeant near the stables, Madelayne had returned to the chamber she shared with Kaspian. The calm she felt was quite eerie, really, a peace that had settled upon her with regard to Nicholas that it was difficult to describe. She was no longer afraid of the man, nor did she have an aversion to him as she had before. All she knew was that she was at peace with what needed to be done and she was quite convinced she was the only one who could do it.

Nicholas had caused so much death and destruction to the people of Lavister, her family and friends, that there was no one left who could avenge them – Kaspian and Reece were away and Thomas had crawled in to a bottle to fester. She didn't even know where the man was; no one seemed to know. Moreover, she was afraid that if Thomas knew what the sergeant had told her, he'd run right to Nicholas to try and kill the man and end up getting himself killed instead. He wasn't in any shape to kill a knight.

But she was.

It was very odd that she would think so because she had never killed anyone before. She'd never even thought on such a thing. In fact, she didn't even like to kill chickens or rabbits for the cook. She just wasn't the killing type. But this was different; Nicholas was going to kill them all, she was sure, and she was the only one who knew of his wicked intentions. She looked at the situation as more than vengeance for Cairn and Ewan and Mavia – she looked at it as self-preservation for those left behind. She looked at it as saving Kaspian's life. It was something she was determined to do, more than she had ever been determined about anything in her life.

It was time for Nicholas to pay.

Something changed in Madelayne that day. Gone was the woman who was rather naïve and stubborn. In her place came a woman determined to fight for her friends and family, to fight for what she believed in. If it meant taking a man's life, then she was willing to do it to save others. The woman who had suffered such loss in her life, the queen of the lost stars that hung high in the heavens watching over her, was about to reclaim some of that sorrow and tuck it away where it could never harm her again. She was going to take back control of her life, to a certain extent, by seeking vengeance against someone who had inadvertently tried to destroy her. There was no more line between those Nicholas had harmed and those he hadn't. Now, they were all one group.

Madelayne was about to fight for that group.

But there were obstacles to that plan. She knew that Nicholas simply wouldn't lie down and let her do as she pleased to him so her only chance against him was surprise. He was much bigger than she was, and much stronger, and she was sure that he believed he was much more intelligent, too. But that was not to be the case – she was going to outsmart him. Since she couldn't overpower him, her only chance was the element of surprise and being just a little bit smarter than he was because she was certain if she didn't seriously disable him with her first strike, she might not get a second chance.

So she plotted what she would do and how she would do it. Up in the bedroom high above Kirk's bailey, she knew what her actions would be. The first strike would be hard and fast, to disable the man. The second would be to kill him. But she wanted him to know why he was suffering, that everything she was doing had vengeance written all over it. Was she an avenging angel? Perhaps. All she knew was that she had to do this. To delay, in any fashion, might cost someone else their life and she was terrified that the someone suffering would be Kaspian.

She couldn't let that happen.

Looking around the chamber, she could see the stick she'd brought with her from the stables. It was actually quite heavy and would make a perfect club to brain him over the skull with. Kaspian had most of his weaponry in the armory but not all of it; they'd come to Kirk with little more than the clothes on their back but Kaspian had possessed numerous small daggers that he had carried on his body and some of those daggers were on a table near the lancet window. She went to the table and picked one of them up, examining it, wondering if she could kill a man with it. It wasn't very large but it could do some damage, at least enough to incapacitate him. After that, she would either have to stab him until she pierced his heart or find something larger to cut him with.

She held the dirk, staring at it, finally feeling some apprehension as she touched the razor-sharp tip. It wasn't fear of Nicholas but fear for herself, perhaps. If something happened to her, then Nicholas would tell everyone that she had gone mad and tried to kill him, and that he had been forced to kill her in self-defense. She knew that Kaspian would not believe him and, in the man's weakened state, he would go after Nicholas and quite possibly lose.

Therefore, she had to win this fight. There was no other option. Therefore, she drew in a deep breath and collected both the dirk and her big stick.

It was time to act.

With every step she took, however, apprehension grew. She hadn't done much with her life; she had lived unspectacularly, doing mundane things, never anything grand. Never anything that would sway nations or save people or contribute to the cause of man. She was, in truth, unspectacular, at least she thought so. But in this chance to avenge people who had been wrongfully taken from this earth, she felt as if, finally, she were doing something important.

She was doing something noble.

The sun was bright in the bailey as she exited the keep, her gaze nervous as she kept an eye out for Nicholas. She wasn't sure what she would say to him when she saw him because she knew he would rush upon her and try to tell her more lies, so it was very important that she be the one to spot him first and not the other way around. That way, she would have time to consider her actions and, hopefully, have the element of surprise. Therefore, she tried to stay in the shadows, watching and waiting for her prey.

This time, she would be the hunter.

A brisk breeze blew through the bailey, stirring the dust and debris, as Madelayne remained at the corner of the keep, standing behind a flying buttress-like feature that kept her somewhat shielded. She stood there for quite some time, watching the comings and goings of the bailey, watching for any sign of the tall, blonde knight who had done so much damage.

Minutes passed into an hour and still no sign of him. She was considering moving to the great hall to see if he might be in there, or even if someone might know where he was, when she suddenly caught sight of him as he crossed the bailey away from the stables.

Seized with the vision of an unsuspecting Nicholas, Madelayne pushed herself against the stone, watching from the shadows as

Nicholas crossed the bailey towards the outbuildings that were housing some of Lavister's troops. The man appeared as if he didn't have a care in the world, moving quite casually, and Madelayne waited until he moved well past her. This way, she could sneak up behind him and club him on the head from behind. Therefore, she was prompted to move as he strolled across the ward away from her. She came out of her hiding place and fell in behind him.

Heart pounding in her ears, Madelayne held the heavy stick in both hands as she stalked Nicholas. There weren't many people in the bailey at this time of day and most of the soldiers were up on the wall, so there wasn't anybody to wonder why Lady St. Hèver was following de Dalyn with a stick in her hands. There wasn't anyone to stop her. That was well and good because Madelayne didn't want any distractions. She picked up her pace, closing the gap between her and Nicholas before coming to within just a few feet of him. He still wasn't aware of her presence and that was exactly what she wanted. Lifting the heavy stick, she clobbered Nicholas across the back of the skull with it. He fell like a stone.

Terrified and thrilled she had struck down her prey, Madelayne circled him at a distance, the club still in her hands preparing to strike him again. She was delighted her plan had worked but apprehensive of what she had gotten herself in to. The reality of the blow was more than she thought it would be and now a man was at her feet, dazed. A man who had killed and killed again.

Still, she didn't want to beat him to death, at least not yet. She wanted him to know why. For Cairn and Ewan and Mavia, she wanted Nicholas to know her motivation, a motivation as old as time itself. To right wrongs. To seek justice.

*To seek vengeance.*

"Can you hear me, Sir Nicholas?" Madelayne asked. When he didn't respond, she kicked his foot. "Can you hear me?"

Nicholas moaned and twitched, rolling his head back and forth and struggling to come around. Madelayne moved closer, standing over him with the stick held high.

"Open your eyes," she commanded. "Open your eyes and look at me, Nicholas. I know you can hear me."

Nicholas lay there a moment before one eye popped open. Then, a second eye popped open, both of them dazed but looking at her. Madelayne realized, as he looked at her, that her fury was returning. Gazing into the face of the man who allowed Cairn to die, any apprehension she might have felt at her actions was vanished. She kicked him again.

"Listen to me, you arrogant swine," she hissed. "I know what you did. I know that you allowed Cairn to die at the hands of the Welsh. Did you think no one would tell me? Did you think no one saw what you did? With God as my witness, you are going to pay for your treachery. Do you understand me?"

Nicholas was becoming more alert. He blinked his eyes but that was all he did; he made no effort to move anything else, not at the moment. His gaze never left hers.

"What on earth are you talking about?" he said, sounding very much as if he were the victim in all of this. "What's this about Cairn? I did what I could for him, lady. I pulled him away from the Welsh. Who would dare to tell you otherwise?"

Infuriated, she kicked him again, right in the thigh. He flinched with pain but made no move to stop her. He didn't move at all. Standing over him, Madelayne was close to striking him with her stick again.

"Soldiers who saw what happened," she snapped. "They saw Cairn beg for help and they saw you stand immobile until it was too late. Are you so arrogant that you would think no one would see such a thing? Worse yet, that they would not tell me what they saw?"

Nicholas gazed up at the woman steadily. He was in a bad position, on his back as she stood over him with a stick. He knew he could easily subdue her but she would fight him and more than likely hurt herself in the process. No one would be sympathetic to a man who hurt a woman, and especially not St. Hèver. Even though Kaspian was still recovering from his wound, he was still formidable. Nicholas wasn't ready yet to face that battle. But he also couldn't let Lady St. Hèver have the advantage over him, now with the knowledge of what really happened at Beeston with Cairn l'Ebreux.

In truth, he never thought anyone would notice what he'd done and even if they did, he didn't think they would talk. It would be his word against rumors.

*Rumors....*

"Are you so foolish that you don't realize they are telling you that to keep you in St. Hèver's spell?" he hissed. "These are St. Hèver's men, for God's sake. They will tell you anything to keep you from knowing the truth!"

That was it as far as Madelayne was concerned. She lowered the stick, cracking Nicholas on the leg and belly as he grunted and rolled to his side, away from her. She was still hitting him as he rolled to his knees before tossing the stick away and yanking forth the dirk she had tucked in her skirt. Leaping onto Nicholas' back, she grabbed him by the hair and lifted the dirk.

"You allowed Cairn to be killed," she yanked on his hair, listening to him groan. "You allowed Ewan to be killed! And Mavia... you tortured her so that she killed herself! You did all of this, you wicked bastard, and their deaths must be avenged. You were supposed to uphold the codes of chivalry yet you upheld nothing – you abused trust. You allowed people to die and then lied about it. I will not let you do it again, do you hear? Not again!"

He had no idea she had the dirk so when she brought it down, it was a stabbing pain near his shoulder blade. No longer willing to stand by and allow the lady to abuse him, which evidently meant she intended to kill him, Nicholas threw her off his back and lurched to his feet, knowing he'd been stabbed but not knowing how badly he was hurt. He could feel the warm, sticky blood trickling down his back as he whirled on Madelayne.

"What have you done to me?" he hissed. "You're mad!"

Madelayne had fallen awkwardly on her wrist and now she couldn't move it without a good deal of pain. But she managed to get to her feet, putting the dirk in her other hand, and moving away from Nicholas. Her biggest fear came to light when she realized that she hadn't disabled him on her first strike or even her second. They were starting to gather a crowd in the bailey and she wondered if anyone would help her. She wasn't sure she could kill Nicholas now that he was on his feet but her determination to punish him had not lessened. It was something she had to do.

"You allowed Cairn to die," she said, pointing the dirk at him. "Why would you do such a thing? You were supposed to be his ally yet you did not help him when he needed it. Why did you not help him?"

Nicholas, too, could see that they were gathering a crowd. Of course, people would sympathize with the lady who had lost her husband in battle and he began to feel just the slightest bit nervous. It was clear that she had been told what had happened but there was no way he was going to show weakness in the face of her accusations.

"You are quite mad," he said, his jaw ticking. Gone was the pleasant attitude he so often put forward. Now, there was a battle going on and he meant to win it. "You are mad with grief and guilt, that is obvious. You should feel guilty, too, for allowing St. Hèver into your bed so soon after your husband's death. But I told you… you know what I told you. He has you under his spell and if you do not break free, he will kill you, too!"

Madelayne's composure was slipping, her fear starting to gain the upper hand. "It is not true," she said. "Why do you lie so? Why would you harm people you are supposed to be allied with?"

Nicholas simply looked at her, a calculated stare. It was obvious that his contention that St. Hèver had allowed Cairn to be killed wasn't registering with her. She was past the point of him being able to convince her. Therefore, he had to silence her. The more she talked, the more people would believe her and turn against him. He could fight the soldiers' rumors but he could not fight against the widow of a man he had allowed to be killed. She would tell St. Hèver what she knew and then, Nicholas knew, everything would turn against him. All that he had worked for, the careful plans he had laid, would be wasted. All because soldiers couldn't keep their mouths shut. Infuriated, his jaw began to tick dangerously as he rushed Madelayne.

She saw him coming and held up the dirk in front of her, as if that would be enough to ward him off, but he slapped at it, knocking it out of her hand and sending it flying. Terrified, Madelayne dodged him as he swiped at her and she ran for the big stick she had tossed away. She could see it several feet away and she dashed in that direction, reaching down to pick it up but Nicholas was right behind her. He grabbed her from behind and she screamed.

Nicholas had her tightly, pinning her arms, but she was still holding the stick. He kept trying to kick it out of her hands although from the angle he was holding her, it was awkward if not impossible. Madelayne held on to it with a death grip, unwilling to release it, all the while trying to twist from his arms.

"Let me go!" she demanded. "*Let me go!*"

Nicholas had his face next to the left side of her head. "I will not let you go," he hissed in her ear. "You tried to kill me. Are you so foolish as to think I would not retaliate? Drop the stick or this will go very badly for you."

She tried to head-butt him. "I will not drop it!" she screeched. "Let me go or you will be sorry!"

He laughed rudely in her ear. "Lady, I have had enough of your idiocy," he said. "You and I are going someplace private where I will talk and you will listen."

He started to walk, carrying her along awkwardly, but she would not make easy prey. She kicked at his knees, squealing and twisting, noticing that the soldiers on the wall were starting to come down from the parapet into the bailey. They were Lavister men; she recognized them. They were pointing at her and discussing the situation between them, obviously very concerned for the lady, and Madelayne held out some hope that they might try to help her. At this point, she would willingly take it. Perhaps they would even hold Nicholas down while she beat him to death with the stick. A pair of the men broke off and headed in her direction, obviously intending to help, but Nicholas saw them.

Quickly, he dropped her to her feet and put an arm across her throat, holding her threateningly. "Come no closer," he commanded the Lavister men. "I will kill her if you do."

Nicholas' release on her arms gave Madelayne the freedom to start swinging the stick again and she did, aiming for his head. He was able to grab the stick with his free hand and yank it away from her, tossing it well away.

Panicked, Madelayne grabbed at his arm, trying to scratch him, fighting him every step of the way as he tried to drag her off. She was terrified of what would happen if he got her alone so she threw her body weight down, trying to dislodge his grip on her, but he ended up releasing his arm around her neck and grabbed her arms instead.

He pulled, she dragged, and the Lavister soldiers followed at a distance, fearful of intervening because they were afraid de Dalyn would follow through on his threat and try to kill Lady St. Hèver if they did. No one wanted to explain that to Sir Kaspian.

Meanwhile, Madelayne was in the fight for her life. It had been reduced to this, a brutal struggle she knew she couldn't win. It was strength against strength and she knew she couldn't match him. Nicholas was dragging her towards the stables where there were nooks and crevices to be hidden from view, places where he could do terrible things to her if he wanted to. But Madelayne just couldn't believe the soldiers of Lavister would let it come to that. This was her fight but, in a sense, it was everyone's fight. What Nicholas had done affected them all. Throwing herself to the ground to try and stop his momentum, she finally turned towards the soldiers who were following at a distance.

"Help me!" she cried.

That prompted the men into action. The lady's request could not be denied. Nicholas, seeing the soldiers advancing, and several with weapons, tried to grab Madelayne around the neck again but she wouldn't let him. She put her hand on his face, pushing him away, digging her dirty fingers into his eyes. When she did that, he abruptly lost his grip because she had nearly blinded him. He growled angrily as she yanked herself free from his grip.

As she backed away, and a few Lavister soldiers put themselves between her and her attacker, Nicholas suddenly lurched forward with a yelp of pain and ended up on his knees. Standing behind him with a sword in his hand, to everyone's shock, was a sight none of the Lavister people ever thought to see. Out of the bottle and into the light, an avenging angel had appeared.

"Thomas!" Madelayne cried.

Thomas looked like hell. His face was pale, his eyes red-rimmed, and even from where he stood, the alcohol could be smelled. He stood there unsteadily, his gaze on Nicholas as he spoke to Madelayne.

"Someone said you might need help," he said, his voice hoarse and harsh. "What did he do to you, Madelayne? Why is he dragging you across the bailey?"

Madelayne had never felt so much relief in her life. She opened her mouth to reply when there was a shout from the gatehouse and everyone turned to see men bearing tunics of Edward charging in on familiar mounts.

Dust kicked up, dogs barked, and men stepped aside so they would not be trampled. The incoming party was very familiar and Madelayne recognized the man in the lead in particular. Her heart leapt into her throat and tears filled her eyes at the realization that her husband had unexpectedly arrived. Kaspian had returned, just in the nick of time.

"*Kaspian!*" she cried.

Kaspian was already off his horse, sword in hand as he charged the group surrounding Nicholas, who was still on his knees. Kaspian was torn between his wife, who was muddy and obviously agitated, and the knight on his knees. It was a perplexing situation, made worse by Thomas standing there with a sword in his hand, the tip bloodied. Kaspian had no idea what he was looking at so his attention moved to his nearly-hysterical wife.

"What goes on here?" he demanded.

Madelayne was already in tears but she had to tell Kaspian what she knew. Tears wouldn't stop her. His appearance was nothing short of a miracle and for a woman who had never had much use for God, she was coming to think that God, in fact, might have had some use for her. In His mercy, He had sent Kaspian just when she needed him most.

Reaching out a hand, Madelayne staggered over to him and he captured her hand, pulling her against him, as she fell into him. He could feel her tremble.

"Madelayne," he pleaded softly, with urgency in his tone. "What has happened, dearest?"

Madelayne pointed to Nicholas, who was struggling to stand. "I discovered that Nicholas allowed Cairn to be killed," she said, her voice quivering "I was told that he stood by and watched as Cairn was killed and then rushed in to collect the body, telling everyone he was too late to help. It simply wasn't true. Many soldiers saw this happen, trustworthy men. I was further told that he put Ewan into an impossible situation, which allowed the knight to be killed. Of course, we all know what happened to Mavia. Kaspian, he is as guilty for their deaths as if he killed them himself. And then he tried to tell me that you were the one responsible for Cairn's death. He said you did it because you wanted to marry me!"

By the time she was finished, Kaspian was looking at Nicholas with nothing short of hatred. Shock, to be sure, but in truth, it wasn't so much shock as it was realization... realization that Nicholas' character was as dark as his soul. Kaspian knew of the man's ambitious reputation, but a murderous reputation... he felt foolish for not having realized it all along. Nothing in his life had ever made so much sense.

"Is this true, de Dalyn?" he asked, his voice rumbling like thunder. "Did you tell her I was responsible for Cairn's death?"

Nicholas was on his feet, dealing with two puncture wounds to his back now and feeling a good deal of pain. He was cornered, caught, but he would not go down without a fight. His arrogance wouldn't let him. He wasn't about to let all of his ambitions, his planning, go to waste.

*He had to fight!*

"It is true," he insisted. "I was at Beeston, St. Hèver; *you* were the one that sent Cairn into a situation where he was overwhelmed by the Welsh. I did not imagine that."

Kaspian lifted an eyebrow. "We were all overwhelmed by the Welsh," he said. "It was your task to assist Cairn while the man was still alive. Did you do that?"

"I did what I could!"

"You did not."

The statement came not from Kaspian but from one of the Lavister soldiers who had come to Madelayne's aid; the man was older, seasoned, and had fought with Edward for years. He had been stationed at Lavister for as long as Kaspian had commanded the outpost; therefore, Kaspian knew the man. He was loyal and brave. Kaspian pointed to the soldier.

"Tell me what you know," he commanded quietly. "What did you see?"

The soldier didn't hesitate. "I was fighting with Sir Cairn that day," he said. "I saw Sir Nicholas ride to the edges of the skirmish and watch as Sir Cairn was killed. He never made a move to enter the fight or even help. He just stood there, waiting. When Sir Cairn was killed, Sir Nicholas rode in and brought the body out. That is what I saw with my own eyes."

A distinct sense of shock settled around those who were listening and accusing eyes turned to Nicholas, who was red in the face with rage.

"That is a lie!" he said. "I did what I could for him! It is Kaspian's fault for sending him to fend off too many Welsh!"

The soldier simply shook his head at Nicholas' denial, looking to Kaspian. "Forgive us for not saying anything sooner, my lord," he said. "We were afraid... we knew... that Sir Nicholas' word would be believed over ours and Sir Nicholas has it within his power to make our lives miserable. I have a son I am responsible for. I had to think of him. But I cannot be silent any longer; with God as my witness, that is what I saw. Sir Nicholas left Sir Cairn to die."

Nicholas simply snarled and hung his head, cursing under his breath. But he was no longer loudly denying the accusation, perhaps sensing there was no use in doing so. "Lies, lies, lies," he muttered. "Men who would *lie!*"

Madelayne heard Nicholas but she was looking up at Kaspian, who seemed rather pale and drawn. It was sickening to realize the depths of Nicholas' betrayal.

"I was afraid his next victim would be you," she whispered to Kaspian. "For Cairn and Ewan and Mavia... I had to avenge them,

Kaspian. I could no longer stand idle and hope you would not be his next victim. I had to do something."

He looked down at her, into that sweet face, and he was both puzzled and astonished. "Do something?" he repeated. "What did you do?"

Madelayne's gaze moved to Nicholas. "I took it upon myself to dispense justice for those we love," she said quietly. "I struck him in the head and knocked him out. I used one of your dirks to stab him but it did not do enough damage to hurt him. I... I was going to kill him."

He was astonished. "For me?"

She nodded, averting her gaze. "For you," she said quietly. "For Cairn, for Ewan, and for Mavia. Nicholas must be stopped, Kaspian. He must be made to pay for what he's done."

He could hardly believe what he was hearing, but on the other hand, he wasn't surprised. Madelayne was fiercely loyal and protective of those she loved. He remembered thinking once how odd it was to have a woman be so protective of him, but it wasn't odd at all, really. It was wonderful. Madelayne had been prepared to risk her life to do away with an injustice, to *seek* justice for those who had been wronged. Kaspian had never heard of anything more noble in his life, coming from a woman, no less.

*A very special woman.*

For a moment, he was actually speechless. He looked at his wife, a million thoughts rolling through his head but unable to think of anything to say. But he did know one thing; she had set out to avenge the deaths of their friends and colleagues. What she had started, he would now finish.

Now, he knew why he had been compelled to return to Kirk, why something had been driving him to go. Some manner of inner voice had him riding at top speed all the way from Shrewsbury like a madman. He thought it had been his overwhelming desire to see his wife, but it was more than that. Perhaps it was God telling him that, at this moment, he was most needed by his wife's side as she struggled with Nicholas. It was God telling him that she needed saving.

That they *all* needed saving.

*... from Nicholas.*

He didn't trust the man; any semblance of trust he might have had was gone, erased forever by the revelation from the soldier. Now, Kaspian had a job to do. For all of their sakes, he would end this.

"Then it is a good thing I returned when I did," he said to Madelayne. "You no longer need worry about Nicholas. I will take care of him now."

Madelayne gazed up at him with all of the confidence in the world. "I fear that I have failed in my attempt," she said. "I know you will not."

He touched her cheek. "Indeed, I will not," he said. "But for trying… know that I love you very much for trying."

"And I love you."

There was warmth in the air between them, both of them feeling the joy and faith and hope that had comprised their relationship. But it was particularly poignant to Madelayne; so much joy had come out of so much darkness, the darkness that had once been her life. The darkness that she had been wallowing in on that day those weeks ago when her son had been born dead and her husband had lost his life.

Such a dark, dark day. But without the darkness, she would have never appreciated the light so much. Gazing up at Kaspian, all she could see when she looked at him was light. Great, bright light. Before she could reply, however, they all heard Thomas growl.

"This is for my wife, you bastard," he said as he thrust his sword at Nicholas. "May you never do another treacherous thing again!"

He was far enough away that Nicholas was able to dodge him and, in Thomas' inebriated state, Nicholas was able to yank the sword away from him and turn it on him. He sliced into Thomas' gut, sending the man to the ground, as Kaspian pushed Madelayne away from the fighting and charged him. Nicholas managed to lift his sword to fend off what would have surely been a terrible blow and from that point, the fight was on.

As the entire ward of Kirk came to a halt, Kaspian and Nicholas went at each other with a vengeance. Kaspian still wasn't completely healed from his injury but he was much better off than Nicholas was, who had two stab wounds in his back. He was losing blood and weakening, but he wasn't going to give in to Kaspian's sword. To do so would be to accept death and he wasn't yet ready to do that.

So he fought back, matching Kaspian strike for strike as their battle moved across the bailey. At one point, Owain and Hawys had been alerted to the battle and emerged from the hall to see the combatants fighting it out. Hawys then quickly retreated back into the hall, unwilling to see men try to kill each other, but Owain was most interested in what was happening. He was also coming to think that the inhabitants of Lavister were, indeed, troublemakers and he made a mental note never to let them back into his castle again. But, for now, there was great entertainment to be had from the two seasoned knights fighting in his bailey. It was truly a sight to see.

The battle was brutal and bloody. Nicholas wasn't wearing any armor; he had nothing on his body but a tunic, breeches, and boots. Therefore, the hand holding the sword was being cut to pieces by Kaspian's sword. Every time the blades would come together, some portion of it was nicking Nicholas' hand. It wasn't long before the blood was streaming, spilling onto the ground in droplets every time Nicholas moved. It was a horrific and messy thing to watch.

As Kaspian and Nicholas battled, Madelayne sat on the ground next to Thomas, who was half-laying in the dirt, watching the fight, as Dolwyd patched up the slice that ran from his midsection up to his chest. The old physic had watched nearly the entire confrontation between Madelayne and Nicholas, having come out of the keep about the time Nicholas put his arm around her neck and threatened her life.

Dolwyd had watched in horror, and then finally hope, when the Lavister soldiers moved to help her. He was considering finding his own dagger and trying to help the lady when Thomas intervened and Kaspian finally arrived. Now, he found himself tending Thomas' wound and thinking, once again, that the inhabitants of Lavister had gone mad.

This time, however, he meant it.

Madness in the form of Kaspian trying to kill Nicholas, who was weakened and bloodied, but simply wouldn't surrender. Madelayne, too, was watching the battle with great fear, praying that Kaspian would soon gain the upper hand. It was torture to watch. But all the while, she couldn't shake the need to help him, to finish what she had started even though he was determined to be the one to avenge the others. Not that she blamed him; he had been through as much as any of them and probably more so; perhaps it was a matter of honor for him since Nicholas was under his command. It was his duty to deal out the punishment to the man.

But as Madelayne watched the pair of knights in their struggle across the bailey, she was feeling more and more as if this were her battle more than it was Kaspian's. It was Cairn that Nicholas had betrayed, after all. It was her husband he had killed.

*Those who were betrayed.*

The old crone's words rang in her head again. Perhaps those souls, those lost stars, were still depending on her.

Leaving Dolwyd tending Thomas, she stood up and began to move, skirting the battle area as the knights fought, her gaze seeking the dagger that had been tossed aside when Nicholas had captured her. No one seemed to be paying attention to her as she shuffled through the dirt, looking for the dagger and finally spying it over near the great hall.

Madelayne ran towards the weapon, scooping it up out of the dirt and trying to conceal it in her hands so no one would see what she had. Now, she would wait for the right moment to do what needed to be done. The longer this battle went on, the more chance there was that Kaspian might be the one injured in it. If that was the case, she knew that the men from Lavister would more than likely tear Nicholas apart but she didn't want to give them that satisfaction. Therefore, she stood there, heart in her throat, and waited for her opportunity.

It wasn't long in coming. Kaspian had managed to back Nicholas up, nearly boxing the man up against the wall of the bailey, but Nicholas was smart enough not to let himself be cornered. He tried to take the offensive against Kaspian, who ended up pushing him back again, only this time, they were over near the edge of the great hall. Madelayne, in fact, was just around the corner from where the men were battling. She could see their feet shuffling around and when Kaspian kicked Nicholas in the knee and the man staggered backwards, like a predator, she was there waiting.

*Now!*

As Nicholas faltered, Madelayne rushed around the corner with the dagger held high. Nicholas was bent over, suffering from the kick to his vulnerable knee, when Madelayne plunged the dagger into his neck as far as it would go. Nicholas stiffened and tried to scream but it was of no use; the dagger had cut through his windpipe, through a major artery, and emerged on the other side.

Wide-eyed, unable to scream or even breathe, Nicholas dropped his sword and fell to his knees as his hands went to his neck, grasping at the dagger. He tried to take it out but it was too late; he was bleeding too badly from the cut artery and as the entire bailey of Kirk watched with shock, he pitched onto his face and bled out into the dirt, never to rise again.

The wild and brutal battle was over in an instant, leaving a brittle calm in its wake. Kaspian watched Nicholas bleed out, startled to realize his wife had delivered the death blow. Breathing heavily from exertion, he looked with shock at Madelayne, who walked up to Nicholas and kicked the man in the shoulder. Kaspian would never forget the look on her face as she did; something between relief and fury and cold-hearted determination.

The expression of a woman who had done something of worth.

"That," she hissed at Nicholas, "was for Cairn. I hope you can still hear me, Nicholas. I hope Cairn's name is the last thing you hear before you pass into hell."

Nicholas didn't move; he was clearly dead. But Madelayne simply stood over him, watching the blood run in rivers through the dirt. Kaspian, exhausted and cut, took a few steps towards her.

"It is over," he said quietly. "Are you well, Madelayne?"

"I am very well."

"Are you sure? Do you feel faint?"

She thought a moment before shaking her head. "I feel fine," she said. "I feel… relieved. Relieved as I have never felt in my life."

Kaspian could see that. Surprisingly, she didn't seem upset by what she'd done in the least. He thought she might be in shock so he lifted a hand to her. "Come with me now," he said. "Let me take you away from this."

Madelayne didn't move. She was still looking at Nicholas. "Forgive me if I upset you by doing this," she said. Then, she finally looked at Kaspian. "Something inside me was telling me that I must be the one to punish Nicholas. I did not mean to interfere in what you were doing, but this… Kaspian, I saw a mystic earlier today. Aye, I did, and you can scold me for it later, but she told me that I was to avenge those who had been wronged. She did not even know about Cairn or Mavia, but still, she told me what I must do. Mayhap… mayhap it was my destiny to do this, to put an end to Nicholas and his treachery. Cairn had to know justice. He was my husband and your friend. Don't you believe he deserved to be avenged?"

She didn't sound like a woman in shock to him. In fact, she sounded quite lucid and Kaspian nodded.

"I do," he said. "I was going to do that for him and for you. But you did not let me finish."

He was smiling faintly as he said it and Madelayne knew that it was his way of telling her he was not angry with her. As shocking as it was for her to have taken a dagger to Nicholas, for there was no doubt the story of Lady St. Hèver and her dagger would become fodder for the rumor mills on the Marches, Kaspian didn't seem to be upset about it in the least.

"I do not think I was meant to let you finish," Madelayne said. "I think this is something I had to do. I have spent so much of my life being helpless to my situation and to events in my life... my children, Cairn... so many things. For once, I had to take control. Does that make any sense?"

Kaspian nodded, reaching out to gently take her arm and pull her away from Nicholas' body. "It makes sense," he said. "It was something that you needed to do."

"It was."

"I understand that need."

She looked at him. "You do?"

He nodded, putting his arm around her as the men collected in the bailey began to break up and a few Lavister soldiers moved, with disinterest, to Nicholas' body. Even Dolwyd was moving towards the knight rather slowly, as if the dead knight was of no matter to him.

"I understand the need to avenge family," Kaspian said quietly. "I understand the need to ensure the safety of those you are responsible for and those you love. Mayhap I understand a wife who is much stronger than I ever gave her credit for, strong enough that she should kill to protect me. Mayhap I understand that you have a little bit of a knight's heart in you, Lady St. Hèver. It would be quite easy to be shocked by what you have done but I find that I am not; I am proud. Proud of a woman who would be strong enough to do what needed to be done."

Madelayne paused, turning her face up to him as the light from the coming sunset caressed her delicate features. The sky above was turning shades of pink and blue and as Kaspian pulled her into his arms, she glanced up at the sky and the brilliant dusk colors. Beyond the shades of pink and blue, she could see a faint smattering of stars beyond. A smile creased her lips as she pointed upwards.

"See the stars?" she said as he looked upward to see what she was pointing at. "My mother once said that the souls of the dead were lost stars. I have seen so many lost stars in my lifetime that there were times I felt as if I was the queen of all things lost. Surely no one has suffered as much loss as I have in my short life. Being the queen of the lost used to have such a sad connotation to me but now, as I look in the sky and see those stars, being a queen also means benevolence and goodliness. Queens protect those that belong to them, do they not? Mayhap I have done that today. I have protected those lost stars by punishing someone who had done them great harm.

Kaspian gazed at the stars a moment longer before looking at her, his gaze gentle. "You are *my* queen," he murmured. "You are my sun, my moon, my stars, and the queen of my heart. Whatever darkness you have known in the past, whatever loss you have suffered, that has ended and a new day will come. For the rest of the days of your life, I will be at your side and you will only know happiness. This I vow."

Madelayne reached up, stroking a stubbled cheek. "I know," she whispered. "And I shall do my best to always make you happy as well. You are my life, Kaspian St. Hèver. Never forget that."

"I won't."

He kissed her sweetly, feeling that instant heat that he associated with her. God's Bones, he had so much to do at the moment – an army to gather, a fortress to regain – but all he could think of was Madelayne. Nothing on earth could consume him more. After the day they had shared, and after what they'd just been through, he needed to spend a few moments with her to collect himself. Her body against his, her flesh against his, calmed and soothed him like nothing else. At the moment, he needed it desperately. He suspected that she did, too.

Taking her arm, he led her towards the keep as the bailey of Kirk began to return to normal. Nicholas was being carted off but Kaspian kept Madelayne turned away so she wouldn't have to see it and Dolwyd went with Thomas to sew up the man's wound. Everything was returning to normal, as if a life and death battle hadn't just taken place, but given the character of the man who had lost his life, there was a sense of relief in the air that Madelayne had spoken of. The man who had brought such chaos into their lives was gone and there wasn't any man who didn't think that his ending, at the hands of Lady St. Hèver, wasn't appropriate.

If anyone deserved satisfaction, it was she.

Aye, there was a new day on the horizon and a fortress to regain. As Kaspian led Madelayne into the keep and passed by the entry guard, she turned to look at Kaspian, seeing that he seemed rather pensive.

"What are you thinking of, Kaspian?" she asked.

He glanced at her, looking at the back of her surcoat. "I am thinking how quickly I can remove you from your dress."

She grinned. "Fairly quickly, I would imagine," she said. "But you have duties to attend to, do you not? The last you and I spoke of such things, you were gathering men to reclaim Lavister."

He nodded, leading her to the narrow stairs that led to the upper floors. "I still am," he said. "But we will not leave until tomorrow. And I suppose that after this, I must send word to Edward about Nicholas' death."

Her smile faded. "What will you tell him?"

Kaspian lifted his eyebrows. "The truth," he said. "Nicholas got what he deserved. Even Edward will not dispute that."

"I hope not. I do not regret what happened."

"Nor do I," Kaspian said, sighing faintly. "But thoughts of Nicholas aside, I must find Lord de Kirk and soothe him of the big battle that just took place in his bailey. The man already thinks that everyone from Lavister is full of mischief and trouble and I suppose today proved him right."

Madelayne could hardly disagree. "We have shown him little else."

Kaspian conceded. "True," he said. "But I will seek him out later. Right now, I plan to spend some time with you."

She paused on the steps, looking at him somewhat reproachfully. "Doing what?"

"What do you think?"

She knew what he meant. "I thought we agreed that we were going to let my milk dry up."

He shook his head. "You came to that decision on your own. I did not agree at all."

She gave him a long look. "You cannot... well, you know... suckle forever."

He frowned. "Why not?"

She looked at him as if he were daft. "You are not an infant, Kaspian. And you are more than well enough to eat solid food. Must I really explain this to you?"

He pursed his lips irritably. "I told you it gives me comfort like nothing else," he said. "I ride to battle tomorrow, Madelayne. Would you deny me such comfort tonight?"

"You have already used that excuse on me."

"Aye, I did, and it worked."

She scowled. In response, he picked her up and carried her, squealing with laughter, up the stairs. Their mood was light when it shouldn't have been; they'd just left a dead man in the bailey and suffered through a particularly brutal battle. But the end result of the battle, the freedom and relief that they felt, warranted the lightness of their mood. They knew that nothing could harm them, ever, knowing the strength and joy and devotion they had found in each other. Knowing that a new day was indeed coming, and the queen of those who had been lost would be the queen of the lost no longer.

Now, she was the queen of the living and of a glorious life she never thought she would have.

Finally, Madelayne had found her peace.

And her stars above twinkled a little bit brighter, just for her.

The avenged had found their peace, too.

# EPILOGUE

*Lavister Crag Castle*
*One year later*

"**W**e must leave, Kaspian," Thomas said. "We should have been gone over an hour ago."

Kaspian stood at the entry level door to Lavister's keep, trying to keep a neutral expression on his face. But the truth was that he couldn't; he was anxious and edgy, dressed in full battle regalia but not making any attempt to utilize that dress. He stood at the door as a six-hundred-man army wait for him in the bailey, growing bored as their commander delayed.

"I know," he finally said, his attention drawn to the keep. "Dolwyd said it would be any moment now."

"I know."

"I promised her I wouldn't leave. She's frightened."

"I know."

"Actually, she's terrified."

Thomas sighed. "Then go back up to the chamber and wait," he said. "Be close to her. Let her know you are near."

Kaspian shook his head. "I cannot be close to the chamber," he said. "I can hear her groaning and it makes me want to vomit."

Thomas chuckled, trying not to let the man see him laugh. "Childbirth is not an event that brings a woman any pleasure, I would imagine," he said. His smile faded. "The outcome will be the same whether or not you stay. We are expected at Holt Castle and I fear the Welsh will not wait. Holt has summoned our help and…."

Kaspian put up a hand to silence the man. "I realize that," he said. Then, he sighed heavily. "I seem to remember having this same conversation with Cairn right before he died. Do you recall? We were heading to Beeston to fend off the Welsh and he was reluctant to leave Madelayne because she was pregnant."

Thomas slapped the man on the shoulder. "I remember it well," he said. "Do you feel badly for rushing the man off now?"

Kaspian rolled his eyes. "I do," he said. "Now, I understand."

A faint smile played on Thomas' lips. He pointed to the top of the keep. "Go, then," he said. "I will hold the army, but if Lady St. Hèver takes too much longer in delivering that child, then you must consider leaving anyway. We are needed, after all."

Kaspian sighed with some exasperation. He almost argued with Thomas but thought better of it. They'd received a request for aid from Holt Castle, something they had been preparing for until Lady St. Hèver, hugely pregnant, went into labor. Madelayne had been laboring to bring forth their first child for twelve long hours. It seemed that all the woman ever did was go into labor when an army was departing. At least, Kaspian thought so. As a result, he hadn't slept all night.

For the first few hours, he had remained with her because she was so frightened. He had held her hand and spoken of the pony he would buy his son, the finest pony in all of England. He told Madelayne he intended to see the boy ride before he could walk, which drew a frown of disapproval from his wife. The labor hadn't been too painful at that point and their conversation had been light, focusing on the excitement and not the fear. But, God's Bones, the fear was great. It was there, hovering over them, even though they hadn't spoken of it. Still, Kaspian could see it in her eyes. The pregnancy itself had been a miracle enough but another dead baby would crush her. Nay, beyond crush. It would destroy her.

And him as well.

So they had spoken of things that stayed away from the end results of her last two pregnancies, the same conversations they'd had since first discovering she was with child. Kaspian wouldn't let her wallow in fear and even when the labor grew more painful and she began to grunt and groan with the pains, he kept the conversation away from the worst. He kept talking until Dolwyd had chased him from the room because the pains had grown so bad that he had turned pale every time she had one. Dolwyd didn't need a nervous father hanging about; he had enough with a nervous mother.

So, he'd gone on with his duties to prepare for the ride to Holt and that included donning his full battle armor. But now he stood in the doorway of the keep, unable to actually make a move to use that armor. He was torn with indecision.

"Kael," he said to Thomas. "If it is a boy, we shall name him Kael."

"A sound name." Thomas gave him another push. "Go and see what is happening so that we may depart."

Like a man facing something terrible, Kaspian turned for the keep and, very slowly, began to make his way up the dusty, stone steps. He truly didn't want to hear Madelayne groaning in pain. He felt so terribly helpless against it. Moreover, while she was fearful for the life of their child, Kaspian was fearful for *her*. Women died in childbirth easily and the thought scared him to death.

Over the past year, Madelayne had come to mean more to him than his own life. There wasn't anything he wouldn't do for her and the love they shared had completely transformed the emotionless, serious knight. Even with his own men, he laughed more and was able to show more compassion. That, among many things, is what Madelayne had done for him.

Love was funny that way.

And then there was the unexpected pregnancy, coincidentally, right after she allowed her milk to dry up. He still suckled her breasts, of course, but purely from the comfort and pleasure it gave him, not from the nourishment. Those days of needing her nourishment were long over and he had finally healed completely, now perfectly sound. The days of his injury, of Cairn's death and Nicholas' treachery, seemed like another lifetime ago. He and Madelayne never even discussed it anymore. Now, it was just him and Madelayne and the world they had created for themselves at Lavister.

It was a wonderful world.

By the time Kaspian hit the second floor, he was reveling in memories of the past year, the most wonderful year of his life. Wrapped up in reflections, he was startled when a female servant came down the stairs from the top floor where his chamber was, where Madelayne was. He recognized the old woman, the old washerwoman who had been at Lavister for many years. She beamed at him.

"Go up, my lord," she said, pointing up the stairs. "Your wife wants to see you."

Kaspian felt as if he'd been hit in the pit of his stomach. His mouth went dry. "Why?" he demanded. "Is everything well?"

The old woman simply smiled and pointed without answering, and Kaspian bolted up the stairs, taking them two at a time, until he reached the top. Heart pounding in his ears, he entered the chamber.

Dolwyd was the first face he saw and the old man slapped him on the chest when he entered, startling him.

"You have a big, healthy son!" he exclaimed. It was more glee than Kaspian had ever seen from the taciturn old man. "He took his time coming because the mother's womb is scarred, but he's finally here. Everyone is doing well enough. Go and see him!"

Kaspian was standing there with his mouth open in shock. He could hardly believe what he was hearing. Dolwyd gave him a shove to get him moving and Kaspian made his way over to the bed where Madelayne was laying down with something in her arms. As Kaspian drew close, he could see little fists waving about. A baby was squealing. When Madelayne turned to look up at him, smiling, Kaspian put his hand over his heart and his eyes filled with tears.

"He came," he whispered hoarsely.

Madelayne was grinning at her overwhelmed husband. "He did."

"Kael."

"Aye, Kael."

Kaspian swallowed hard, trying to swallow away his tears. He was overwhelmed. He had tried not to let himself expect this moment but now that it was here, he was having a difficult time believing it. All of his dream and hopes and passions were nestled in Madelayne's arms, wailing away in the form of the loud little boy his wife had just given birth to.

*His son!*

"He... he's a handsome lad," he said hoarsely. "He's very loud."

Madelayne could see how emotional he was. She peeled back the swaddling to let him see the boy's head, shoulders, and arms. She gazed at the child adoringly. "He looks like his father," she said, soft tones of a woman who had much love to give her child. "He even sounds like you."

Kaspian bent over the bed, looking at the boy. His eyes drank in the sight of his firstborn. He never knew he could feel such love. At that moment, he was swimming in it, every possible measure of joy and adoration he could feel. It was engulfing him. He put a big hand gently on Madelayne's forehead.

"I am speechless," he finally said. "I... I do not even know how to say what is in my heart. All I can seem to think of is to tell you how proud you have made me. From the bottom of my heart, I thank you. This child… my son… will be the most cherished child on this earth."

Madelayne gazed up at him, tears filling her eyes. She remembered once when he had told her that he'd never longed for heirs, but she had known it wasn't true. She'd always known it. Hearing the awe and reverence in his voice nearly undid her. She reached over and grasped one of his hands, watching as he lifted her fingers to his lips and kissed them.

"Aye, he will," she said softly. "He has the greatest father in England and a powerful legacy to live up to. He will make you proud, Kaspian. He will be a great man like his father."

Kaspian lowered himself onto the edge of the bed, watching the baby fuss. "I was thinking…."

"Of what?"

He paused a moment. "I was thinking of changing his name."

"To what?"

"Kairn. We shall spell it with a 'K' so that it is spelled with the same letter my name is spelled with."

Madelayne grinned, so broadly that it split her face in two. She was deeply touched by his suggestion. "What a lovely tribute that would be," she said. "Are you sure?"

Kaspian nodded. "Aye," he replied. "I have been thinking… Cairn never had a son. And it was his tragedy that brought you to me. I would like to honor him if you are agreeable by naming our son after him."

"I think it is a lovely gesture."

"You do not think it strange to name our son after your first husband?"

She shook her head. "He was your friend, too."

Kaspian nodded, his gaze on the infant. Then, he smiled. "He was, indeed," he said. "I am quite accustomed to having a Kairn by my side. I shall look forward to little Kairn being my shadow."

Madelayne simply smiled at him, thinking that his desire to name her son after Cairn to be one of the sweeter gestures she'd ever known. But, then again, Kaspian St. Hèver was one of the sweeter men she had ever known. A man who had grown so much over the past year that she couldn't even remember the man he'd been before they were married. That man didn't exist any longer. Taking his place was a man of great compassion, love, humor, and understanding.

Now, he had named their son after his dead friend in a touching tribute to the man who had given him everything in his life worth having – a beautiful wife and a healthy son. None of that would have existed had Cairn not become one of those lost stars in the heavens. Aye, it was a fitting tribute to the man who had given both Kaspian and Madelayne everything.

After all, all Cairn had ever wanted was for Madelayne to be happy. Finally, she was.

**THE END**

Do you want to read more about the House of St. Hever and other related family groups? Here are the other novels in the House of St. Hever/Dragonblade Series:

# About Kathryn Le Veque

*Medieval Just Got Real.*

KATHRYN LE VEQUE is a USA TODAY Bestselling author, an Amazon All-Star author, and a #1 bestselling, award-winning, multi-published author in Medieval Historical Romance and Historical Fiction. She has been featured in the NEW YORK TIMES and on USA TODAY's HEA blog. In March 2015, Kathryn was the featured cover story for the March issue of InD'Tale Magazine, the premier Indie author magazine. She was also a quadruple nominee (a record!) for the prestigious RONE awards for 2015.

Kathryn's Medieval Romance novels have been called 'detailed', 'highly romantic', and 'character-rich'. She crafts great adventures of love, battles, passion, and romance in the High Middle Ages. More than that, she writes for both women AND men – an unusual crossover for a romance author – and Kathryn has many male readers who enjoy her stories because of the male perspective, the action, and the adventure.

Kathryn loves to hear from her readers. Please find Kathryn on Facebook at <u>Kathryn Le Veque, Author</u>, or join her on Twitter <u>@kathrynleveque</u>, and don't forget to visit her website at <u>www.kathrynleveque.com</u>.

<u>Kathryn Le Veque on Smashwords</u>

Made in the USA
Middletown, DE
16 March 2018